Praise for the

"A strong story with a lot

"A wondrous adventure, full of action and suspense, which will enchant readers." —*RT Book Reviews*

"The history, the characters and the plot blended flawlessly for a well-rounded story and hard-won happily ever after."
—*Night Owl Reviews*

"I couldn't put this book down once I started it. I highly recommend [it] be added to your must-read list." —*Fresh Fiction*

"A fast-paced, romantic adventure filled with laughter and danger . . . The pages turn very quickly and their story of adversity keeps the reader absorbed." —*Romance Reviews Today*

"A delightful western romance . . . The story line is at its best when it concentrates on the lead couple, especially during humorous interludes." —*Midwest Book Review*

"[Cindy Holby] takes us on an incredible journey of love, betrayal and the will to survive. . . . Ms. Holby is definitely a star on the rise!" —*The Best Reviews*

"Like no other book you'll read, and you owe it to yourself to experience it." —*EscapetoRomance.com*

"Ms. Holby has created a delightful and fast-paced medieval fantasy full of characters that felt real and poignant."
—*Romance Reader at Heart*

Angel's End

Cindy Holby

B
BERKLEY SENSATION, NEW YORK

THE BERKLEY PUBLISHING GROUP
Published by the Penguin Group
Penguin Group (USA) Inc.
375 Hudson Street, New York, New York 10014, USA

Penguin Group (Canada), 90 Eglinton Avenue East, Suite 700, Toronto, Ontario M4P 2Y3, Canada
(a division of Pearson Penguin Canada Inc.) • Penguin Books Ltd., 80 Strand, London WC2R 0RL,
England • Penguin Group Ireland, 25 St. Stephen's Green, Dublin 2, Ireland (a division of Penguin
Books Ltd.) • Penguin Group (Australia), 250 Camberwell Road, Camberwell, Victoria 3124, Australia
(a division of Pearson Australia Group Pty. Ltd.) • Penguin Books India Pvt. Ltd., 11 Community
Centre, Panchsheel Park, New Delhi—110 017, India • Penguin Group (NZ), 67 Apollo Drive,
Rosedale, Auckland 0632, New Zealand (a division of Pearson New Zealand Ltd.) • Penguin Books
(South Africa) (Pty.) Ltd., 24 Sturdee Avenue, Rosebank, Johannesburg 2196, South Africa

Penguin Books Ltd., Registered Offices: 80 Strand, London WC2R 0RL, England

This is a work of fiction. Names, characters, places, and incidents either are the product of the author's
imagination or are used fictitiously, and any resemblance to actual persons, living or dead, business
establishments, events, or locales is entirely coincidental. The publisher does not have any control over
and does not assume any responsibility for author or third-party websites or their content.

ANGEL'S END

A Berkley Sensation Book / published by arrangement with the author

PUBLISHING HISTORY
Berkley Sensation mass-market edition / May 2012

Copyright © 2012 by Cindy Holby.
Excerpt from *Colorado Heart* by Cindy Holby copyright © 2012 by Cindy Holby.
Cover design by George Long.
Cover art by Tony Mauro.

ISBN: 978-0-425-24841-6

BERKLEY SENSATION®
Berkley Sensation Books are published by The Berkley Publishing Group,
a division of Penguin Group (USA) Inc.,
375 Hudson Street, New York, New York 10014.
BERKLEY SENSATION® is a registered trademark of Penguin Group (USA) Inc.
The "B" design is a trademark of Penguin Group (USA) Inc.

PRINTED IN THE UNITED STATES OF AMERICA

10 9 8 7 6 5 4 3 2 1

ALWAYS LEARNING   **PEARSON**

*To Peggy, who said in seventh grade,
"Let's write a story." I miss you.*

ACKNOWLEDGMENTS

There are so many people who helped me along this journey. My wonderful husband who was very patient during the struggle to sell again and the deadline days. I love you so much. My two sons who always inspire me. My parents who are always there when I need them. Dad, I miss you so much and I'm glad I made you proud.

A special thank-you to my wonderful agent, Roberta Brown, who always believed in me and to Kate Seaver, for asking for a project that was a perfect match for my writing style. We never gave up on each other and I'm thrilled to be writing for her now.

A special shout-out to my neighbors, who are absolutely the best. I really believe that our little community is paradise.

And of course, to all my werearmadillos. Alesia, Barb, Eileen, Marianne, Michelle and Serena. I love all of you more than dark chocolate and peanut butter together, and could not have written one word of this without your constant support. We rock!

ONE

Cade Gentry was not one to ask for forgiveness. Life was what it was and it was best just to deal with it. He'd done a lot in the past ten years that he wasn't proud of, acts he thought he'd have time to atone for. He just needed the opportunity to succeed, to set the record straight. He'd always thought there was still time.

That was before he'd been shot.

He supposed he was lucky because the bullet passed straight through his gut, tearing its way through his belly and bouncing off his ribs before it blew its way through his back. If this was luck, then it was the first time he'd ever been graced by its company. He could only hope that it would hang around until he froze to death. That had to be less painful than bleeding out.

Or so he hoped.

Cade took a moment to survey his surroundings. He stood deep in a copse of aspens that led down to a frozen stream. He'd lost his horse hours ago, a full day after they'd both been shot. The animal finally gave out from the bullet in his lungs, but not until Cade had escaped his pursuers. He hated losing that horse. He'd been his only friend for as long as he could remember. At least he had the satisfaction of knowing he'd taken out several of the men who'd chased after him.

The air was so cold that it burned his throat as he sucked it in. Still he felt hot, sweaty and clammy since he'd awakened shivering from the hour of sleep he'd allowed himself at dawn. Cade pulled his hand away from his stomach and his shirt moved with it, clinging to his glove with tiny flakes of ice. The bleeding had slowed down to a trickle, but he had no way of telling if it was because of the cold, or because he didn't have any left to give. The only thing he did know was that he couldn't stop. If he did, he'd be dead for certain, because the bastards who shot him were bound to finish the job.

Desperation, always close at hand, grabbed him by the throat and held him until he couldn't breathe. The moments of his life, especially the last few wasted years filled his mind. Was this it? Why bother living if there was nothing to this existence but loneliness and desperation to fill each passing moment. Why bother at all? He should just sit down in this beautiful, peaceful spot and die alone. His body would freeze solid and lie there until the animals got to him. There was nobody to know, nobody that would even care, except a brother he hadn't seen in ten years.

"Please God," Cade said to the silent trees. "I'm not ready to die." Why did he bother to pray? God had never heard him before. And why should God care? It wasn't as if he was worth saving. But suddenly the golden leaves that stubbornly clung to the branches of the aspens, despite the quick approach of winter, rattled with the quickening wind. It wasn't much of an answer, but it did bring the scent of burning wood. Maybe after all these years God finally heard him. There was a fire close by, and hopefully warmth, a horse, and a way out of his latest predicament.

Cade pulled his .45 from his holster and checked the load. He had three bullets left. His belt was empty. He could only hope the three would be enough. He opened his mouth to pray again, and then clamped it firmly shut. No use tempting fate or God. He didn't need any help killing. That was something he was good at.

He holstered his Colt and staggered a few steps down the slope. The ground wavered and he had to grab onto an aspen to settle his spinning world. Cade closed his eyes and leaned his forehead against the gnarled bark. It felt cool against his skin, but there was only a moment of relief. He took a deep breath and the smell of burning wood filled his lungs, along with the scent of meat sizzling on a fire. He opened his eyes and saw a trace of smoke hanging just above the trees on the opposite bank.

"If you want it," he reminded himself, "you're going to have to get it yourself. There are no handouts in this world." With a determined step he moved onward.

The sun, weak in the wintry sky, was gone, chasing the horizon that hid behind the mountains. The air around him grew colder, so sharp that it felt as if you could break it off in great chunks and shatter it against the ground. It was so quiet that Cade could hear his heart beating in his chest. Each thump-thump weakened him, like a spinning top that slowly lost its momentum and finally spun over on its side.

The soft glow from the fire kept him moving. Somewhere in his mind he knew the heat he felt on his skin was from a fever and not the fire. That didn't keep him from shivering. He wrapped his arms around his body and kept trudging onward, not even caring when his foot slipped off a rock and splashed into the icy cold water of the stream. He was so desperate to get to the fire that he kept stumbling onward until his instinct for self-preservation, always so strong, screamed *slow down, look around, and make sure you know what you're getting into.* He had to take a moment to remember what he should do. Finally his mind caught up with his instincts. Cade changed his angle of approach and moved from tree to tree until he was able to crouch down and observe the site, with gun in hand, from behind a deadfall of pines.

"You are most welcome to join me brother," a voice boomed out.

A man stood before the fire, fully exposed to Cade's shot, if he decided to take one. Cade could not make out his features. The entire scene wavered in his vision, as if he were dreaming. The man wore a long heavy coat and held his arms outstretched to show he was unarmed. In his left hand he held a book. The fire snapped and popped behind him and the scent of coffee filled his senses. A pale horse stood off to the side with his ears pricked toward Cade's hiding place. Whoever he was, he'd chosen his site well. It was close to the trail and within a copse of evergreens that grew beside a huge boulder that had probably lain there for an eternity. When the snow finally came, he'd have the benefit of some shelter and the reflected warmth of the fire off the boulder.

"I have food, coffee and an ear for listening if you are so inclined," the man continued.

Cade wiped his forehead with his sleeve. He had two options before him. He could shoot the man down, eat his food, drink his coffee and steal his horse. Or he could holster his gun and join him.

"I may be a lot of things, but a murderer isn't one of them." He holstered his gun and stood with his hands up. *Liar,* his conscience said as he stepped forward into the light. Cade looked side to side, to make sure it wasn't a trap, but for some strange reason his eyes couldn't focus. If it was a trap, there wasn't much he could do about it. It took every bit of strength he had to walk the ten paces that led him to the fire.

"Welcome brother," the man said. He extended his right hand. Cade looked at it, willing his mind to accept the fact that there was no danger here. Slowly he lifted his hand to grasp the one offered. It floated before him as the fire burned brighter. The trees spun around him as he finally gave in to the fever and his wound and sank to the ground.

It was the dream again. The one that haunted him ever since Sand Creek and the death of his mother and baby sister. The one where he ran through the smoke and the falling bodies while the sound of the howitzers drowned out the screams. He tried to escape the dream but something held him back, suffocating him, just as the smoke had that day. Something grabbed him, held on to him, and he swung out, fighting his father who held him as they watched his mother struggling beneath a soldier . . .

"It's a dream!"

Cade slowly opened his eyes. His lids felt heavy and the weight upon him was oppressive. He looked down and saw that he was covered with a heavy coat. A man knelt by his side and smiled encouragingly at him. "You were having a bad dream," he said.

"Who are you?" Cade managed to get the question out, even though his mouth felt as dry as sand.

"Reverend Timothy Key of Chillicothe, Ohio." He offered Cade a canteen. "And the Baptist church." Cade took it and Timothy helped him sit up so he could drink. The water inside was so cold that his head seized up as he gulped it down.

It was full dark now. Thick clouds hung just above the treetops, waiting with indecision to drop their heavy load of snow. "What are you doing out here in the middle of nowhere?" Cade returned the canteen.

"I'm on my way to my flock." Cade looked around. Flock? This man wasn't foolish enough to bring sheep into cattle country was he? He was relieved to see his gun belt lay close at hand. The movement also made him realize that his abdomen was tightly bandaged. He put a hand to his wound.

The preacher smiled as he doused his handkerchief with water. "I'm referring to the people of Angel's End." He motioned to the north and west with one hand as he dabbed the wet handkerchief on Cade's forehead. "I was called to be their minister." He handed the handkerchief to Cade and picked up his book. One glance confirmed that it was a Bible. Cade wiped his face and grimaced as he moved.

"I have my letter of introduction right there." Timothy pointed to the pocket of the large overcoat that covered Cade. "A recommendation from Bishop Henderson himself. Unfortunately the stage driver didn't believe me when I said the snow would hold off until we got there," Timothy further explained. "And since there won't be another stage until the spring melt I bought a horse and struck out on my own."

"Trying to beat the storm?"

"Wherever God leads me."

"Looks like he's brought you to the middle of nowhere," Cade grunted. His wound pained him and the fever was enough to make him wonder if he were still caught up in a dream.

"Or perhaps he's brought us together."

Yes. He was dreaming. Or else the preacher man was crazy.

"God led you all the way from Ohio?"

"To this very place." Timothy smiled. Cade studied his

eyes. If he *was* crazy, the eyes would be a sure indication. But all he saw was a feeling of peace in the warm brown that was a shade lighter than his own.

I wonder what he sees when he looks into my eyes?

"Do you think you can handle some food?" Timothy turned to the fire. He had to be cold. He was dressed in a black frock coat, just like his father used to wear. He'd thrown his heavy overcoat over Cade, who'd had nothing but a short jacket over his shirt, pants and long johns. It wasn't as if he'd had time to prepare when all the bad showed up.

Timothy looked expectantly over his shoulder. The man had to be crazy, turning his back on a complete stranger who showed up in his camp. Or was he?

Cade tried to recall the last time he'd eaten, and whether he should try to eat now. There was no telling if the bullet had nicked any of his internal organs. If they had he was dead anyway so he might as well go out with a full stomach as opposed to an empty one. "I'd appreciate it," he said and Timothy once more graced him with his peaceful smile.

Timothy handed him a large slice of bread wrapped around a thick chunk of ham. "The cook at the stage stop was most generous," he explained. Cade didn't bother to reply as he sunk his teeth into the sandwich. Timothy handed him a cup of coffee. He'd thought when he'd started that he'd eat the entire thing but after a few bites and one swig of coffee he was exhausted.

"Thanks," he said when Timothy took the remnants of his meal. He sank back to the ground with his head propped on the saddle and pulled the coat up beneath his chin. He knew he lay on the only blanket but the thought of getting up, and giving up this small comfort was more than he could bear at the time. "For the food, and for the doctoring."

"Brother, you were lucky the bullet passed through," Timothy said. "I'm afraid my skills of surgery are quite lacking, even with the power of prayer." He raised what was left of Cade's sandwich in a toast and finished it off as he sat cross-legged by the fire on the cold hard ground with the Bible by his side.

"You really believe in that stuff?" Cade asked.

"Don't you?" Timothy's eyes seemed to see more than Cade wanted to reveal. How could he know that he'd just prayed for help? He'd been across the stream on the opposite side of this small valley when that occurred. It seemed like it happened days ago instead of moments.

"Not a bit," he lied. "Every time I pray God laughs."

"Really?" Timothy quirked his head to the side as if he was contemplating Cade's statement. "What makes you think that?"

He was warm, and as long as he didn't move too much the pain was bearable, so he decided to humor the preacher. It had all happened so long ago that it felt as if it were someone else's life. Or so he kept telling himself.

"I lived in an orphanage from the time I was ten years old. My dad dumped me and my little brother there after our mother died. Every night I prayed that he would come back and get us. After a while I realized he wasn't coming back, so I started praying that a nice family would adopt us." Cade looked up at the night sky, recalling the many nights he used to do the same when he was a boy. Praying to the heavens in hopes that God would hear him better without the interference of a roof or wall. And sometimes wishing on a falling star because his mother always did so. There were no stars to be seen through the heavy clouds. Maybe a prayer or two could get through the dense cover, but none of them would be his.

"When I was fifteen and my brother was eleven someone did come and adopt us. We couldn't believe our luck. They were going to Oregon and needed a couple of strong boys to help them work their homestead. So we went with this *nice couple . . .*" He almost choked on the words. "I remember climbing up in the back of that wagon and being so excited I could hardly stand it." Cade looked at Timothy to make sure he was paying attention. He was.

"That night when we made camp another man was waiting for us. I thought it was kind of strange, especially the way he looked us over, checking to make sure we had all our teeth and were healthy. Then he said he'd take my brother, Brody. And just like that he loaded him up on his horse and took off. I tried to follow them and the man who was supposed to be my new father caught me, tied me to the wagon wheel and beat me with a leather strap until I bled. Then he said if I ran off, or ever did anything that he didn't like, he'd have his friend kill my brother."

As he expected, Timothy looked appropriately shocked.

"Not exactly an answer to my prayers now was it, *brother*?" He sneered the word and a tiny bit of his conscience flared up for being an ass toward the man who helped him.

Timothy smiled. "We have no way of knowing where God's path will lead us," he began. "For instance the last thing I expected tonight was to be keeping company with a wounded man but here I am, listening to your tale and very grateful to the Lord for the company, as I imagine you are?"

"I already said so and I'll say it again. Thank you for helping me."

"So what happened to the people who adopted you?"

He didn't want to think about those three years. The worry every day about Brody and if he was as scared as he was that he was going to die. About the things Jasper Middleton taught him to do and made him do. The things his wife Letty whispered in his ear and did to him when Jasper wasn't around until he had to lock what used to be the good part of his soul up into the deepest recesses of his mind. He'd have been better off dying with his mother and sister. At least that way he'd have had a chance of getting into heaven. Instead he was sure to go to hell, a place he was very familiar with.

Cade summed it up for the preacher. "He killed his wife. Then I killed him."

"Bless you brother," Timothy said. "The Lord will forgive you. All you have to do is ask."

Obviously the preacher wasn't listening. It was hard to argue with a man when he was practically flat on his back. Cade shifted and sat up. Timothy moved to help, adjusting the saddle so Cade could sit comfortably. Cade explained things to the preacher one more time.

"God doesn't have the time, or the inclination to listen to me ask for forgiveness for all my sins." He gritted his teeth as a pain shot through his abdomen. "And believe me, *brother*, the list is long. There is no doubt in my mind that I've broken every one of the Commandments."

Timothy crouched beside him. "And yet God led you to this place at this time in your life. Did you ever stop to think that perhaps God's answer was *not now*? To wait and be patient and see where he leads you?"

"God sure has a roundabout way of doing things if all he wanted me to do was to talk to you."

"You never told me your name you know. When I introduced myself, you never mentioned your name."

Cade had nothing to lose by telling him. Fortunately he'd managed so far to avoid getting his name on a wanted poster, or so he hoped. "Cade Gentry."

Timothy smiled again and poked at a log in the fire. It popped as it settled and he added another piece of pine, which burned quick and bright. "So tell me, Cade Gentry, what did you pray for when you were stumbling around out there, gut shot, without a horse, with a blizzard bearing down on you." Timothy looked at him. "You did pray." It wasn't a question, just a statement of certainty.

Yes he did. But what exactly did he say? Cade found he could not remember the words.

"Maybe God knew what you needed before you knew what to ask for."

"Are you like this with everyone you meet?" Cade asked.

"God said to feed his sheep."

Cade looked incredulously at Timothy. Not because he didn't believe him. It was because his father had said the same thing before he packed up his wife and three young children and brought them out west to minister to the Cheyenne.

"I take the responsibility personally," Timothy added.

As usual, if God was listening to Cade, it was only because he needed a laugh.

The fire popped again. A log broke and sparks sprayed up. Timothy turned toward the deadfall and stared into the darkness. Cade sensed movement in the woods and his hand went instinctively to his hip. His gun wasn't there, but it was within reach. He yanked the belt over and pulled his weapon from the holster.

A shot rang out. The impact of the bullet hitting Timothy's chest spun him around. He looked down at his chest, at the blood spurting out from where his heart had been struck. He looked up at Cade and spoke three words before he fell, facedown, into the fire.

"Feed my sheep."

Cade rolled to the side and fired. The first bullet missed. He grabbed the saddle and scrambled behind it. Timothy's horse jerked against the hobble.

"I knew I'd run you down eventually." A man walked into the circle of light cast by the fire.

"It took you long enough Davis." He had two bullets left and a fever that made him shaky. Plus the smell of burning flesh wasn't making things any easier for his stomach.

"Fitch said to bring you back alive. He's got plans for you."

"Tell him no thanks." He had to draw Davis in closer if he wanted a good shot at him. He also had to hope that the gunfighter was on his own. He probably was. Davis was a selfish bastard. He'd want the bounty Fitch offered all to himself. "Tell him I was dead when you found me." If Davis thought he was weak enough he'd come in real close. The man never was one to take chances. "Dead from that gut shot one of you gave me when I ran."

"I'm betting you're out of bullets too," Davis said. He paused by the fire and nudged Timothy's leg with his boot. As if Timothy could be playing possum with his face in the fire.

"That's an easy bet," Cade said. "How many did I take out?"
Closer . . .

"Enough that my cut is going to be real nice. You're good with a gun Gentry, I'll give you that. One of the best I've ever seen. But an empty gun ain't going to do you no good now, no matter how fast you are."

Cade slowly settled back against the saddle. He had to make Davis think he was done. It took every bit of his will-power to stay still, to be patient until Davis took the last few steps toward Cade. Davis had the audacity to smile at him when he finally came face-to-face.

Cade dropped him with the first shot to his chest. He followed up with his last bullet just to make sure. Davis fell backward against the rock from the close and sudden impact, and slowly slid to the cold, hard ground.

Standing up was harder than Cade anticipated. Dizziness just about put him back down, but he fought through it. When he could finally stand without the world spinning around he kicked Davis in the ribs. He was dead. Cade took Davis's gun and stuffed it in his belt.

"Damnit!" Timothy's body smoldered in the fire. Another

one of God's jokes. Cade grabbed his ankles, pulled him out and flipped him over. His face was burned and unrecognizable. Gone. He didn't deserve to die, especially not like this.

It could have just as easily been me . . .

A sudden thought hit him. Was it divine intervention or straight from the devil himself? With his fever it was hard to tell if he was thinking straight. Timothy's hair, what was left on the back of his head was the same dark brown as Cade's. The preacher had to have been close to his age, perhaps a little older. His eyes were definitely the same basic color. He might be a few inches shorter. It was hard to say since Cade couldn't recall standing next to him. Whatever discrepancies there were could be taken care of by the fire, the coming snow and the pack of wolves he heard howling in the distance. They could always smell death.

"I should bury him." It was a weak protest at best. The ground was frozen hard, he had no shovel and the snow would start at any time. Cade looked at where Davis lay. Even with his fever he realized that it was feasible. Whoever found the bodies would think he and Davis shot each other. All he had to do was put Davis's gun in Timothy's hand.

Cade shucked off his jacket and traded with Timothy's corpse. Timothy's black frock coat was a bit charred around the collar but it would have to do. He'd think of some lie to cover it. Hell, he was great at lying. He flipped Timothy back over and was about to return him to the fire when he realized there was one more thing he had to do. His jacket had a bullet hole in the back. Cade had no choice. He flipped Timothy over and shot him in the general vicinity of his own wound. A trickle of blood oozed out. Something else he could only hope nature and time would take care of. The bullet wouldn't go through but he figured no one would take the time to look and see if it was still in him. All that was left to do was put his gun in Timothy's hand and place him back in the fire.

Cade wiped his forehead with the back of his hand as he crouched by the fire. Timothy's clothing began to smolder but that did not stop him from placing his gloved hand on Timothy's shoulder.

"I'm sorry brother. Sorry that you got caught up in my problems. But like you said, maybe God put you in my path for a reason. I'd hate to think that this was it. But like *I* said, when it comes to me, God doesn't exactly listen. So maybe our prayers kind of canceled each other's out. Whatever it is, I know you're standing before him now with a big old smile on your face as the devil will be with me when I finally get down to his place."

That was as close to a benediction as he was going to get. As Cade turned away he saw Timothy's Bible, open on the ground with the pages flipping rapidly with the growing wind. Cade picked it up and stuffed it in the pocket of the thick long coat that Timothy had covered him with. He placed Davis's gun back in his hand, and with the last ounce of his strength saddled Timothy's horse. He put on the heavy coat and managed to drag himself into the saddle. He pointed the horse's nose up the trail and dug his heels into the animal's sides. The snow started just as he lost sight of the fire.

"Feed my sheep."

He would, if he could find them. He heard them calling, heard them bleating, but the wind howled and the snow swirled and he couldn't find them. They were lost.

He was so cold. But he was hot. His body shook and the sweat poured beneath his hat and coat, mixing with the snow that hit his face. He wanted to take off the coat; it weighed him down but he was too weak to shrug it from his shoulders. All he could do was hang on to the reins with his fingers twisted in the horse's mane. It wasn't his horse. His horse was lost.

"A lost sheep," Cade mumbled. "The shepherd will leave the ninety-nine to search for the one who's lost." A scripture he recalled from his childhood. From one of his father's sermons. He could see his father, standing in the smoke, his hands covered with his mother's blood. Then he couldn't see anything. The snow was too thick. The horse kept moving, plowing onward, in hopes of finding shelter from the storm.

"Gotta keep moving. No hope. No sheep. No shelter from the storm." He kept it up. Kept talking because it was the only way to keep the ghosts at bay. The only way to keep the horse moving through the storm. He talked until his voice was gone, barely rasping out the words.

The horse stopped. Cade realized they weren't moving and looked up. His lashes were frozen to his cheek and he had to blink several times to break them loose. He untangled his hands from the mane and slid from the horse into snow deep enough to cover his ankles. He kept his hands on the reins and struggled forward, his feet dragging through the snow as if each one weighed a ton, until he stood by the horse's head. The animal stood with his head down, blinking against the snow, and blowing from his labors. Cade looked up and saw an angel standing before him with its hands reaching for him, as if it would swoop him up into her arms and fly him to heaven.

"You're wrong," he said. "I'm going to hell."

TWO

"**D**odger! What are you barking at?" Leah Findley wiped her hands on the towel tucked in the apron she wore around her waist and walked down the narrow hallway to the front door of her house. Dodger, her black and white dog, whose mother was a shepherd and father was a traveling man, stood on his hind legs with his nose pressed to the glass. He looked over his shoulder and wagged his tail as Leah approached. He wanted out. Now.

Leah looked through the glass. Snow poured heavily onto the small town of Angel's End and made it impossible to see anything out in the street. The roads would be impassable by morning if not already. With the rate that the snow piled up outside, the small valley where Angel's End was located would be cut off for a while. Luckily this was not Leah's first winter in the Colorado mountains. She had worked very hard through late summer and into early fall to make sure she was well provisioned for the winter.

Firewood, nearly half of it split with her own hands, was neatly stacked and close at hand, and her root cellar was full of enough food to last until spring. Or so she hoped.

"If you want to go out and freeze your tail off then be my guest," Leah informed Dodger as she opened the door. "Just make sure you wipe your paws before you come back in."

Dodger, who was very used to her wry humor or immune to it, took off with a grateful yelp and bounded into the street. Thank God for Dodger. With him around she didn't feel quite so vulnerable. His barks sounded over the howl of the wind and the rattling of the windows. No doubt he was after some sort of creature looking for a place to ride out the storm. Dodger. Her protector. She was blessed.

I hope it's not a skunk. . . . The wily critters were notorious for coming out when the weather changed. If one was looking for a place to winter in town, they'd all suffer in the coming months.

"Thank you God, for Dodger and for this warm shelter from your storms," Leah said by way of a prayer. She tried to make it a habit to be grateful for her blessings every day. Some days it was easier than others to find things to be grateful for. However there was one very special blessing that she was consistently thankful for.

Leah stood in the doorway that led into her small parlor. Her six-year-old son, Banks, stretched out on the rug before the fire. He played with a battered set of painted wooden soldiers, busily lining them up only to shoot them down again with a toy cannon. His book lay forgotten on the floor next to him. The firelight cast an angelic glow upon his tousled golden hair. In Leah's vast experience with Banks, and his father, dead for four long years, firelight could be very deceptive.

"Did you finish your schoolwork?"

"Yes ma'am." He didn't look up from his play.

"Do your reading?"

"Five pages, just like you said." Banks looked at her side-ways with a half smile on his face. It was so much like his father's that Leah's heart flipped in her chest. It wasn't fair that Banks would never know his father or that Nate was murdered before his son was old enough to remember him. At times it was hard to be grateful. But at least she had Banks. She would never forget Nate or the love they shared. How could she when she saw him every time she looked at her son's face.

"Clean up your toys and get ready for bed." Morning would be here soon enough, especially for her, since half of the town would be expecting their breakfast at the Devil's Table café where she worked as a waitress and cook since Nate died. Being the widow of the town's sheriff didn't come with a pension. At least Nate had the foresight to ask for the rights to a piece of property in town and to build them a house which he finished right before Banks was born. It was a sturdy house with four rooms, two chimneys and a loft, along with a shed that housed a small flock of chickens and a root cellar. It wasn't the same as having a husband, but it was a comfort to know that as long as she stayed in Angel's End, she'd never be out on the street.

Instead of going about his tasks, Banks went to the parlor window that looked out onto the street. "What is Dodger barking at Momma?"

Leah lifted the curtain and peered out the window. The snow blew sideways now. Even though the snow was thick, Leah saw the glow of lamplight coming from the rooms above the café where Dusty, her boss, and owner of the Devil's Table, lived. Down the street the light from the Heaven's Gate Saloon was brighter. Leah couldn't see Dodger but she heard him, barking earnestly, as if he had something treed.

"I better get him before Bettina complains about the

noise." The grocer's wife was prone to complain about everything, from the temperature of the coffee Leah poured into her cup, to the color of cloth she bought to make a new apron.

"I thought she said the saloon made enough noise to wake the dead," Banks said. "Could she hear barking over that?"

"Bettina can hear everything," Leah said. "She has *special* ears."

"Don't you mean big, Momma?"

"I do," Leah said and yanked on a wayward lock of her son's bright hair. "But don't go telling anyone that."

Banks flashed his father's grin at her as they walked to the door. Leah grabbed her shawl from the hook and threw it over her shoulders. As soon as she stepped onto the porch she wished she had taken the time to put on her heavy winter coat. And her hat. And her gloves. The wind hit her with a blast of stinging ice that took her breath away. Leah pulled the shawl up tight around her neck and called for Dodger. He stopped barking, gave a high-pitched yip, and then started up again. She could hear him, but could not see him through the blowing snow.

"Stay here," she instructed Banks and stepped off the porch into the street. The wind was stronger now, swirling around her skirts and grabbing at her shawl. Tendrils of hair escaped the pins that held it captive and teased her face with their freedom before falling flat with moisture and sticking to her cheeks.

The main and only street of Angel's End sloped downhill. The entire valley was nothing more than a bowl, broader on the down end and narrow at the top. A stream tumbled down from the mountains and ran through the valley. Angel's End sat on the north side of it. Leah's house was on the upper end, with the only thing past it being the brand-new church. They'd found someone to come be their pastor, but so far, after four years, there'd been no takers on the sheriff's job.

Having your last one murdered in the street by a drunken outlaw wasn't much of a recommendation.

From the looks of things, they would be going a bit longer still without a pastor. There'd been talk that he'd be here before winter set in, but it was only talk. No one had heard from Pastor Key since August, when he'd accepted the job via letter. Leah had mixed feelings about his arrival. She was to provide room and board in exchange for a small pittance from the town. It wasn't much, but it would be enough to keep Banks in new shoes and a nice winter coat every year. She was anxious for the income, but not happy about having a stranger living in the house Nate built for her, even if he was a minister.

Leah wiped the snow from her face and plodded through the foot-deep snow to the stone statue of an angel that sat directly in the middle of the street. Luckily she still wore her knee-high boots or she would have floundered after the first few steps. The snow drifted badly, especially on her side of the street. She'd have to dig their way out of the house come morning.

A dark form that had to be Dodger stood on her side of the statue. The base, which the townspeople had built from piled stones to raise their angel up to a more heavenly height, was covered with a thick drift of snow. Leah's skirts drug with each step and grew heavy with moisture. Her shoulders were already covered with white, and her lashes stiff with frost.

"Dodger! Come here!"

Dodger ran a lap around the statue and yipped.

People were funny, Leah mused. Hauling a six-foot-tall stone statue of a winged angel out west only to abandon it in the middle of nowhere. How did they think they would get it over the mountains? Did they have no concept of how big the Rockies were when they struck out in the first place?

Leah didn't think they were any more foolish than those

who came along later and erected a town around the statue and then went so far as to name the town after it. The same people who, seven years ago, hired Nate to be sheriff. Angel's End, Colorado, located somewhere in the Rocky Mountains, just short of nowhere. Her home now. Dodger ran to her and whined. He crouched before her, his head on his forelegs and his rear in the air, and then with a bark he turned and ran ahead. Leah put her hand over her eyes to block the stinging snow. She saw something, a movement on the opposite side of the statue. Was someone there?

Leah looked toward Heaven's Gate. Light poured forth from the saloon but any sound that came from within was lost in the howl of the wind. She saw a few lights farther down the street. Most everyone was in their homes with their doors barred against the storm. All of the small businesses, the general store, the telegraph and stage office and bank, the assayer's office, the livery, were dark. Only the saloon showed signs of life. So what was moving around the statue?

Dodger came back for her again. If there was a threat he would have attacked. Leah rounded the statue to find a horse standing patiently. The animal's coat was covered with snow, but enough of it showed that she could see that it was either white or dappled. Which made it practically invisible in the storm. It jerked its head at her approach.

"What are you doing out here?" Leah cooed. She held her hand out beneath its nose and he nibbled at her palm. She didn't recognize the animal as belonging to any of the townspeople. "And where is your rider?" The horse wore full gear. Leah looked toward the saloon once more. When she found the idiot who left his horse out in this weather to suffer, he would definitely get a piece of her mind.

Leah took the reins. She pulled on them, determined to get the horse to the shelter of Martin's livery, but they were stuck. Dodger yipped again and dug at the snow that surrounded the angel. Leah yanked on the reins again. Were they frozen to the ground?

"Oh my goodness!" They were attached to a hand. Someone was buried in the snow. Leah dropped to her knees to help Dodger dig. Her hands, already chilled, turned to ice as they both flung the snow away. Dodger whined and stuck his nose in the man's face.

"Is he dead?" Dodger couldn't answer her. He looked at her expectantly. Leah pushed him out of the way. She shook her hands to relieve the numbness, slid them under her arms to warm them, and then touched the man's face. It was covered with frost, yet she felt heat coming from his skin. "He's burning up with fever." Leah was so accustomed to talking to Dodger as if he were human that it was second nature to her. She brushed the snow away from the man's head. His hair was dark, soaking wet and plastered around his face. He wore a heavy wool coat that reached to his knees. Even though he was crumpled in the snow she could tell by the breadth of his shoulders and length of his legs that he was big. Too big for her to move on her own.

Leah gathered her skirts and quickly made her way to the saloon. The wind gusted as she pushed the door open. It flew out of her hand and hit the wall behind with a bang. Ward Phillips, the owner of Heaven's Gate and Jacob Reece, a local rancher, both reached for their guns with the noise but relaxed when they saw it was her. Priscilla, who waited tables, gave her a friendly wave and Bob the bartender nodded from behind the bar. Leah recognized a few of the cowboys from Jake's ranch and some of the miners who were scattered about as frequenters of the Devil's Table.

"I need help," Leah said.

Jacob jumped up so quickly that his chair fell over backward. "What's wrong? Are you hurt? Is it Banks?" Concern flashed across his handsome face as his gray eyes looked her over for any sign of injury.

Once more Leah felt the guilt of not being able to return Jake's feelings for her. How could she ever love another man after what she had with Nate? Yet Jake didn't want to take no for an answer, as he'd made it very plain that he would wait her out until she came to her senses. "N-n-no." Her teeth chattered. "There's a m-m-man in the snow." Jake looked past Leah into the night. He took the time to grab his coat from a hook and place it over Leah's shoulders before he went out.

"What kind of man?" Ward was a few years older than Jake and far more jaded. His coal black eyes avoided her gaze as he asked his question, searching out the window. Even though she'd forgiven him, he had yet to forgive himself for not being there the day Nate was shot down on the street.

Leah pulled Jake's coat close and immediately felt warmer. "A sick man," Leah replied with a shrug. Ward gave Bob a look that said *don't give away the place while I'm gone* and followed Jake.

"As if it makes a difference," Priscilla said, "what kind of man it is." She was sweet to everyone, no matter what the situation. "Obviously he's hurt and needs help." She put her tray on the bar and went for her coat.

"It could be an Indian," one of the miners volunteered.

He wasn't Indian. Leah wouldn't dignify that statement. "He's burning up with a fever," she said.

"Hope he don't have the pox," another miner said.

Miners. They stuck together like glue, yet were afraid everyone was after their claims. There was nothing more to say. Leah went back out into the night and Priscilla followed with a lantern.

"Holy Mother of God," Priscilla exclaimed when the wind hit her. "It's colder than a nun's lonely bed out here." Pris had been raised in a Catholic orphanage. She'd left it behind when she was sixteen and headed west. She knew at a young age that her personality was better suited to the atmosphere of a saloon than a convent. "Hard to believe it's only the middle of October."

"I was just thinking the same thing," Leah admitted. Dodger stood in the snow, halfway between the statue and the saloon, anxiously awaiting her return and yet not giving up on his rescue. Jake and Ward were already with the man. Ward took something from the man's pocket and walked to a pool of light that poured from Heaven's Gate's window.

Priscilla held the lantern over the man while Jake turned him onto his back. He unbuttoned the thick coat, and pushed aside another one beneath. The lamplight was not needed to see the dark frosty patch of blood that covered his shirt.

"He's been shot." Jake's diagnosis was quick, yet accurate. "We need to see if the bullet's still inside him."

"You can put him in my bed," Priscilla volunteered brightly.

"Pris," Leah chided.

"Have you looked at him? He's gorgeous."

Leah couldn't admit in front of Jake that she had. Not that it meant anything. Jake was as handsome as sin if you liked the carved from stone type.

"Pris, you are going straight to hell," Ward said. "According to this letter I found in his pocket, this is our new pastor, Timothy Key."

"What a waste," Pris sighed. She tilted her head to get a better look. "If the priests back in Boston had looked like this I might have stuck around."

"Maybe he'll inspire you to repent," Jake said as he tucked the coat back around Pastor Key. "That's supposed to be his job after all." Jake scooped up a handful of snow to clean his hands as he stood.

"From the looks of him he might not live that long," Pris said.

"God only knows." Ward stuck the letter inside his coat. "I guess we best take him to Leah's place."

"My place?" Leah's heart jumped in panic against her breast. The wind swirled around the statue and picked up her skirts.

"Isn't that where he's supposed to live?"

Visions of Nate when he was carried into their home, blood pouring from his chest, staining his clothes, the sheets, the mattress, and even the apron she wore filled her mind. Memories of the frustration that no matter what she did, she couldn't stop the flow of blood. Of knowing he was dying right before her eyes. Of keeping Banks from the room so he would not be haunted with nightmares of his father's death. The plaintive sound of Dodger howling when Nate finally gasped out his last panicked breath.

Dodger looked at her hopefully and gave a slight wag of his tail. "Bring him on," Leah sighed. "It's not as if we've got a doctor to take care of him."

"Leah, are you sure you want to do this?" Jake asked.

The plain and simple truth was, there was no place else to take him. There was no way they could take a preacher to the saloon, especially a Baptist preacher. God would surely strike them dead. The Swansons, even with all of Bettina's posturing, were not that charitable, although she did deign to let the schoolmarm, Margy Ashburn, live with them. Jim Martin, the blacksmith, and his wife, Gretchen, were generous people, but had no room in their house next to the livery since they were the parents of three sets of twins and had Gretchen's grandmother living with them.

Jake's ranch was too far away. He'd likely be staying in one of Ward's rooms tonight. Zeke Preston, the assayer, was about as friendly as a rattlesnake. There was Dusty . . . but Dusty was Dusty and about as predictable as the weather. The other few families that lived close to Angel's End were full up, another reason Leah was chosen to board the preacher in the first place.

They were waiting on her. As they waited for her mind

to stop its dithering, Pastor Key could freeze to death. "I'm sure."

"Pris, take the horse over to Jim's," Ward instructed as he and Jake picked up the preacher. "Dang," he grunted. "He's pretty solid for a preacher."

"Go tell Gus too," Jake said.

"What if his wife answers the door?" Pris complained. "I'm not walking all the way down there in this weather in these shoes just to be left out on the step freezing my backside."

"He's the mayor, Pris," Jake said. "He should be told." He shifted Pastor Key's shoulders into a better position with his knee. "I wonder how he got shot." Jake grunted with his heavy burden.

The wind whipped against Leah's body and she practically had to bend over to make any headway up the street. With Dodger bounding excitedly ahead of her, she let her mind race with the impossible task set before her.

Bandages. She'd need bandages. And hot water. *What else?* Something for the pain; no doubt Ward would recommend whiskey. Well then he could supply it. *Oh my goodness, I can't give whiskey to a preacher.* If only she knew more about herbs and such like the Indians used. What if the bullet was still inside him? They wouldn't expect her to dig it out would they? Not after she'd failed with Nate. It had been in too deep and she couldn't get a hold of it. He'd screamed in agony when she tried. Why, oh why, Lord, didn't they have a doctor in town. Wouldn't it make more sense to save lives instead of souls? Or course, it wasn't that often that men showed up shot on the streets of Angel's End. Only twice to her knowledge.

She'd been expecting a boarder, not a patient. She'd hoped Pastor Key would spend his time visiting the ranchers and miners that lived around Angel's End and his limited time at her house would be used for private prayer and preparation for his Sunday sermons. Dusty had begrudgingly agreed to feed him his three meals a day. Maybe both of them needed a lesson in giving. *And who better to deliver it than a preacher?*

His room was sort of ready. She'd been postponing moving Banks up to the loft, certain the preacher would not show up until spring. Jim was supposed to hang doors to the bedrooms, once he got done making them. She could only hope that it wouldn't take him too long to finish them.

Banks stood on the porch. Luckily he had enough sense to put his coat on but the door was open, which meant the house was filling up with cold air. Dodger barked joyfully. Obviously proud of his success, he waited on the porch for Leah to congratulate him. All she could do was touch his head as she hustled Banks inside.

"Go get your stuff from your room," she instructed. "The new preacher is here and he's hurt."

Banks watched wide-eyed as Ward and Jake stomped on the porch and into the house with their burden. "What happened to him?"

"He got shot," Ward said.

"Ward!" Leah hissed.

"Hey, it's a fact of life. You think he's going to grow up out here and not know what guns do?" They stood in the hallway as wind brushed by them from the open door.

"Ward, Banks is Leah's son. She gets to decide how to raise him," Jake said.

"Where are we putting the not-shot patient?" Ward asked dryly.

"In here." Leah led them to the second bedroom, behind the parlor and across from hers. She threw back the blanket and quilt. Turned up the lamp that hung from a hook over the bedside table, out of Banks's reach.

"Banks. Stuff. Dodger. Out." Everything was happening too fast. There were six bodies in the room, counting

Dodger. Jake, Ward and their burden seemed impossibly big in such a small space. It was all too much. More than she could handle.

"Let's get these clothes off of him or he'll wind up soaking the bed when he thaws out," Ward said. "We'll hold him and you strip him." The preacher was propped between the two men with his head lolling forward, oblivious to everything. Even bent over as he was, Leah could see that he was taller than both Ward and Jake.

"I'll do it." Jake pulled the coat down over the side he held.

"Geez, Jake, Leah was married. I'm pretty sure she's seen a naked man before." Ward seemed to be enjoying himself at both Leah and Jake's expense. He was usually busy snarling and being the voice of doom and gloom. "Or have you decided to go sweet on the preacher man?"

Jake didn't dignify Ward's comments with an answer. "I swear Ward, I'm going to strike you dead unless God does it first." Leah hissed. "Banks is standing right here." Indeed he was. His bright blue eyes looked between the three men and Leah with concerned fascination. "Take your stuff to my room sweetie, you can sleep with me tonight." She knew she wouldn't be in her bed this night and it was freezing in the loft. "Take Dodger with you."

Between the two of them Jake and Ward managed to get the heavy coat off, and followed that with a black frock coat. They held him up and looked at Leah. With a sigh she attacked his shirt. "Sit him down on the bed so I can get those clothes off."

"Woohoo!" Another cold draft of air accompanied Bettina's arrival. Leah didn't bother unbuttoning the preacher's shirt, instead she jerked it, and the thick undershirt beneath, over his head.

"For heaven's sake Leah, what are you doing to our minister?" Bettina cried out from the hallway.

Leah looked down. Blood gushed from his wound. In her haste to remove his clothing, she'd torn off the bandage frozen to his skin. Dang it all! Leah moved quickly to stop the flow of blood. She refused to let another man die under her care.

THREE

"**P**lease God . . . I can't do this. Not again." Leah stood in the doorway, looking in on her patient. How long she had stood there she couldn't say. She needed to move, to do something else for him. But what? Her grandmother's cuckoo clock, which hung between Banks's room—*no Pastor Key's room*—and the parlor, popped out of its tiny door and announced the time with twelve quick repetitions of its song. The door to its house snapped shut and the clock resumed its steady tick-tick-tick. Outside the wind still howled and tiny shards of ice pelted against the windows along the back of the house. Behind her she heard the softly comforting breathing of her son as he slept. Dodger lay at the foot of the bed, gently snoring in time with Banks.

The scene before her was not so peaceful. Pastor Key had been lucky, according to Jake. The bullet had gone straight through, evident when they found the exit wound in his back. It hadn't been too difficult to get the bleeding stopped, even though she was as nervous as a cat in a room full of rockers, what with Bettina telling her everything she did was wrong and Gus wringing his hands at the new minister's unexpected arrival and impending death. Thank goodness they'd both gone home, and Ward soon after them.

She'd done all she could for the wound. The trouble was, she didn't know what more she could do for the fever. Her patient wrenched his head back and forth on the pillow with jerking motions. She could only imagine that he was lost in dreams of some sort, brought on by the fever.

Jake came through the back door with another load of firewood and Leah ran to push the door shut behind him. "You don't have to do this, Jake."

"You've got enough on your plate without having to worry about the fire going out." Jake walked down the hall and into the parlor and dropped his load on the already overflowing wood box. "By the way, I found a rattler curled up in your stack." He looked over his shoulder at her while he returned a few stray pieces. "He's not feeling the cold anymore."

Leah suppressed a shiver. She hated snakes with a passion. And once more she was indebted to Jake. The side of beef in her cellar was courtesy of him. She was shameless where Banks was concerned and Jake well knew her weakness.

"Are you sure you don't want me to stay here?" he asked.

"I'll— We'll be fine," she assured him. "You've got a ranch to take care of."

"There won't be much ranching going on while this snow keeps up." Jake stood, brushed off his hands and looked at her, his clear gray eyes, as always, looking for some sign from her.

Leah gathered her shawl around her shoulders.

"Yeah . . . well . . . I guess I'll be going." He pulled on his heavy coat, hanging over the back of a chair. "I'll be at Ward's if you need anything."

"Thanks, Jake." Leah quickly looked away. The constant disappointment that showed in his eyes was more than she could stand at the moment. She leaned her forehead against the door when it closed behind him. No matter how much Jake wanted it, she couldn't bring herself to love him. She respected him, liked him, enjoyed his company, but the only thing she felt for him was friendship. Was it wrong of her to think he deserved more in a wife? He was a wonderful man, strong, generous and handsome. He should have a woman who was madly in love with him.

I'm just being selfish. Was it greedy of her to want the same love she'd had with Nate twice in one lifetime? Or had she lost her one chance of a happily-ever-after ending to an outlaw with a gun?

He'd be such a great father for Banks . . .

"NO!"

Leah ran to Pastor Key's bedside. He struggled beneath the weight of the sheets and blankets. He pushed them down below his waist and his arms flailed at his hips, searching for something seen only in his feverish state.

"Shhh," Leah said. She smoothed his damp, dark hair back from his broad forehead. He responded to her touch, turning his face into her hand. He inhaled against her palm as if he were Dodger, tracing a strange scent. He murmured something in an unrecognizable language and fumbled with the blankets.

Leah rinsed out a cloth from the bowl of melted snow on the bedside table and placed it on his forehead. It quieted him somewhat, so she moved the chair closer and sat down to study her patient in peace.

The lamplight cast a small circle of light over his head

and chest. His hair was a rich dark brown, and long, as if he'd missed a few haircuts. It curled in more directions than she could count, wild from his snowy ride and fever. His forehead was broad, his eyes deep set beneath thick dark brows.

I wonder what color his eyes are . . . Brown?

His nose was long and straight, perfectly proportioned to the shape of his face. She took it all in as she wrung out the cloth once more; his fever was so hot that the cloth dried almost as soon as she put it on his forehead.

"No," he said again.

Leah stared at his mouth. The flash of teeth when he spoke showed them to be perfectly aligned and surprisingly white. His lower lip was thicker than the top and his mouth mobile, moving in interesting ways as he drifted into his conversation with whatever demons haunted his dreams.

I wonder what he looks like when he smiles . . .

Leah wrung out the cloth again. His chest was covered with sweat so she wiped across it, amazed at the breadth of it, and the smoothness. Nate's chest had been sprinkled with crisp blond curls so the absence fascinated her. He was dark too, his chest, back and arms tanned olive, contrasting greatly with the white bandage she'd wrapped around his abdomen and the flash of pale buttocks she'd seen when Jake and Ward finished the job of stripping him before placing him beneath the blankets. The tan had to be from physical labor as he was covered with muscles, each one well defined, even the corded ones on either side of his taut belly that trailed down beneath the sheets. She could well imagine him being the type of minister that held barn raisings, swinging a hammer and easily lifting beams, all with his shirt off.

Leah felt her cheeks flame. "You're having lustful thoughts . . . about a preacher." She put her fingers to her lips, embarrassed that she'd chastised herself out loud. Had he heard her? Did her words register in his subconscious? Would he look down at her from the pulpit and scold her for being a woman of loose morals?

"No . . . no . . . stop . . . please stop . . ."

Leah placed the cloth on his forehead once more.

"Is he going to make it?" Pris asked Ward as he entered the Heaven's Gate Saloon. Ward walked directly to the bar and poured himself a shot of whiskey.

"I reckon that's up to the good Lord and Leah Findley," he said after he'd tossed back the shot. He poured another one to chase off the bone-chilling cold that came from standing in the street talking to Gus Swanson about the preacher's dramatic arrival to town. "Hand me another glass," he said to Bob. "Jake should be here soon."

He looked around the empty saloon. "We rent out some rooms?" he asked.

"Two," Bob replied. "The miners took one and once those cowpokes figured out Pris wasn't interested they took another." He wiped a towel down the bar. "I'm turning in."

Ward tipped his glass toward Bob as he went into his room in the back. Pris yawned and laid her head down on the bar.

"Go on to bed," Ward said. "Nothing else is going to happen tonight."

"Are you sure Jake's coming here?" Pris thought her crush on Jake was a secret and it mostly was. But Ward knew how to read people better than most, and Pris showed the same signs of yearning for Jake that Jake showed for Leah. It was a big old circle of unrequited love that kept Ward well entertained.

"Leah won't have Jake to stay if that's what you mean." Ward poured a shot into Jake's glass and pushed it toward Pris. "Why should tonight be any different?"

"That good-looking preacher is there."

"Are you thinking about switching religions Pris?"

Pris grinned. "A girl can dream, can't she?"

"Go to bed. Jake won't be in a mood to talk when he gets here."

Pris drank the shot and climbed the stairs to the second floor. There were eight rooms above, two of which were Ward's, one belonged to Priscilla and the rest he rented out on nights like tonight. Ward made a decent living with Heaven's Gate and for the most part he enjoyed it. There was no better place to study your fellow man than a saloon.

The wind grabbed the door and banged it back against the wall. The half doors, used only in summer slapped back and forth as they came loose with the abruptness of Jake's entrance. Jake wrestled them back into place, jerked off his gloves, threw them on the bar and threw back the shot Ward poured for him.

"That was an interesting turn of events." Ward poured them both another shot. A cold draft swirled around their legs as both men leaned against the bar.

"He's a bit younger than I expected," Jake said.

"He's a bit more shot than I expected," Ward replied. He knew Jake was already worried about the competition for Leah's heart, but he was feeling generous so didn't say anything about it. "I wonder what happened to him."

"He ran afoul of someone, that's for sure."

"Bad night for it." Ward studied Jake over his glass. How much longer before he realized that Leah just wasn't interested in him? "Leah felt like she could handle it on her own?"

"What's to handle?" Jake replied. "The bullet passed through, live or die, now it's up to God, not Leah."

"She'll do what she can for him."

Jake shrugged. "That's all anyone can ask of her." His voice was tight and his words clipped. Yep, she'd shot him down. Ward opened his mouth to speak.

"Don't," Jake said. "Just don't." He jerked on his gloves. "I'm going home."

"In this mess?"

"I've got a ranch to run."

"Yeah, good luck with that when you're frozen and the wolves are chewing on your bones."

"Not all of us have saloons to hide in Ward." Jake stomped out not bothering to close the door behind him. The wind caught it once more and kicked it back against the wall. Ward put the lid back on the whiskey bottle and shivered as he pushed the door shut. It was a bad night out, but Jake was a grown man. He'd make it home, just out of pure stubbornness. Ward went back to the bar and opened a locked cabinet beneath the till. He took a cigar from a wooden box, clipped its end and lit it. He looked around the empty saloon, at the polished bar, the mirror that hung behind the tables scattered about and the staircase that led to the rooms. Satisfied that everything was as it should be, he went to the battered piano and sat down to play.

He couldn't fight her alone. She was too much for him, just as she'd been too much for him when he was younger. Cade tried to push Letty away but she wouldn't go. She clung to him like a tick. She crawled on top of him, pulled at his shirt, and clawed his chest. He was hot, slick with sweat and she used it to move her body against him like a snake slithering through a puddle. If Jasper came in and found her on him he'd kill them both for sure and then tell his friend to make sure Brody died. Why wouldn't she leave him alone?

"I know what you want." She took his earlobe in her mouth and bit down.

"I don't . . . stop . . . please . . ." The things he felt, it couldn't be right. The way his body reacted. It had to be wrong. Cade saw it happening. He was outside himself, watching his sixteen-year-old self from above, yet he still felt the evilness of her touch. His skin crawled. If only he could make her stop. He had to get away. He had to get away from Letty, yet he felt paralyzed, helpless, and trapped.

No more. Never again. He wasn't a boy now. He was a man. Wasn't he? How could he be both?

Hell . . . I'm in hell . . . It had to be. He was dead and in hell. He heard the screams of the condemned howling around him. He was burning up and his punishment was to watch his sins, each one as he committed it, over and over again. There was one comfort at least. If he was in hell then Letty and Jasper were too.

She's here . . . she's here . . . God. Please. No. He had to get away from her. He had to. He couldn't live it again. He'd fight her. Like he should have fought her before but he was too damn scared at the time. Scared for himself, and scared for Brody.

Cade pushed at her with arms that had no strength. He willed his legs, legs that felt as if they were no longer connected to his body, to move. He felt himself, in two different places, one on the bed beneath Letty and the other floating on the ceiling, watching. Surely the two Cades could fight her together. Surely the two of them could move as one.

Letty laughed. She kissed his neck, then moved her mouth down his chest, licking and nipping his skin. The bed held him prisoner. The blankets twisted around his legs, holding him like chains. His gut twisted in pain and his chest ached with the effort. He had to get away. He must. *I must!*

Leah's chair tipped, startling her from her troubled sleep. She blinked and jerked quickly to attention. "Banks?" She was in his room, next to his bed. The lamp was turned down low and showed the empty sheets torn loose and rumpled as if a wrestling match had occurred. Awareness hit her like the cold wind that howled outside. Not Banks. Banks was safe and asleep in her bed with Dodger by his side. *Pastor Key.*

"No."

Leah stood and turned up the lamp. The glow lit the upper part of the tiny room, casting a circle of warmth to fight the cold darkness that seemed to creep through the walls with the blizzard that still screamed outside. Her patient stood in the corner, next to the window, on the opposite side of the bed. He trembled, with his arms crossed before his face, his palms facing outward, his head bent, as if he were waiting for a heavy blow to strike him down.

Leah took a cautious step toward him. "Pastor Key?"

"No. I won't let you." He turned to her, his eyes dark, unfocused, seeing something within. Something terribly frightening by the look on his face. "No more. Never again."

"You're safe," Leah said. *I should have let Jake stay . . . I can't handle this . . .* She took a step around the bed. "Oh my goodness."

He was naked. His flanks, starkly white against the planked walls took her by surprise. It shouldn't have been a shock; after all she knew he was naked before, when he was under the blankets. It was just that male part of him, that very male part of him, was where her attention was drawn.

"God forgive me," Leah said. Heat flooded her face and she put her hands up to cover her cheeks. It was not as if he knew, he was out of his head with fever. If he made it . . . *God please let him make it . . .* she'd never be able to look him in the eye. She'd seen Pris make the sign of the cross on her forehead, chest and shoulders when she did something that she knew was a sin. Leah would have done the same now, if she hadn't been so scared she'd do it wrong and offend the Lord even more.

She swallowed hard. "Pastor Key?"

He jammed his palms to his eyes. "No. Not him. No." He dropped his hands and turned to her. His eyes were brown, as she'd expected. But more than brown, they were sad, as if there was no hope left in the world. "He's not here." So very sad. He gazed at her, unseeing and a tear trickled down his cheek. "Please don't let him be here."

Leah took the last few steps and caught him as he started to slide down the wall. "You need to lie down. It's all right. You're safe. Everything will be fine." She didn't really know what she said; she just knew she needed to soothe him to get him back into bed. She grabbed his arms. He was so solid and much taller than she was, but she was strong from hard work and she managed to get a grip and sling his arm over her shoulder.

He fought to stay upright and she placed her arm around his waist to steady him. He was bleeding again. She was a horrible nurse. Horrible. It would be a miracle if he survived.

"Let's get you back to bed," she said. They staggered forward the few steps until she was able to drop him none too gently on the bed. Leah straightened the sheets and blankets and tried her best to keep her eyes averted until she was able to cover him. She checked his wound by pulling the wrapping back. All she could do was place more padding against it and hope it would be enough to curtail the bleeding. She wrung out the cloth again and turned to place it on his forehead. He was looking at her with his very brown, very sad eyes.

"Who are you?" His voice cracked on the words.

"I'm Leah."

"What did you do?" He closed his eyes once more.

"Angels can't be in hell." He gasped and his head dropped to the side with an exhalation.

Oh my God. He's dead. Please God, don't let him be dead. Leah leaned in closer. She bent her head, her ear close to his mouth, and near his chest. Was he breathing? "Pastor Key?"

He sighed deeply and then spoke again. "No."

Why was she here? The angel. The angel who found him in the cold. But if she was an angel, why did she take him to hell? Maybe she wasn't. Maybe she was just more of the punishment. But maybe, just maybe she could get a message to Timothy. She could tell him he was sorry. She was close by. He couldn't see her, but he knew she was there.

"Tell him I'm sorry," Cade said. Was it possible that she could reach him? Tell him?

"It's hell . . . anything is possible." Jasper leaned over him and laughed.

"You might have gotten me but you didn't get my brother."

"Yes I did." Jasper stepped back and swung his arm out, just like he used to during his cons with the medicine show. The insidious smile was definitely the same, so what came next would be evil. It always was in the past. What was he up to?

Cade saw himself as a boy, much younger this time. He was with Brody and his father stood behind the two of them. His father smiled, the same generous smile he'd give before he began one of his sermons. He placed his hands upon their heads, one on Cade's, one on Brody's. He ruffled their hair. Then he knelt down between them, slid his hands down their backs and shoved them. Cade felt his body stumble forward. He spread his arms out to catch himself but Jasper caught him instead and another man came in and snatched up Brody and ran with him.

"Poppa! No! Please Poppa come back for us." Cade watched as his father shook his head, turned and walked away. He left them. Even though Cade knew it happened many years ago, he felt the terror and loneliness all over again.

Because he was in hell.

FOUR

"What do you see in your dreams that are so horrible?" Leah stood over her patient's bed, jammed her fists in the small of her back and stretched. She'd kept up her vigil in the chair all night, terrified to sleep lest Pastor Key leap from the bed again and do more damage to his wound, or worse, scare Banks with his worrisome fretting. "What could a minister do that was so horrible that he has nightmares?"

Her patient tossed his head in response, his words lost in a quick mumble. Heat still radiated from his body. How long could a body survive such a fever? The water in the bowl was tepid and the cloth stale. Fortunately there was plenty of snow available.

Leah was stiff for the first few steps into the hall. Dodger greeted her with a yawn and a stretch as he jumped from her bed.

"Don't get used to it," Leah reminded him. As if she could stop him. Dodger slept at the foot of Banks's bed every night. She looked longingly at the bed, and at Banks curled beneath the quilts. If only she could crawl beneath their warmth and sleep for a week. But she couldn't. There was too much that needed doing. Dodger padded down the hall to the back door and even though the fire needed stoking, Leah agreed that the call of nature should come first.

The door was frozen shut. It took quite a bit of determination and stubbornness on Leah's part to finally wrench it open. Dodger tried to help by scratching at the doorjamb. A wall of snow, as high as Leah's waist, greeted them. Luckily it was frozen so hard that it remained in place. Leah looked mournfully at the outhouse that stood some thirty paces away next to the shed. The rising sun was hidden behind a heavy cover of clouds. The snow and wind were gone, leaving behind a quiet emptiness and a strange foreboding.

"It's going to be a long, long day."

Dodger whined and touched the wall of snow with his paw.

"Tell me about it." Leah picked the dog up and with a grunt, sat him on top of the snow. "I think Banks has finally passed you on weight," she said as she once more stretched her back. Dodger's paws scrambled for purchase as he slid about a foot down the drift but the snow held him and he made his way on skittering feet past the porch posts and out toward the shed.

Leah went to the kitchen for the pail and grabbed her coat from the peg. She should have brought in the washtub before the snow fell, but she'd forgotten with all the other preparations she made, and now it was buried under a three-foot, frozen blanket. It would have made for less work in melting the snow for water.

Leah checked on Banks, who had not moved and on her patient, who had rolled over on his side with his back toward the door. She studied the long length of his spine for a moment. The width of his shoulders. The definition of the muscles that showed beneath his tanned skin. *How is it a man who's traveled all the way from Ohio in autumn can spend so much time in the sun?* Maybe it was a good sign that he'd rolled over. Maybe he would rest easier now and find some escape from his fevered nightmares.

Leah briefly debated going outside at all. She knew she could take the easy way out and use the chamber pot but she figured the exercise and the frigid air would do her a world of good and would wake her up enough to deal with the tasks that awaited her. Leah put on her gloves and chiseled some steps in the snow with her hands, throwing the excess snow in the bucket. Using her makeshift staircase, she climbed to the top of the snowdrift. Dodger, done with his business, ran back and greeted her as she slid down the opposite side.

Leah grinned as she rose to her feet and looked back at the way she'd come. Getting back in might not be so easy. A shovel stood against the porch rail and she wrenched it free. Walking to the outhouse was a balancing act and she was thrilled that she made it without falling. Even more so when she was able to free the door after a few sharp jabs with the shovel.

She came out to find Dodger rushing around on top of the snow, searching for familiar scents, wagging his tail when he found a new one. Leah closed her eyes, turned a slow circle and breathed in the crisp, cold air. "We made it through the night Lord, and for that I am grateful. Please give me the strength and wisdom I need to make it through this coming day." She opened her eyes and stared up at the thick gray clouds. They weren't done with Angel's End.

Nature was taking a rest, gathering its strength for the next onslaught. Just as she was. But first she needed to check on her chickens.

The drifting wasn't as bad around the shed door. Plus she had the added benefit of it opening inward. The chickens stirred when she came in, raising sleepy heads and staring at her with their black beady eyes. Her little banty rooster rushed over to investigate the intrusion. He swelled up the speckled feathers on his chest and stretched his head up, trying with all his might to appear larger than he really was. "Go on Roscoe." Leah nudged him with her foot and he strutted away with his shiny black tail feathers twitching with indignation.

Leah laughed at his antics and grabbed the dipper from the hook, stuck it in the bag and scattered feed on the floor. The hens quickly abandoned their nests to join in the scramble for every last bite. Leah took her basket from the shelf and gathered the eggs that were left behind. Leah checked the water pan. The top was frozen over so she chipped it free and left, satisfied that the chickens would survive another day of bad weather.

"Momma!" Banks's cry was shrill, panicked. Leah took off at a run. She slipped, and fell forward on her hands. The basket landed on the snow and the eggs tumbled out and cracked except for one that bounced and rolled away. Leah ignored the mess. Her boots gave her no traction as she fought her way forward. Finally she was able to stand and move. Dodger bounded toward the door with a sharp growl, scrabbled his way over the drift and disappeared just as Leah slid under the porch overhang.

Banks called out again. Leah went through the door headfirst and landed on her outstretched arms. Her coat and skirts flew up around her waist as she flopped over and scrambled to her feet.

"Banks?"

"In here." His voice came from his room, not hers. Leah grabbed on to the door frame as she skidded to a stop. Dodger stood in the room with the ruff of his neck standing straight up. A low growl rumbled in his throat as he stared up at Banks and Pastor Key.

"You've got to get away Brody," Pastor Key said. "It's not safe here." He stood in front of Banks, who peered around his naked hip with his eyes as big as she'd ever seen them. Pastor Key's deep brown eyes held the vacant stare from the night before. He was dreaming again, once more fighting his unseen demons.

"Banks," Leah said gently. "Come here."

God please don't let Banks get hurt . . . please . . .

Banks tried to step out and Pastor Key pinned him against the wall with his arm. "I won't let him take you."

Dodger lowered the front half of his body and snarled.

"He won't let me," Banks said.

"Dodger! Down!" Leah was afraid that Banks would get hurt if Dodger attacked. Dodger growled and flattened his ears but stayed in place.

"Pastor Key." Leah spoke slowly and quietly, even though her heart raced. "I need you to let my son go."

He tilted his head and his eyes focused on her for a moment. "Mother?"

"Yes, I'm his mother." Leah stretched out her hand. "Let my son come to me please."

"You came for us." A smile lit his face. His mouth widened and deep creases showed in his cheeks and around his eyes.

"Yes . . . I came for you. Now let him come to me." Leah motioned for Banks with her hand. Banks slipped by the pastor and ran to Leah. Leah grabbed him to her and turned away, taking him from the room and across the hall into hers. Dodger followed, jumping up against her side to sniff Banks, making sure in his own way that he was unhurt.

"Are you all right?" She sat down on the bed and rocked him, more for her benefit than his. *He's fine, he's fine, he's fine . . . Thank you God, he's fine . . .*

"He didn't hurt me," Banks said. "I think he was scared of something."

"You stay away from him until he's better."

"I'm sorry Momma. I went to get my book."

"Next time ask me to get anything you left in there."

"I will."

She heard the crash; she knew Pastor Key would eventually fall when she left the room. She couldn't be so lucky to hope that he'd find his own way back to bed, but she really didn't care. Banks was fine. That was all she could concentrate on at the moment. Leah knew she'd eventually have to get Pastor Key back up by herself and could only pray that his wound hadn't started bleeding again.

She stood Banks on the floor. "Can you go stoke the fire for me?"

"Yes Momma."

She straightened his blond curls with her hand. "In the stove too."

"I will."

Leah touched his cheek. "I'll come fix your breakfast in a minute."

Banks nodded. "Is the preacher going to die like my daddy?"

"I don't know sweetie. All we can do is help him the best we can, pray and leave the rest up to God."

Banks nodded. "I'll say a prayer for him when we have grace."

"I think that would be a good thing." She grabbed him to her for a hug and kissed the top of his head. "Go and do your chores."

"I gotta go to the outhouse first."

"Put your coat on and be careful. It's slick out there."

Leah helped Banks and Dodger out the door before she turned once more to her patient. He lay curled on his side on the floor, still slick with fever. "Pants," she said as she went to his side. "The man definitely needs some pants."

FIVE

Pastor Key did not look well at all. Leah caught her bottom lip between her teeth as she studied her patient. Luckily his morning escapade had not resulted in more bleeding but his fever seemed to be hotter than ever. She'd tried dribbling some water into his mouth but that had only resulted in most of it spilling onto the sheets. "You are stubborn, that's for sure," she said as she looked at him. "Handsome and stubborn. How did someone like you wind up being a preacher?"

His head moved restlessly on the pillow as he mumbled. Either he was getting weaker or his nightmares weren't as bad. She was afraid it was the former.

"Here's more snow, Momma." Banks carried the pail with both hands. Leah had put him to work scooping the snow at the doorway. The chore served two purposes. One, it would make it easier for them, especially Dodger, to get in and out, and two, it was an easy source of water. Plus it kept Banks busy while she took care of her patient.

"Thank you sweetie. Just leave it by the door." She didn't want Banks anywhere near the preacher until she was certain he'd regained enough of his senses not to accidentally hurt her son.

Leah picked up a handful of snow and placed it in the bowl to melt. Her hands, already chapped from the cold, burned from the frosty snow, so she blew on them in a feeble attempt to relieve the pain. Residual moisture dripped from her fingers. She looked at her hand, then at the snow. An idea formed in her mind so she scooped up a handful, opened the preacher's mouth and dropped it inside. "There," she said with some satisfaction. "Water." Just to make sure, she put her finger beneath his chin to keep it closed. "At least it will be eventually."

The corners of his mouth turned up in a quick smile and a soft sigh sounded in his throat.

" 'For I was hungry, and you fed me; I was thirsty, and you gave me drink; I was a stranger, and you took me in.' " Leah wiped his feverish brow. "I'm not sure of the wording but I know it's a scripture. Perhaps when you're feeling better you can tell me what chapter and verse."

"Momma, the Martins are here." Dodger's deep bark confirmed it.

Now that was surprising. The snow was so deep that Dusty hadn't opened. He just yelled across the street for her to stay home and take care of the preacher. Funny how word got around, even in the middle of a blizzard.

Leah wiped her hands and went to the door. Jim and Gretchen came in, Jim with a steaming pot in his gloved hands and Gretchen with a basket. "How is he?" Gretchen asked.

"Still alive."

"That's a good sign," Jim said. Leah followed them into the kitchen. Jim put the pot on the woodstove and Gretchen took off her gloves and went immediately to work, unpacking the basket. Jim went down the hall to get a peek at the new preacher. Banks stayed by the table, and watched each item that came out of Gretchen's basket hit the table. Dodger did the same from the floor, his dark eyes hopeful that something would fall his way.

"Nonnie said we're going to get ice starting this afternoon." Nonnie was Gretchen's seventy-year-old German grandmother. Gretchen's mother had died soon after her daughter's marriage, so Nonnie had made the trip west with Gretchen and Jim, riding the entire way in the back of Jim's wagon, along with his smithy supplies. She'd also delivered all three sets of Gretchen's twins and Banks. If Nonnie said an ice storm was coming, then Leah was inclined to believe her.

"We brought soup for your patient, fresh bread, butter, some jam and Nonnie's apple strudel." Gretchen continued, "Also Nonnie made some of her salve. She said it cures everything from dry skin to foot rot."

Leah made a face. "I'm pretty sure that's not an issue, although I haven't really looked at his feet." Leah picked up the small jar. "But I will try it on my hands."

"From what I heard, it's his face that needs looking at." Leah looked at her in confusion. "He's handsome?" Gretchen said when she realized her attempt at a joke had failed.

"I'm beginning to wonder if I missed a party last night," Leah said as she rubbed the salve into her hands. She held them beneath her nose and smiled as she smelled the faint scent of roses. Gretchen has a climbing rose on the side of her porch, carefully carried out west from Pennsylvania and tenderly nurtured. Its blossoms were the palest of pinks and when it bloomed during the summer months the scent was glorious. Leah had tried many times to start cuttings from it but they always died before they took root so she had to satisfy herself with visiting Gretchen's every chance she could. Nonnie collected and dried the spent petals and used them in her salve and soaps. "How does everyone know all the details about Pastor Key?" Banks picked up the jar so he could have a sniff.

"So he is good-looking," Gretchen said. "Pris said he was, when she brought his horse by." She laughed. "Actually she couldn't stop talking about his looks."

"I wonder how Dusty found out." Leah changed the subject so she wouldn't have to admit what she thought about the preacher's looks. "From what I could see he hasn't stirred from his place."

Gretchen shrugged as she folded the cloth that had protected the goods and placed it in the basket. "Life in a small town. Word gets around." She stuck her finger in the jar to get a dab of the salve and rubbed it into her own hands. "We also wanted to know if Banks wanted to come spend the day with us."

"Momma I want to go play with Sam."

Leah's first instinct was to keep Banks close at hand, especially since the weather was going to get worse. But then again, she didn't want to go through another scare with Banks like this morning. What would she have done if the preacher, in his feverish state, had actually hurt Banks? Even in his weakened state, Pastor Key was still strong, much stronger than she was.

"I think that's an excellent idea," she said.

"Why don't you pack some things in case the weather gets really bad," Gretchen suggested.

"Whoop!" Banks jumped in the air and shouted. Then grimaced as he put his hand over his mouth. "I'm sorry," he whispered. "I forgot."

"I'm sure you didn't wake him." Leah ruffled his curls. "Go get your things. And don't forget your book. Just because there's no school doesn't mean you don't have to read every day."

"Yes ma'am!" Banks yelled. "Oops sorry."

The women grinned at Banks. "Are you sure he won't be any trouble?"

"I already have six children under twelve in the house. What difference will another one make?" Gretchen smoothed back a strand of Leah's hair. "Rough night?"

"You could say that. I'm scared that I really don't know what I'm doing."

"Shame on Ward and Jake for putting you in this position," Gretchen said.

"There really wasn't anyplace else for him to go," Leah admitted. "His fever is pretty bad."

"What are you doing for it?"

"Trying to keep him cool."

"Can he eat or drink anything?"

"No. He's too out of it. Really out." Leah felt a sudden rush of relief. She didn't have to worry about Banks, and she had someone to voice her concerns to. "It's strange. It's like he's seeing things in his sleep. Having horrible nightmares."

Nonnie says when you're sleeping the demons have an easier time getting to you."

Leah knew about demons. She fought them all the time. Loneliness, jealousy, anger, fear, and self-doubt. But she was weak. She had always been weak. "What kind of demons would a minister have?"

Gretchen shrugged. "None of us are perfect. I guess he is the only one that knows. I would hope that he's better equipped to fight them than the rest of us."

"Are you going to be all right with him?" Jim asked as he came back into the kitchen.

"I don't know why not," Leah said.

"He's a big guy," Jim said. "Bigger and younger than what I expected." Jim, along with Bettina, Gus, Jake and Margy, had been on the search committee for the new minister. The search had taken the better part of a year. "I guess it's a good thing that he's not a weakling. He seems younger than thirty-seven too."

"That probably comes from clean living," Gretchen teased. Jim had celebrated his thirty-fifth birthday early in September. His dark hair had a few strands of gray at the temples and the skin around his eyes showed wrinkles, whether he smiled or not.

Leah shrugged. "We all look younger when we're sleeping."

"I've got to see him for myself," Gretchen said.

"I'm surprised you haven't already." Jim rolled his eyes and Gretchen went down the hall with Leah behind her and Dodger padding after them.

Pastor Key's head made quick jerking motions on the pillow and his mouth moved with unspoken words. "He does look young," Gretchen said as she looked down at him. "I wouldn't say a day over thirty at the most."

Leah studied his face while Gretchen spoke.

"And he is good-looking in his own way."

Gretchen touched his forehead. "He *is* burning up with fever."

Leah automatically picked up the cloth from where it had fallen to the side, dipped it in the bowl of melting snow, wrung it out and placed it on his forehead. She scooped up some of the remaining snow and put it in his mouth, once more holding a finger beneath his chin to keep it closed.

A fleeting smile moved across his lips. "I thirst . . ." He sighed.

"Sounds like he knows his scripture," Gretchen said. "I'll ask Nonnie about his fever."

"Thanks," Leah replied. "I'm afraid I don't know what else to do for him."

Banks stood at the door looking in. He wore his coat and held a bag with his things. Leah knelt and took him in her arms. "I will see you tomorrow," she assured him. "Have a good time."

"I will."

"I'll check on you later," Jim said.

"I'll send Dodger down if I get into trouble," Leah replied. "Thanks for taking Banks."

"Try to get some rest," Gretchen added.

If only I could. Stillness filled her ears with their departure. With Banks gone, it felt as if all the light and life had left the house. Leah stood at the kitchen window and watched the three of them stagger through the snow. Jim carried Banks and Gretchen hung on to the tail of Jim's coat as he led the way, trudging through the same path he'd cut on the way to her house. The sound of tiny ice pellets hitting the roof suddenly filled the air. *Once again, Nonnie is right.* A log popped in the stove. The cuckoo clock ticked away. Dodger lay down with a huff on the hall rug and put his head on his crossed paws.

Leah checked the pot on the stove. Chicken and dumplings. It smelled heavenly, not only because Gretchen was a good cook, but mostly because Leah didn't have to prepare it herself. She opened the stove door and stuck a few more chunks of wood inside. She moved the pot over to the side so it would not bubble over. She wrapped the bread Gretchen delivered in a towel and put it on the shelf over the stove, along with the strudel. Both would stay warm until she was ready to eat. At the moment she was too tired to even think about it.

"Hmmm," Leah sighed. She wiggled her rump closer to the solidness pressed up against her. Just the pressure against her back made the ache dissipate. The arm around her waist, holding her close, felt so safe and warm, especially with the sound of the ice hitting the roof. The scent of warm bread and chicken and dumplings filled the air. The only thing that needed doing was the fire. Nate would take care of it. He'd make sure she was warm.

Nate . . . Leah opened her eyes. Strange clothes hung on the hooks next to the window. She was in Banks's room, but the arm wrapped around her did not belong to her son, and it certainly didn't belong to Nate.

"Stay with me angel," a voice whispered in her ear.

Her eyes widened with shock. "Oh my goodness." Slowly, and most carefully, she eased out from beneath the arm. Her escape was not graceful in the least. She ended up on the floor on her rump and scooted away by propelling herself with her arms and legs until her back was against the wall. She felt the icy cold from outside come through the wall and chill her back through the woolen fabric of her dress and the cotton chemise beneath. Somehow, in her sleep, her hair had come loose. She found the pins hanging in the tangles and quickly twisted the long strands back in place. Her hands shook with cold and nerves. She placed them on her cheeks to cool the telltale flush that heated them. She saw her shawl, still on the bed, caught beneath Pastor Key's shoulder. She vaguely remembered being tired and deciding the best place to rest and still keep an eye on the pastor was on top of the covers next to him. Amazing what a sleep-deprived brain could construe was a good idea!

Leah heard the click of Dodger's nails on the wood floor. He came to the doorway and gave a questioning wag of his tail.

Pastor Key rolled onto his back, taking her shawl with him, and flung his arm over his face. Leah leaned forward, grabbed her shawl and pulled it slowly until it was free. She held it before her like a shield until her heartbeat slowed to a normal pace. It was damp with sweat. She tiptoed to the bed and quickly touched his forehead. It was moist but cool.

His fever had, miraculously, broken and he seemed to be sleeping peacefully. *Thank you Lord.*

"If I had known that sleeping in the same bed with him was all it would take to break his fever I would have done it sooner." She spoke quietly to Dodger, who carefully watched her every move. "I think the best course is to pretend like this never happened." Leah straightened her skirts and gathered the clothes hanging on the peg. She'd forgotten about them in her worry over Pastor Key's wound. The blood needed soaking from his shirt and she wanted him back into pants as soon as possible. She'd wash them out and have Jim put them on him tomorrow morning.

His boots stood in the corner with a pair of socks hanging out of them. Wasn't it strange that Pastor Key wore the same type of boots as Jake and his cowhands? You would think that someone from Ohio would have regular shoes. They were well worn too. Curious. But she already knew from his physique that he wasn't what a person would consider a typical pastor.

Dodger whined. Leah scooped up the socks and let Dodger out. The world had changed while she slept. Night was quickly approaching and the storm had yet to abate. Ice covered everything. Icicles hung from every eave. Dodger slid down the drift on his stomach with his legs splayed in four different directions. He managed to find his feet and shook himself indignantly before cautiously lifting his leg against the clothesline post.

"I really should have dug out the washtub," Leah said mournfully. Dodger scrambled back up the drift, sliding back down twice before he got close enough for Leah to haul him in. "Guess I'm stuck with the chamber pot."

Dodger shook the ice from his coat and followed Leah to the kitchen. She dropped the pastor's clothing on the table and built up the fire in the stove. She went to the parlor to add more to the fireplace, which was almost out.

A quick look out the parlor window showed the streets to be deserted. Everything was covered with ice. Lights glowed in Dusty's upstairs window and down the street at the saloon. She'd expected Jake to stop by during the day. He could have, when she slept, but Dodger would have barked and knowing Jake he would have been comfortable enough to come inside to check on her whether she answered the door or not.

"More than likely he's punishing me for telling him to go last night." He did get moody at times. He and Ward could have drunk the night away and slept all day. Ward was known to be a bad influence, a reputation he enjoyed way too much.

The drifting wasn't as bad on the front of the house as the back. Leah was able to scoop up several bucketfuls of snow and filled all her pots. She ate a quick and filling meal while the water heated. Then she went to work on Pastor Key's clothes.

She put his shirt and his long johns in the sink to soak. It should be a simple task to mend the bullet holes.

"I wonder if he has any other clothing."

Dodger yawned from the rug. Clearly he could not care less about the preacher's wardrobe.

"I'll ask Jim if he had anything with his rig."

Leah went through his pants pockets. She found a few coins that she dropped in a crock and a wide blue ribbon. It was wrinkled and dirty, as if Pastor Key had found it on the ground and then stuffed it in his pocket. Leah extended it between her hands. It was long enough to tie back hair. What a strange thing for a minister to keep. Was it any stranger than having him show up shot? Leah put the ribbon in a wooden bowl she kept on the table and put the pants aside to wash.

She held up the frock coat. It needed a good brushing. The collar looked like it was charred. Had he dropped it in a fire? That would need some work, but maybe with some of the black velvet she had in her quilt fabric she could repair it. She turned it over to search for the bullet hole but there wasn't one. So he'd been shot when he had his coat off, then put it back on before he got on his horse? Leah dropped the frock coat and grabbed the big coat from the hook. It was heavy. She searched the pockets, and found the letter Ward had read and a Bible. She put both aside and turned the coat over to see if there was a bullet hole in the back of it. There wasn't.

"What happened to you?" Leah placed the letter inside the Bible and went to the preacher's room.

The room was dark except for the dim glow of the lantern hanging over the table. Leah put his Bible on the bedside table, turned up the wick on the lamp, and studied her patient.

He was definitely resting easier now. His chest rose and fell with long, steady breaths. He lay on his back with one strong arm thrown over his head, revealing the curve of the muscle. The sheets and blankets were pushed down to right below his chest. His skin was dry, and the fever gone.

His mouth was slightly open, showing the tips of his teeth. He needed a shave and a haircut. His hair was wild.

Leah picked up the bowl of water she'd used to cool him with. "Sleep well Pastor Key." She turned down the lamp.

"Amen . . ." He sighed as she left the room.

SIX

There was a dog staring at him. Cade opened his eyes and found himself eyeball to eyeball with a black and white dog. The light was dim, a shade of bluish gray that told him it was either morning or evening, he had no way to tell. The dog sniffed him, and then got downright personal by licking his cheek before voicing a gentle "wuff" as a greeting.

"Pleased to meet you." His voice was hoarse and cracked and his throat dry. "I think." He held his hand out beneath the dog's nose and it sniffed him again, and then opened its mouth in a friendly grin with its tongue lolling out. Cade rubbed its ears. "Where am I?"

He rolled over on his back, weak from the small bit of exertion. He could make out a wood plank ceiling above him. His entire body hurt like hell, especially his gut. He put a hand over his wound. Yes, he'd been shot. Shot by Fitch and his bastards because he had helped the girl and her husband escape.

"I should be dead." Cade closed his eyes. Was he grateful to be alive? That all depended on where he was. If this was prison, or worse, Fitch's place, then no, he wasn't. It could just be another one of God's jokes. Yes, I saved your life but what I've got in store for you now is worse than death. God did seem to enjoy playing with his life.

What happened after he got shot? His memory was fuzzy, lost somewhere among strange dreams that seemed as if they belonged to someone else. Cade felt like he'd been asleep for a year. Wished he had. Wished he could wake up to find the last ten years nothing but a horrible nightmare.

Cade opened his eyes again and stared at the wooden planks of the ceiling. He was in a small room, in a comfortable bed, with a dog. A lantern hung from a peg off to one side. It was turned down low. *Morning then.* He rubbed the dog's head again. There wouldn't be a dog in prison or at Fitch's. Most dogs, or at least the smart ones, stayed far away from Fitch. Maybe he'd been taken to a doctor. Which meant they probably didn't know who he was. How could they? He'd had nothing on him that said his name, or where he was from. *That he was running from dangerous outlaws* . . .

Cade still had no answers. All he knew for certain was he was warm, he was dry, and he was alive. He was also naked and the pegs on the wall didn't hold anything that looked like it would fit him. Where were his clothes?

Cade closed his eyes again. He sent his mind back to the last thing he remembered. *There was an angel* . . . Images flashed through his mind. Were they real or dreams? He heard footsteps. Cade kept his eyes closed and willed his body to relax, and his breathing to stay even.

"Dodger," a voice whispered. "Come here." He felt the

strapping under the mattress shift as the dog jumped from the bed then the soft snick of toenails on the wood floor. Was it her? The angel? Was she real? A door opened and a blast of cold air moved through the room. It smelled fresh and clean.

Snow? Bits and pieces of memories came to him. Flashes of faces moved quickly by, gone before he could center on them. Footsteps sounded once more, coming closer. He wasn't ready. He didn't know where he was or whom he was with. He kept his eyes closed as the footsteps came closer and finally stopped by the bed. They were light. They had to be the woman's. *Who is she?*

Her touch was light and quick. Just the barest hint of her fingertips on his forehead, and the scent of roses as they pushed the hair back. It took every bit of his willpower to stay still beneath it. He wanted more. Beyond the roses, he smelled fresh bread. It filled him with a sense of peace. Roses and bread. What a combination.

"Sleep is the best medicine now," she said. "I imagine you'll be hungry when you wake up."

He was. Starving. His stomach nearly growled in response. He felt her move, heard the gentle swish of her skirts and the soft sound of her feet on the hardwood floor.

"Sleep well Pastor Key."

Cade opened his eyes. It all came back to him. Fitch, the escape, being shot, stumbling around in the forest after his horse died, finding the camp, Davis showing up and the ensuing gun battle. *Pastor Key's dead because of me . . .* The man who helped him. The man who thought he'd been put in Cade's path by God to help him. Timothy Key. Another one of God's practical jokes, on both him and Timothy Key. And this woman thought he was the pastor.

"I've got to get out of here."

He looked around the room once more. There was no sign of his clothes. The only thing that looked remotely familiar was the book on the bedside table. Cade attempted to reach for it and realized how weak he really was. It didn't matter. He could see it now. It was Timothy's Bible. An envelope stuck out of it.

"I have my letter of introduction right there." Timothy *pointed to the pocket of the large overcoat. "A recommendation from Bishop Henderson himself."* He'd taken Timothy's overcoat and his Bible. Whoever had found him, assumed he was Timothy Key.

Isn't that what you wanted? It had been his hope that whoever else was trailing him would find the bodies and assume that the burned one was his. That he and Davis had killed each other. That they would think he was dead and would leave him alone. It had never been his intention to assume Timothy's identity.

Wasn't it? He'd taken his coat. Because it was warm. Because Fitch and his gang knew he didn't have a coat like that.

"I took his Bible." Why? Fitch knew he didn't have a Bible. But more than that, he wanted to protect it. He didn't want any of Fitch's gang laughing over it. Kicking it around. Throwing it in the fire. They would have. *You used to be one of them . . .* But he wasn't now. He'd drawn the line. There were some things he simply would not do. Murdering the husband of a woman Fitch wanted, then delivering the woman to Fitch so he could take their land was the something he could not do. Not under any circumstances.

Did he draw the line at impersonating a minister? That depended upon whether or not it would save his life. And how long it would take him to get out of this place, wherever he was.

Cade decided he was too tired to think about it now. He closed his eyes and fell back asleep.

The scent of roses awakened him. Cade blinked his eyes against the light until a face came into focus.

"Welcome back," a woman said. "I'm Leah Findley."

She was the angel in his dreams. The lamplight glowed around her head, highlighting her light brown hair with copper and gold. She wore it pulled back, but a few curls had pulled loose and danced around her shoulders. Her face was lovely, with a pert nose, a wide mouth with perfect teeth, and large green eyes surrounded by dark lush lashes. She smiled and turned to pick up a cup from the table. When she handed it to him he noticed there were gold flecks within the green of her eyes.

"It's water," she said. "You must be parched after your fever."

He was. Cade drank thirstily, draining every drop. He wiped his hand across his mouth to spread the moisture over his chapped lips. "Where am I?"

"Right where you're supposed to be. In Angel's End."

I was called to minister to the people of Angel's End . . . Timothy's words. *Feed my sheep.* His last words to Cade before he died. And here he was in the one place he shouldn't be. He needed time. Time to figure this out. Memory loss might be a convenient side effect of his wound and fever. When in doubt, play dumb. It had served him well in the past.

"What happened?" he asked.

"You don't know?" She returned the cup to the table and sat down in the chair.

Cade rubbed his jaw. He needed a shave, and a bath would be downright wonderful. He quickly looked at Leah's profile while she turned away. He wouldn't mind if Leah gave him a bath. Not at all. *You're supposed to be a minister. They don't go around asking women to give them baths.* Cade tried to recall what Timothy had told him.

The stage wouldn't take me any farther, because of the weather. So I bought a horse and struck out on my own. He looked at Leah with what he hoped was confusion.

"You don't remember getting shot?"

Cade looked down at the bandage and shook his head. "I don't." He was in it now. He just needed to play it out until he got his strength back. Until he could leave town.

"I found you a couple of nights ago. Your horse brought you to town during the blizzard. You must have fallen off. You were in the snow, in the middle of Main Street, by the statue."

A statue of an angel? Was that what he saw that night in the snow? Or was that all a part of the nightmares he'd experienced during his fever? Cade kept his face blank. Things really were fuzzy, the line between what actually happened to him and what Timothy told him blurred.

She smiled at his hesitation. "Actually, Dodger found you."

"Dodger?"

"My dog." The dog appeared in the doorway as if he'd heard his name. He gave a slight wag of his tail. "Since you're supposed to live with me we brought you here. Angel's End doesn't have a doctor."

"I don't remember any of it."

"Well, you were very sick." She stood and fussed with the blankets, straightening them and tucking them in at the foot of the bed. "You didn't have any money on you. I'm guessing that you were robbed."

That meant she hadn't found the money he kept in his boot. Or maybe she had and was using his memory loss as a reason to keep it?

"Maybe it will all come back to you." She pulled her shawl up and crossed her arms. "Hungry?"

"I am," he said.

"I'll be right back." She touched the top of the dog's head as she walked by.

When did you get so jaded? How could he think someone who more than likely saved his life could steal from him? Not everyone in the world was bad. It was just that the good were so few and far between that he sometimes forgot they existed.

Dodger stared at him. Cade waited. It seemed as if the dog wanted to say something to him, which was a pretty crazy notion. Dodger moved beside the bed, sat down and placed a paw next to Cade.

"What?" Cade asked the dog. He wagged his tail in response. The trouble was, he knew what. He was in it now. Masquerading as a minister. "She's the one who said I was supposed to be here."

Cade picked up the Bible. Its weight made his arm drop and he had to drag it across the bed to his lap. "Dang, I'm as weak and helpless as a baby."

Dodger whined.

"Also good for nothing," he added.

Dodger turned a circle before lying down on the small rag rug next to the bed. Cade heard the sounds of Leah in another part of the house: footsteps, the heavy sound of a plate being placed on a table, the clank of a pot lid.

The leather of the covering on the Bible was worn smooth. There was an indentation in the spine. Cade recognized it as the result of years of wear and tear, from a palm holding it open so that it eventually warped the spine. He remembered the sight of Timothy holding it in his hand and waving it like a banner as Cade approached his fire. It was apparent the book had been read many times throughout the years.

Cade tested the heft of it and a vision of his father appeared before his eyes. In it he held a Bible in one hand and thumped his other on a pulpit. Cade quickly blinked his eyes to chase away the image. His father had abandoned him, why should he waste a minute of his life thinking about him now?

Cade flipped the Bible open. A verse was written on the inside cover.

Because he hath set his love upon me, therefore will I deliver him; I will set him on high, because he hath known my name.

With it was written the chapter and verse: Psalms 91:14. Obviously this verse was of some importance to Timothy or a former owner of the Bible.

Cade read it again. Since it had been made quite clear to him through the years that he was not privy to God's love he dismissed the verse with a shrug. "To each his own."

A rather extensive family tree filled the next few pages. At the bottom he noticed Timothy's name and the date of his birth, followed by the birth of brothers and sisters who all died young. One sister, born several years after Timothy, did not have a death date next to her name. Cade studied the handwriting. There were notations of Timothy's parents' deaths in a different hand. He flipped back a page to look at the scripture again. It matched. Cade could only assume that Timothy wrote the deaths and the scripture since this was his Bible. He checked the date next to Timothy's birth again. He was thirty-seven years old when he died. Twelve years older than Cade was now. Did he look thirty-seven? The town must know how old their new preacher was supposed to be.

There are days when I feel like I'm a hundred and seven . . .

Footsteps in the hall alerted him to Leah's return. He snapped the Bible shut and it slipped from his hands. The pages flipped open, and several flattened envelopes and folded pieces of paper escaped just as Leah entered the room with a tray in her hands. Cade made a grab at the letters but missed most. Dodger jumped up, instantly alert.

"Oh my goodness!" Leah quickly put down the tray and bent to retrieve the sheets of paper from the floor just as Cade turned and weakly stretched his arm to the floor. His hand contacted soft flesh. *Her breast?* He yanked his hand back and it tangled in her arm. Leah jumped at his touch and the top of her head cracked on the underside of his jaw, knocking his head backward and into the headboard.

"Ow!" He saw stars and his stomach heaved in response. Luckily there was nothing in it to come up.

"Oh. My. Goodness. I'm so sorry." She babbled. Her cheeks turned scarlet and she covered them with her hands before reaching for him, then pulling her hands back as if he were a pot of scalding water. "Are you hurt, of course you're hurt, I am such an idiot at times. I can't believe I did that." She knelt down and gathered up the papers.

Cade opened his mouth and then snapped it shut. Even that hurt. *Think man, what would Timothy say?*

She was turned away from him, her upper body level with the bed as she straightened the papers. Cade hesitantly reached out and after a tentative pause, placed his hand on her head, cupping it within his palm. Her hair was soft and silky and he had to force himself not to pick up a lock and run it between his fingers. Leah stopped her dithering and turned to look at him. Her eyes widened behind the thick dark lashes and the gold flecks shimmered around the dark center. They drew him in. There was sadness in her eyes, and loss, both emotions he easily recognized. Emotions that were his constant companions. He pulled his hand away, surprised by the connection he felt between them.

"No harm done." Cade nodded his head toward the tray. "And that food smells wonderful." He straightened his blankets and pulled them up around his chest, suddenly conscious of his lack of clothing.

She smiled and bit her lip. She handed him the papers and the Bible. Cade shoved the papers inside the Bible and put it on the table. His mouth watered as she placed the tray on his lap.

Chicken and dumplings, warm bread and something with apples in it. Cade couldn't remember the last time he'd had a meal like this. His appreciation must have shown on the first bite. He closed his eyes as the succulent chicken settled onto his tongue.

"Gretchen made it," Leah quickly said. She dithered about with his clothes on the peg. His clothes were back. She must have brought them in while he was sleeping. She straightened his shirt. Flicked an imaginary piece of lint from the black frock coat. *Timothy's coat.* "She's Jim's wife. Jim Martin? On the selection committee."

Was he supposed to know whom she was talking about? The selection committee? Something to do with Timothy and his letter of introduction. Who was he supposed to be introduced to? Maybe he should read that letter, and the rest of the papers that were stuck in the Bible.

"She's a wonderful cook," he said after he swallowed. He might have been an orphan for most of his life but he well recalled the manners his mother had taught him. "Please tell her I said so."

"You can tell her yourself," Leah said. "Jim and Gretchen should be here soon. They promised to have Banks back by suppertime."

"Banks?"

"My son." Leah stood at the foot of the bed with his long johns folded over her arm. "He's six."

The second bite was as good as the first. Cade chased it down with a piece of the bread. It was lightly toasted and spread with a soft creamy butter. *Heaven . . .* Or as close to it as he was going to get.

"What about your husband?"

She stiffened. "He died four years ago." She put his long johns and pants on the end of the bed. "I thought you might want these now. I'll be back for your tray in a bit." She left without another word.

Cade watched her go. *I wonder what happened to her husband.* Was he supposed to know already? Dodger padded around to Cade's side of the bed. He placed his paw on the mattress and gave a slight whine.

"Go get your own," Cade said. He could hardly wait to sample the apple treat. As for the arrival of Jim, Gretchen, Banks and the selection committee, he was more than willing to wait on that treat.

SEVEN

"Nate's been dead four years." Leah swiped at the tears that clung to her lashes. Why was she getting so emotional now? "He's a minister for God's sake." She laughed at her play on words.

The rattle of the kettle let her know the water was hot. She poured some into her teacup to let it steep and the rest into the sink for the dishes. She looked mournfully at the pump. It was broken, thus the need to melt the snow for water. That was the one good thing about all this snow. Shoveling it into a pail sure beat hauling water from the stream.

Nate would have fixed the pump in a heartbeat. He was handy about things like that. This house was proof of it. He'd carefully planned it, laid out the four rooms for efficiency, gave it a center hall, with doors on both sides so the air would flow through and cool it in the dry summer months and two chimneys between the sets of front and back rooms to keep it warm in the winter. If only he'd pursued a career building houses instead of being a sheriff.

Leah scraped the scraps from her dinner into a bowl for Dodger and added some milk from the crock. A bit sloshed over as she sat it on the floor. She didn't worry about it. Dodger would take care of it. As always there was no sense in crying over spilt milk. Nate was Nate, he wanted, no, he *needed* to do good. He thought he could accomplish it best by being a sheriff. If he had known he'd wind up dead, leaving a wife and son . . .

"Maybe he should have been a minister." Leah tried to imagine Nate standing in the pulpit, wearing a black frock coat like Timothy's, quoting scripture. She couldn't see it, couldn't even see his face. She usually didn't have any trouble picturing him.

Leah took a sip of her tea. Banks should be back soon. Maybe she was just feeling melancholy because she missed her son and she was still so bone tired. That was why she couldn't see Nate's face when she closed her eyes. Four years wasn't long enough to forget the way someone looked, was it?

Or it could be guilt because of the way she felt when Pastor Key touched her hair. "What's wrong with me?" It was just that it had been so long since she'd been touched by an attractive man. Of course she'd feel a spark of attraction. *You don't feel it when Jake touches you.*

Leah looked out the window. The ice and snow had ceased earlier in the day, trailing off with a few remaining bursts as if the clouds shook themselves out like a rug before moving onward. The sun was weak in the sky and cast an odd shine on the ice-covered streets. The barest hint of her reflection showed in the glass and stared back at her with recrimination. Leah told herself she was attracted to Pastor Key because it had been so long since she'd been loved. That explained the knot in her stomach, her raw and tender emotions and why she got emotional when Pastor Key asked her about Nate.

But if that was the case, why didn't she feel the same thing when Jake touched her, or when he kissed her? She couldn't remember ever feeling this unsettled and restless. "I must be losing my mind."

A movement caught her eye. Dusty stood on the porch step of the Devil's Table, waving his arm. Leah hurried to the door and stepped out into the frigid air.

"How's the preacher?" Dusty yelled.

"Better. His fever broke and he's eating."

"Good." He stomped on the porch boards and swung his arms about in an effort to keep warm. Leah had the benefit of some shelter from the parlor wall that jutted out even with the porch and protected her from the wind. "I'm opening in the morning."

"I'll be there," Leah called back. Dusty always sounded crotchety even when he was saying something simple. He waved at someone down the street before ducking back inside the café. Leah grabbed her broom from the hallway to beat the snow from her porch back into the street.

"Momma!" Banks plowed through the snow with Jim behind him. Both were bent over against the wind that gusted down from the mountains. The confusion that plagued her earlier disappeared at the sight of her son. Banks was all she needed to think about. Banks was what she had to live for. Nothing else mattered. Now if she could just figure out what he was carrying in his hands. He struggled mightily, breaking through the drifts with great determination. Joy oozed off him. Obviously he'd had a great visit.

He was carrying a kitten. Not really carrying, she realized, as he got closer. It was more like he had it trapped beneath his coat. Its little head was stuck up under his chin and its meows rang in her ear as Banks got closer. Jim looked apologetic behind him.

"Momma, look." Banks stomped onto the end of the porch.

"I see."

"We found them in the barn. Nonnie said the momma cat was looking for a place to hide them before the snow."

"And why isn't this baby still with its momma?"

"Oh they're plenty old enough to be on their own," Jim said sheepishly. "And considering how many were in the litter . . ."

Leah took the kitten from Banks. It was gray and fluffy with bright green eyes. "Oh it"—she lifted it higher—"she, is precious." Leah tucked the kitten up under her chin and a purr rumbled loudly against her throat. "How many were there and how come I get a girl?"

"Seven," Jim said. He tickled the kitten's cheek with a finger.

"And the brood decided there was one for each of them?"

"With this one left over for Banks." Jim laughed. "Gretchen is not happy. She's determined to find homes for at least four of them."

"Poor momma kitty. I wonder where she came from?"

"Probably one of the mining camps. I'd never seen her before. I found her curled up in one of the empty stalls, exhausted from ferrying all her babies. I don't mind having her around. We haven't had a good mouser since the coyotes got Blackie."

Banks's eyes swelled wide and his mouth formed a perfect O. "Momma?" he gasped.

"The coyotes don't come close anymore because the town is too busy." Leah gave Jim a look that let him know how unhappy she was with his directness. "But that doesn't mean that you don't have to watch her carefully when she's outside." Visions of tiny kitten puddles and other presents on her floor suddenly filled her mind. "I need a box."

"I'll send one of the boys back with one. I guess I should

have thought of it before we came down here." Jim grinned a little sheepishly.

"It's the least I can do after springing the animal on your household. So how's our preacher?"

"Take your kitty inside and fix her a bowl of milk." Leah handed the kitten to Banks. "And stay away from the pastor's room."

"Yes, Momma. Will you help me name her?"

"I will." Leah waited until the door was firmly shut behind her and she could see Banks through the kitchen window. "He's awake and he's eating."

"That's good news," Jim said. He leaned against the wall with his hands jammed in his pockets.

"Yes, but there's also something strange. He doesn't remember what happened to him. The last thing he recalls is getting on his horse and striking out for town. As far as getting shot . . ." Leah shrugged. There was something else that bothered her about Pastor Key's story but she couldn't put her finger on it. She didn't want to voice her concerns in case they were tied up in the strange feelings she'd been having since his arrival. "He didn't have any money in his pockets. Did he have any belongings on his horse? A change of clothes. Anything?"

"Nope. Not a thing. Not even a bedroll. But he could have been robbed, or it could have fallen off in the storm. Or he could have left his trunk at the stage stop for them to bring on when the weather breaks."

"I guess you're right," Leah said. Should she mention his boots? If that was all he had to wear, Jim would see them for himself soon enough.

"He was shot, sick and got lost in a blizzard," Jim said. "He's bound to be a bit confused. It's not exactly the welcome he was expecting."

Leah nodded as she chewed on her lower lip. "I'm kind of surprised Jake didn't come around to check on him."

"I'm not. Jake is back at his ranch."

"He left in the middle of the blizzard?"

"There's only so much rejection a man can take Leah."

"So it's my fault that he didn't have enough sense to wait out the storm in town or at least wait until daylight to go home?" Darn that Jake for making her into the villain. She never asked him to care about her. Was she supposed to feel guilty because Jake chose to act like an idiot at times? Did he think that would change her mind, or her heart?

"Can we take this inside? I know I'm cold." Jim rubbed his hands over his arms. "How about you?"

"Apparently I'm made out of ice and my heart is solid rock." Leah went inside and Jim followed her. "And my love life, or lack thereof, is excellent fodder for the town to gossip about."

"Now wait just a minute," Jim protested. "I wouldn't call it gossip, I'd say it's more like people are genuinely concerned for your and Jake's welfare."

"I know," Leah said in exasperation. "I'm sorry. Jake's a wonderful man and any woman would be lucky to have him." They moved into the parlor.

"But you don't love him."

"It's not because I haven't tried."

Jim put a comforting hand on her shoulder. "You shouldn't have to try to love someone. You just do. You just know."

Leah sighed in relief. "If only I didn't feel so guilty about it, or the lack of it."

"Jake would be the first to say he doesn't want you because you feel guilty. He's just stubborn, you know? He's too used to getting his own way. For fighting for what he wants and not backing down."

"You're a good man Jim Martin."

"Remind Gretchen of that will you? She just about clubbed me with the skillet before I left."

"Too many kids and kittens underfoot?"

"The husband is always the last to know and the first to go."

"Yeah I can see how much you're suffering."

"It builds character you know."

Leah punched his arm. "I wouldn't necessarily call it character."

Jim put his hand over his heart. "You have wounded me to the core."

"Yeah, I'll tell Pastor Key to pray for you."

"I'll tell him myself." Jim walked down the hall to the preacher's room with Leah close behind him. Timothy was curled on his side with the blankets pulled up over his shoulders. His pants and long johns rested where she left them and the dinner tray occupied the opposite side of the bed. Dodger lay on the rug next to the bed with the bowl between his paws, licking the finish off the inside.

"I guess eating wore him out." Leah tiptoed in and got the bowl from Dodger. "Sleep will do more for him than I can." Dodger stood and gave a slight wag of his tail. "Go on," she whispered. She could only hope that his meeting with the kitten would be a quiet occurrence.

Jim shrugged. "I guess I'll try again tomorrow. Are you good with firewood?"

"Yes, Jake brought in a bunch before he left." There it was again. That pang of guilt with Jake's name on it.

"All right." Jim went to the door. "Let me know—"

"If I need anything," Leah finished for him. "A box for the kitten will do for starters. And tell Gretchen she has my undying gratitude for looking after Banks."

"Yeah, about that. May I sleep in your shed if things get out of hand down my way?"

Leah pushed him through the door. "I'm certain the chickens would love it." She heard Jim's hearty laugh as he stepped into the street.

Leah went into the kitchen to find that Dodger had met the kitten. The tiny ball of fluff had taken shelter in a chair and had its fur puffed up, making it look twice its size. It peered through the spindles on the back of the chair and hissed mightily at Dodger, who whined and looked hopefully, between the kitten and Banks.

"She doesn't like Dodger," Banks informed her.

"She'll get used to him," Leah said. "She's got a lot of spunk."

"What does spunk mean?"

"It means she's brave." Leah ran her fingers through her son's hair. His blond curls stood straight up and the skin under his eyes was blue. Banks leaned into her hip and yawned. "I'm guessing you and Sam stayed up late last night."

"Uh-huh."

"How 'bout you go ahead and wash up and get ready for bed."

"Do I have to?" Why did children always complain about having to go to bed? Leah found she couldn't wait to climb beneath the covers and close her eyes.

"Yes you do. Go let Dodger out and I'll heat up some water. Feed the chickens and check for eggs too." She'd forgotten about them with all her worry over her patient. "Did you have dinner at the Martins'?"

"Yes ma'am."

Good, that was one less thing she'd have to do. "Make sure you're quiet so you don't wake up Pastor Key. When you're done, watch for a twin to show up with the box for the kitten."

"Is he ever gonna wake up?" Banks wasn't in a hurry to do his chores.

"He was hurt really bad and was very sick. He needs lots of sleep to recover." Leah yawned as Banks and Dodger finally went down the hall. She picked up the kitten from its perch and rubbed the tiny head. "You're the last thing I need right now, you know that?" The kitten purred and Leah sat down, closed her eyes and tucked it up under her chin.

"Momma, here's the box." Leah blinked.

Had she actually fallen asleep? "That's it. We're going to bed." A half hour later the fires were stoked for the night, Banks was as clean as a quick washing could get him and they were both in Leah's bed with the kitten huddled between them and Dodger banished to the rug on the floor. The sky had finally cleared and the half moon cast a gentle light through the window even though the wind whistled around the house.

"So what should we name her?" Leah asked as they watched the kitten wash its face.

"I don't know." Banks yawned and rubbed his eyes. "I can't think of anything."

"Well she's fluffy and gray." Leah touched her finger to the top of the kitten's head. "She looks like a puff of smoke. Or a pile of ashes."

"I like Ashes," Banks said.

"Ashes it is." Ashes squeaked out a tiny yawn and moved closer to Leah. She stuck her paws against Leah's stomach and pressed them in and out. Banks's even breathing let her know he was already dreaming.

I should have checked on Pastor Key, was the last thought that went through her mind before Leah drifted off to sleep.

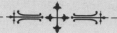

EIGHT

At last. Cade didn't think they'd ever get to sleep. And he had to go. Bad. He tentatively placed his bare feet on the floor and stood, hoping all the while that the floorboards would not creak. Standing was harder than he thought it would be. He wavered dizzily for a moment, squinted his eyes and willed his head to stop spinning. His gut felt like it had been kicked by a mule. He was so weak that his legs were actually trembling. It took a couple of attempts to pull on his long johns. More for his pants, especially since he was trying to be quiet.

Cade stood at the foot of the bed for a moment, to gather his strength before going outside. He stared dubiously at his shirt, which hung on a hook on the opposite side of the bed. Given that he was doubtful about how long his legs would actually support him, he decided to go without. He didn't plan on being outside that long.

Dodger met him in the hall. He looked up at him with his mouth open, in a semblance of a grin and his black bushy tail swished back and forth.

"Shhh." Cade put his finger to his lips. He glanced into the room and saw two lumps in the bed. Leah, and the boy. She lay on her side with her arm flung over her son in a protective gesture that left a strange lump in his throat.

Dodger followed him outside and Cade found he enjoyed the company. After he relieved himself, he leaned against the porch post before he went in. His body shook with the cold; still he looked around. He'd been cold before, plenty of times. So cold he thought he'd never get warm again. There was a door behind him, shelter and heat. He could stand it for a few minutes.

Dodger stood beside him, waiting patiently, in the way that dogs do. Cade rubbed the top of his head. He loved dogs, had always wanted one. The Cheyenne camp they lived in had several and the orphanage his father left him at was a working farm with dogs. Unfortunately his way of life wouldn't work for a dog. It certainly hadn't worked for his horse. Dang he hated losing that horse.

How would his life have turned out if the Middletons hadn't shown up at the orphanage? He'd only had a few years left when they arrived. He was smart and had already finished his schooling. He would have found some sort of job close by, on one of the local ranches, so he could stick around until Brody aged out. They would have had the entire world before them. They could have started their own place with the money he'd earned. Found some nice girls. Gotten married. Started families. Things would have turned out better.

He couldn't tell how big the town was from the back of her house. Dang, it was cold, but he needed to get the lay of the land. He had to leave, as soon as he got his strength back.

Behind Leah's house the land faded and dipped; most likely there was a stream back there. On the other side was a copse of evergreens that trailed up into a mountain. From what he could see they were pretty deep in the mountains. Snow-covered peaks glistened in the moonlight in every direction. That would make for hard, slow traveling. He best make sure he had plenty of supplies before he took off. And a gun.

"Let's go get warm." Cade turned, expecting Dodger to follow. Instead the dog walked out from under the porch eave and stared at a point to the left of the shed. Cade looked out into the darkness. Dodger took a step and growled. The fur behind his neck stood straight up and he lowered his head.

"What is it?" Cade bent to get on Dodger's line of sight. He saw a shadow dart behind the shed. Coyote, or possibly a wolf. Nothing to be done about the animal now.

"Come on boy, let's go inside." Dodger looked at Cade, then back at the shed. "Come," Cade said more firmly. Dodger cocked his head, paused for a moment and then with a wag of his tail he followed Cade.

Coming inside made Cade realize how cold he was. He rubbed his arms briskly. His feet were absolutely numb. It felt as if he stood on the stubs of his shinbones with nothing beneath. He went into the kitchen, knelt before the stove and placed a couple of sticks inside, leaving the door open so the heat touched his skin. A lamp sat on the shelf, turned down low, in case someone had to come into the kitchen during the night. Was that a common occurrence, or just the result of his being here? The room was neat. The stove against the inside wall so the stone chimney would heat the room behind it. A cabinet with a sink and a window above, with shelves on either side on the outside wall. A table pushed against the front wall beneath the window with three mismatched chairs around it. A rag rug in the middle.

Curtains pulled against the cold at both windows. An old blanket tucked into the corner by the stove for the dog. All very homey and cozy.

Cade's feet began to thaw and they burned with a pain so intense that he had to stand to flex them. Moving was the only thing that would help so he hobbled around, crossing from the kitchen into the parlor while trying desperately not to make any noise from the pain. Luckily Cade had a lot of experience at walking silently. The cold seemed to intensify everything and his wound felt as if someone had just poked a red-hot lance through his gut.

Dodger padded into the hall and watched him with bright and curious eyes. The wind stopped its incessant howling for a moment and the sound of a clock ticking filled his ears.

"Doors," Cade said quietly to Dodger. "What this house needs is some doors." The house was solidly built and laid out well, but the absence of doors was a problem. It didn't offer much privacy. Something he'd need if he was going to successfully continue his charade until he could make his escape.

Would Leah notice if he put a few more pieces of wood in the fire? At least she had enough sense to stock up before the blizzard hit. Cade moved the screen and placed another log on the embers. It flared to life and he instantly felt better. The braided rug beneath his feet was thick and warm.

Cade scratched his jaw. His beard felt coarse. How long had it been since he shaved, or even bathed? What he wouldn't give for a big tub to soak in. To get good and clean and let the heat take the aches away. All the aches. Suddenly he felt so tired, so much weaker, as if the last few moments had sucked away his remaining strength. Yet the thought of climbing back into bed without washing repulsed him.

Dodger followed him back into the kitchen and lay down

in the corner with a huff. Cade stuck another small log in the stove and shut the door. He shouldn't have left it open in the first place. He didn't want to repay Leah's kindness by burning down her house.

The effort of picking up a large pot and setting it in the sink nearly undid him. He wouldn't survive five minutes if he had to leave now. He wrapped one arm around his abdomen for support and used the other to work the pump. Nothing happened. He gave it a few more attempts but he could tell by the feel of the handle that there was no pressure in the pipes.

Cade propped his arms on the edge of the sink and wearily leaned against them.

"It's broken."

If Leah had been one of Fitch's men, he'd be dead right now. He had not heard her over the noise of the pump. His instincts, usually so finely tuned, had failed him. Cade turned around, and suddenly became more aware of his lack of a shirt.

Leah stood in the door of the kitchen in her flannel gown and woolen socks. Her braid was tossed over her shoulder and covered one of her breasts. The other one peaked with cold and Cade found that he could not tear his eyes away from it.

"Leah," she said. "Remember?"

He forced himself to focus on her face. Her green eyes were heavy with sleep and her dark lashes shaded them seductively. She was totally unaware of how appealing she looked. She had to be.

Cade cleared his throat. For once things were going his way. His body was too weak to show what she was doing to his insides. "Yes. Leah," he managed to choke out.

"Are you looking for something to drink?" She crossed to the counter by the sink. "I have cold milk." She poured some from a heavy crock into a cup. "I'm sorry, I was so tired, I didn't check on you before I went to bed." She stood before him and held out the cup.

Cade blinked. She gazed upward through her thick lashes. Without the light to show them, her eyes were as dark as the evergreens. She was the angel from his dreams, the one who gave him water when he thirsted. Cade wanted nothing more than to wrap his arms around her, bury his face in her hair and hold on. She was so close, just an arm's length away. There might as well have been a canyon between them.

What was he thinking? Needing people was a sign of weakness. He couldn't afford to be weak. He'd learned a long time ago that weak only led to one thing and that was dead. *You're supposed to be a preacher.* What would a preacher do?

He took the cup. "Thank you." His fingers brushed hers as she released her hold. "I'm sorry to be such a bother." The milk was soothing on his throat and so cold that a shiver gripped him and goose bumps appeared on his skin. Funny, the cold didn't usually bother him. He'd gotten immune to it long ago. He had to, to survive. He just didn't think about it.

She was staring at his chest. He noticed as soon as he lowered the cup. She caught her bottom lip with her perfect teeth as she looked. Cade was suddenly aware that he'd lost weight during his illness. That walking in the snow had dampened the legs of his pants and helped them sag lower on his waist than they should. Apparently she was aware of it too as her cheeks reddened and she turned away.

Cade cleared his throat again. "So what do you do for water since your pump is broken?"

She busied herself with the crock, wiping imaginary drips from the lip, placing the lid back on, and putting it back in its corner where it would stay cool and fresh. "Luckily we have snow," she said. "Or I haul it from the stream." He took advantage of her distraction to hitch up his pants.

"Would it be too much trouble for me to wash up some? And shave?" He smiled at her. "The thought of going back to bed feeling this way . . ."

She looked at the pot he'd put in the sink. "Oh my goodness, of course not." She whirled around, grabbed the pot from the sink, then picked up a bucket from beside the stove and dumped the contents in the pot. It was melting snow, no doubt carried in before she went to bed. "Unfortunately the washtub is buried on the porch. I forgot to bring it in when the blizzard hit. But I can heat enough water to give you a quick bath . . ." The bucket hit the floor with a clang. "Er . . ." She stumbled over her words. Funny how she must have read his mind. He wouldn't mind her giving him a bath at all. And then joining him.

Dodger sat up, suddenly interested in the goings-on in the kitchen. Leah quickly ducked to the woodpile, picked up a few sticks to feed the stove and shoved them inside. She caught her fingers in the door as she slammed it shut. "Damn!" she exclaimed as she grabbed her injured fingers with her other hand. "Oh. My. Goodness. I am so sorry, I don't usually . . ." Her voice trailed off.

Cade grinned. She stared up at him with her face all flushed and guilt showing at having cussed in front of a preacher. He scooped a handful of snow from the pot, and took her fingers in his hand, wrapping the snow around them. "I think it was warranted, considering the circumstances." He gently massaged the snow into them and she lowered her eyes to watch their entwined hands. He could see the glint of green and gold through her lashes.

Oh he was *so* going to hell. An evil thought took him. If he was going, he might as well enjoy the journey. Cade closed his eyes, gripped her hand and pulled it up against his chest. "Lord I ask for healing for Leah's hand. She injured it trying to do your work Lord. Amen."

"Amen," she said after him.

Cade resisted the urge to kiss her fingers. He wasn't in that much of a hurry to get to hell. "There's no rush," he said. "I've got no place to go at the moment." He didn't bother to tell her that God wouldn't help her fingers because of anything he'd done. He would more than likely have them fall off her hand.

"Why don't you sit down and I'll get a towel and washcloth."

"I don't suppose you have a razor around?"

"I do. It was my husband's. Nate's." She pulled a chair from the table and moved it to the counter by the sink.

"What are you doing?"

"It's on the top shelf. I put it up there so Banks couldn't . . ."

"Show me where. I'll get it."

She pointed to the cupboard on the far left corner next to the stove. Cade opened the door. A shaving brush stuck up from a small wooden box. Cade easily reached it and saw the contents, a brush, razor, soap and a strop. He handed it to Leah and turned to shut the door. There was a shadow on the shelf, behind where the box had sat. A shadow that looked very much like a rolled-up gun belt and the ivory handle of a .45. He shut the door quickly and quietly and gave Leah a perfect smile of contentment.

Her cheeks flamed. His pants were sagging again. Cade casually hitched them up and she turned away to pull out a chair.

"Sit down, please," she said. "I'll just be a minute getting the towels."

Cade wearily settled at the table as she darted from the room. He was so tired, he needed to sleep, and to plan, but there was no way in hell he was going to pass up a bath, especially from Leah. The water hissed in the pot with the melting snow. His eyes darted to the cabinet. Dodger let out a huff of disgust.

"What?" Cade said to the dog.

Dodger lay down on his bed and stared at him with his dark, incriminating eyes.

NINE

"I cannot believe I cussed in front of him." Leah lectured herself as she gathered the bathing supplies from the cabinet in her room. She didn't worry about waking Banks as she spoke in hushed tones. Banks could sleep through anything. The kitten, however, was disturbed and meowed sleepily from the pillow by Banks's head.

"Go back to sleep Ashes." Leah rubbed the tiny head between the upturned ears and the kitten yawned before closing its eyes. Leah grabbed her comb from the washstand and caught a glimpse of herself in the mirror. "Oh my goodness." When she woke to hear Cade in the kitchen she wasn't thinking about propriety, just that he might need something, that his health may have deteriorated again. She'd stood before a man of God wearing nothing but her old, faded gown. If nothing else, she'd given Pastor Key plenty of fodder for a sermon. If he judged the entire town by her standards, it would be a miracle if he didn't light out as soon as the snow melted.

"Which won't be till spring," Leah grumbled as she yanked on her robe and tied the sash with a sturdy bow. He'd seemed very casual about standing bare-chested in her kitchen with his pants slipping around his hips. "Still he might decide to live somewhere a lot more holy than my place." She couldn't resist a grin. "Good luck in finding a place like that around here." They were no saints in Angel's End, unless you wanted to count Bettina, and just the fact that she considered herself one put her out of the running in Leah's mind. "Judge not . . ." Leah looked in the mirror again. Straightened her braid. Ran her fingers under her eyes to chase away the shadows. Winced when she used the injured fingers.

"I've really got to bone up on my Bible verses," she said with a sigh. The one about lust came to mind. Lust at seeing Pastor Key standing in her kitchen with his bare chest and his pants sagging dangerously low and revealing a trail of dark hair and well-corded muscle. She had even lusted after him while he was praying over her hand.

"I guess I best get used to spending some time on my knees." It had been pretty simple to let things like reading the Bible and worship get away from her since she hadn't been close to a church in the years since Nate brought them to Angel's End. Sure the circuit preacher came around occasionally, performed weddings, baptisms and funerals, along with the obligatory prayer meeting. But the daily things that one should do had just slipped away in the battle to just make it through another day with a roof over their heads and warm clothes on their bodies. Yes, she prayed, but they were more like arrows that she shot into the heavens when she thought about it, not actual worship. Pastor Key would have his hands full with all the backsliders in Angel's End, including her.

"Lord give me strength." For what, she wasn't sure. Leah gathered her supplies and went back to the kitchen.

The pastor's head was bent forward and his arms wrapped around his body. Was he praying? He moved with a start when she came in and the sight of his bare chest once more shocked her senses. She would just have to get used to having a man about the house again. *A minister* . . . Leah reminded herself.

"Aren't you cold?" she asked. "You must be freezing."

He shrugged. "I just don't think about it. I taught myself a long time ago to ignore physical pain as much as possible."

Now that was a strange thing for a preacher to say. Or was it? It wasn't as if she ever knew one personally. Sure she'd gone to church when she was a child, but the extent of her relationship with her minister had been passing the potatoes when he came to dinner and repeating the vows when she married Nate. He quirked an eyebrow at her in question. He thought she was stalling. Was she? Leah placed a towel around his shoulders. "This should help with the cold."

A lopsided smile lit his face. "Thank you." He pulled it around in front. He might say he ignored the cold, but he wasn't immune to it. He was just like every other man, pretending to be stronger, smarter or warmer. He was just a man, after all. A man who needed her help.

Leah quickly arranged the shaving supplies on the table. She crossed to the stove and checked the water. It was warm. She dipped some out into a bowl and dropped a small towel into the pot. She wrung it out and carried both towel and bowl to the table. "I thought you could start with a shave while the water warms up enough to bathe."

"Sounds wonderful," he said. He raised his head obligingly while she wrapped the warm, moist towel around his jaw. He tilted back and his eyes closed in contentment. She had thought that he'd shave himself, but by the looks of him, he was quite willing to let her do it for him. As if he read her mind, he said, "I'm so weak that I'd more than likely drop the blade and cut off my toes."

Leah looked down at his bare feet and the long toes that seemed to want to bury themselves into the braid of the rug as if they were seeking warmth. His pants were damp nearly up to his knees and she realized he must have gone outside that way. Not only did he think he was immune to the cold, but also to pneumonia. Or maybe he just believed that God would look out for him. As he had, since he survived being shot.

Leah placed the soap in the water, swished it around and scrubbed at it with Nate's brush to create lather. Behind her, Dodger yawned loudly and then settled into his bed. The stove cracked and popped with the heat from the fire and the water hissed in its pot. The quick ticktock of the cuckoo clock kept time in the background. Leah removed the towel and scrubbed the lather into the thick dark bristles that covered his lean jaw. While it soaked in she got the lamp from the shelf, turned up the wick and placed it on the table.

She picked up the razor and checked its edge. Four years of disuse had not dulled it, still she ran it across the strop just to make sure. One dark eye opened to watch her.

She couldn't help herself.

"Are you afraid I'm going to cut your throat?"

"You wouldn't be the first woman who wanted to." He closed his eyes once more and sighed deeply, as if he'd resolved himself to what was to come.

She smiled at his quick rejoinder. Once more, he didn't talk like a preacher, or how she thought a preacher should. She placed the blade against his cheek and scraped. Leah studied the angles of his face while she worked. Without opening his eyes he knew the placement of the razor and moved his face to line up with her strokes. His lips were mobile and expressive, even while he was relaxed. It was as if his thoughts were connected directly to it and each one caused a different reaction to show itself upon his mouth. Leah had never shaved a man before. Nate had never given her cause to.

She quickly realized it was all a matter of trust. The fact that Pastor Key trusted her not to hurt him made her all the more careful with the way she moved the razor over his face and then down around his neck.

Just one slip and she could hurt him. Why did he trust her? Was it because he was a man of God, and therefore saw the good in everyone?

"Tell me about your husband," he said.

The blade hovered at his neck. *Relax . . . It was an innocent question.*

Why shouldn't he want to know about Nate? It wasn't a secret. Anyone in town could tell him about Nate.

"He was the sheriff," she said. "He died four years ago."

"I reckon you were a child bride." He cocked one eye open and looked up at her.

A sense of relief washed over her when he didn't ask about how Nate died. It was too painful to talk about. Pastor Key's coming had made it fresh again, brought all the memories to the surface. "I was seventeen," she said with a smile. "Nate was twenty. The town advertised for a sheriff and Nate got the job."

"Twenty years old and he got hired as a sheriff?"

Every time the pastor spoke she raised the blade so she wouldn't nick him.

"His father had quite a reputation from the border wars. The town figured Nate had to be just as good."

"Kansas?"

"Yes. His father was against slavery. And not afraid to fight for what he believed in. Nate was a lot like him."

"So he packed up his bride and brought her west."

"Yes. We left the day after our wedding." She couldn't

help remembering it all. The trip west in the wagon with the things she'd inherited from her grandmother, the way Nate made love to her in the back of the wagon when they camped at night. The realization that she was pregnant with Banks almost immediately, and how Nate cared for her after that, not even letting her lift a bucket of water. A thousand memories or more ran through her mind.

The water for his bath bubbled on the stove. Leah wiped the remaining soap from Cade's face and examined her work. He smiled lazily with his eyes closed as if he knew she was studying him. The smile created deep creases in his cheeks, and lines fanned out around his eyes.

"I could get used to this," he said.

Leah picked up a towel, wrapped it around the handle of the pot and moved it from the heat. She looked over her shoulder at him. The look of contentment on his face was sweet, like a kid who'd gotten way more than he asked for at Christmas. "It's a onetime service," she replied. "Because you're so weak." *And because I don't trust myself around you.*

"How do you know I'm not playing possum?" His eyes were open now and he watched her as she tested the water with her finger.

Was he teasing her? Leah stopped what she was doing and turned to look at him. "Because a few hours ago I wasn't sure if you were going to live or die."

His dark eyes were hidden beneath his deep brow and shaggy hair. She should trim it for him, after she washed it. His expression turned serious. "I wasn't so sure either." His mood seemed to be ever-changing and it confused her, made her feel off balance. "You saved me," he said.

Her skin heated at his steady perusal. Leah felt the flush rise from her neck and over her face. She turned back to the stove and tested the water once more. It was tolerable. "I really didn't do anything." She tossed the line carelessly over her shoulder.

"For I was hungry, and ye gave me meat; I was thirsty, and ye gave me drink: I was a stranger, and ye took me in." He looked away from her, as if he were suddenly shy, or even embarrassed.

"We look out for each other around here," she explained. "We take care of each other."

His voice was husky when he spoke again. "You are lucky to have that. Not everyone does."

"Is that why you left Ohio and decided to come here?"

He blinked, and momentarily looked off balance, then he smiled. "God said to feed his sheep."

"He also moves in mysterious ways." Leah carried the pot of warm water to the table. "I bet you didn't count on being shot and robbed before you got here."

"Just like you didn't count on being a widow with a son to raise," he returned.

His comment, so out of the blue, stunned Leah. Did he understand how hard it was for her to be a widow? How lonely she sometimes felt. How she missed having someone to share her life with. A man to help around the property, to laugh at Banks's antics as well as take pride in his accomplishments. "You can't predict the future," she finally said. "There's no way of knowing anything for certain. All you can do is step out in faith."

His eyes turned distant, as if he were trying to remember something.

"Wherever God leads me." He said it quietly, as if Leah wasn't there.

As if contemplating the odd events that led him to be sitting in her kitchen as an injured man.

"You still don't remember what happened to you?"

He looked away again. "No."

"Maybe a good night's sleep will bring it all back."

He studied her. "Does it matter? Whoever did this is probably long gone and his trail lost in the blizzard."

"I guess it doesn't," Leah agreed. "Although I hate to think of a killer being out there somewhere."

"The town is safe," he said as if that was all there was to it.

Leah wasn't so sure. What about Jake? He'd left town the same night that Pastor Key was found. What if Jake, on the way home, had come across whoever it was? He could be dead or hurt and buried under the snow. Leah shook her head at her foolishness. Her mind was looking for trouble while the water was getting cold. She could tell by the set of his shoulders that Pastor Key was nearly done in. She'd best get him bathed before the poor man fell asleep in the chair.

"As long as we're at it I'll change your bandages." Leah knelt by the chair. The bandages were tied in place under his arm. He lifted his elbow and watched her as she concentrated on untying the knot. Her fingers continually brushed against his smooth skin. She must have touched him a dozen times before, when he was unconscious, and never felt awkward. But now with his watchful dark eyes on her she felt self-conscious and clumsy. She looked up at him apologetically as her hand slipped.

"You must have gotten pregnant right away," he said.

Leah blushed. It was such a personal observation. Nursing him was one thing, sharing the intimate secrets of her life with Nate, quite another.

He studied her face. "I'm sorry," he said. "None of my business." She didn't want things to be awkward between them, she felt strange enough as it was, so she decided to plow forward. "I did," she said and it wasn't as personal as she thought it would be. "Nate was beside himself with joy, especially when Banks was born."

"He wanted a son?"

"What man doesn't?"

He gave a slight humph in agreement. "Where did the

name come from? I've never heard of anyone named Banks before."

"It was my grandmother's last name. She raised me after my parents died. They drowned. We decided to name our baby after her. Sarah if it was a girl. Banks for a boy."

"I like it," he said. "It's a good name." His eyes studied her again, the anguish she thought she'd seen earlier now hidden. "A strong name," he added. "Not that you need my approval."

Finally the knot on his bandage came loose and she was able to unwind the length of linen. The padding on the back pulled off easily but the front was crusted with blood. "I'll have to soak that off."

He studied the wound. "I guess I was pretty lucky." He placed his hand next to it. "I think the bullet nicked a rib. I feel like I got kicked by a mule."

"I'll make sure to rewrap it tighter." Leah rolled the bandage and set it aside. "You must have a guardian angel."

"I never would have thought so before."

Once more his response was cryptic and totally unexpected. Leah lathered up a washcloth. "Lean forward," she instructed. He obliged by folding his arms, placing them on the table and then resting his forehead upon them. One side of his face was turned up and the set of his jaw was tense, as if he dreaded what was to come. Leah moved behind the chair. She stopped, suddenly, as she went to place the cloth on his skin. His back was crisscrossed with long and faded scars. *Oh my goodness . . .* She hadn't noticed them before. She'd kept the light dim in his room and most of the time he'd been on his back. How did he come to have such scars? It looked as if he'd been beaten, but it had to have been several years ago, when he was much younger.

He shivered. Leah shook her head. It wasn't her place to ask. She quickly rubbed the cloth across his back, unaware at first that she used each stroke of the cloth to trace the line of a scar. Did he realize it? Or were the wounds so old that he didn't even think about them? He must have been barely more than a child when he got them. Why? *It's none of your business.*

He sighed and his face relaxed. Leah pushed harder with her palm and used the cloth to knead the muscles that followed the long line of his spine. He arched against the pressure and she consciously felt his body give in to the sensation. Leah rinsed the cloth in the bowl, dipped it once more in the clean water and wiped the soap from his skin. After lathering the cloth again, she touched the back of his right arm and he lifted it. She took his wrist in her hand and scrubbed from his shoulder down to his fingertips. He relaxed into her hold and she turned his arm back and forth, to cover every inch of his skin.

Time ceased to move for Leah. The only sounds were the ticking of the clock, the slosh of the water and Dodger's soft snores. She did not think of anything beyond the section of skin that she washed. When she finished with his arms she decided to wash his hair. He kept his eyes closed when she tilted his head back. She placed a bucket behind the chair and poured water over his hair to wet it. She used the almond shampoo that Nonnie made and worked it into his thick locks.

He groaned with pleasure as she massaged his scalp. He wrinkled his nose when some of the soap escaped and trickled in the groove between his nose and cheek. She quickly captured it with the towel, rinsed and then dried his hair until it hung in thick waves. It needed a trim, but that could wait until she was done with his bath.

She moved beside him, her knee against his thigh as she faced him. He raised his head, opened his eyes and the look he gave her was so tragic, and so very, very lonely, that her heart shattered.

What was wrong with her? She shouldn't be doing this.

She was playing Delilah, tempting him, or maybe he was tempting her, she didn't know. She did know she was in way over her head. She wasn't thinking clearly. Not thinking at all.

"I'll let you finish up." She stepped away, and left the cloth within easy reach. "Don't worry about the mess, I'll get it in the morning."

Leah fled to her room and sought the comfort of her bed. Ashes greeted her with a sleepy meow and wrapped her tiny body under her chin. Leah listened to the sounds the pastor made. The slosh of the water as he finished washing. The heavy gurgle as he dumped the pail in the sink, and then saw darkness descend when he turned down the lamp.

I didn't bandage his wound. I didn't change his sheets. Those were the least of her recriminations, but she felt too guilty to risk seeing him again so soon. Instead a litany of her faults ran through her head as she listened to his slow step down the hall, then Dodger's as he followed him. She lay, stiff as a post when she heard the squeak of his mattress, and then the heavy huff Dodger let out at the many disruptions that had kept him from his sleep. Even though the pastor was in a different bedroom hearing him so close felt oddly intimate and Leah cursed to herself.

I need doors she thought once again. Sleep was a long time coming.

TEN

He didn't expect to wake up to find a kitten staring at him. Why not? Dodger had had his turn already. The gray ball of fluff extended a paw and touched his cheek. Cade sneezed. It startled the kitten, which laid its ears back and stared at him with wide green eyes. It seemed to think about leaving for a few seconds, then relaxed, kneaded its paws into his bare chest and purred.

"Hello." Cade looked toward the sound and saw a boy with tousled blond hair and huge blue eyes staring at him.

"You must be Banks. Where's your mom?"

The boy seemed scared of him. He hung back in the hall as if he were afraid to come in. "At work."

So they were alone in the house. "What does she do?"

"She's a waitress." Banks swiped his sleeve across his nose. "At the Devil's Table."

Cade grinned. A restaurant called the Devil's Table in a town called Angel's End. Whoever named it that had a wicked sense of humor, something he always appreciated. "Where is the Devil's Table?"

Dodger appeared by Banks's side. The boy wrapped his fingers into the thick scruff of hair of the dog's neck. "Across the street."

Cade put his finger under the kitten's chin and scratched. The kitten stretched his neck out to follow his finger and then rolled over on its back to give Cade better access. Cade looked at Banks. "So I reckon we're the only ones here?"

Banks's eyes grew wide, and he nodded nervously.

"Which means you're in charge." Cade kept his face serious.

"She said for me to tell her if you wake up before it's time to go to school." He hitched up his pants. "Can I come in and get Ashes?"

"I take it this is Ashes?"

"Yes sir."

"You may." Cade waited until Banks had grabbed his kitten and hurriedly stepped away. "Don't bother your mom. I'm going to go right back to sleep."

"You are?"

"Just as soon as I take a trip to the outhouse."

"Um . . . all right . . ."

A bell rang out, clang-clang, as it was jerked back and forth on its rope. The kitten sank its claws into the front of Banks's shirt and laid its ears back at the noise. Dodger looked at Banks and the kitten and whined hopefully. The kitten hissed at the dog and climbed up Banks's chest with its claws still extended. It had to be painful, yet Banks bore it, showing nothing more than a grimace at the discomfort. He was a good kid. Tough. Losing a parent usually did that to you. Made you grow up before you had to. Babying him wouldn't help him. It wouldn't give him what he needed to survive in this world.

The noise had to be coming from the building next door.

He recalled seeing a steeple when he looked around the town last night. "Is that the school bell?"

"Yes sir."

"Then you best be on your way. You don't want to be late."

"Yes sir, I mean no sir . . ." He stood there for a minute until Cade moved his head toward the front door. Banks whirled around, put the kitten on the bed in Leah's room, scooped up his bag and ran to the front door. It slammed behind him. Cade slipped from the bed and went to the front door with Dodger padding along beside him. He stood to the side of the window and peered out. There was no sign of Banks, which meant he either ran as fast as he could to get across the street or else he'd gone directly to school. Cade hoped it was the latter.

The snow on the street was windblown and drifted. It piled up on the buildings, rooftops and windowsills like a sugar coating. The sky, clear the night before, had turned gray and ominous with the promise of more bad weather to come.

There were a few tracks in the snow, mostly foot traffic, and smoke poured from the stovepipe across the street. Two horses stood at the hitching post outside, their heads hanging wearily, proof that whoever had ridden in on them had come a long way on a hard trail.

The building was two stories with a huge sign that went all the way across the porch roof. The top parts of the letters were visible above the snow that piled against it. Devil's Table was written in big, bold, black print. Beneath it were the tops of swirling letters, impossible to read because of the snow. The windows on either side of the entrance were covered with condensation, definite proof that there was a crowd of people inside.

"And I'm betting the weather isn't the only thing they're talking about." Leah had mentioned the search committee.

One of them had already come calling and would no doubt be back soon, especially if Leah told him he'd been up and talking last night.

Last night . . . Cade had never felt anything like that before. He could not recall a time since his mother died when anyone had given him such tender care. Never had anyone touched him in such a way that he felt it, inside, deep in his soul.

It's because she thinks I'm a preacher. That's all. If she knew who I really was and what I am, she wouldn't be leaving her kid alone in the house with me. She'd have me out on the street in a heartbeat. He couldn't think about it. Couldn't let it affect him. Thinking about things like that made him weak and vulnerable. His only thought should be about how to get out of town, and how soon he'd be able to travel.

His wound felt raw and his ribs bruised and tender. Cade put a hand to his stomach and immediately pulled it away. It was too sore to touch. He looked down and saw the wound, red and raw, along with an ugly bruise radiating from it. He reached around and found the exit wound on his back. He'd been lucky. *God's plan?* Timothy's words haunted him and he shook them off.

Leah said she'd bandage him after the bath, but she didn't. She'd left so abruptly, leaving him to finish his bath on his own and fall wearily into a bed that still stank with his fever. What made her run? He hadn't done anything to scare her, had he? He had to admit he'd enjoyed it when she bathed him. He could have done it himself, but why should he when he had someone willing to do it for him. The memory of her touch was still with him.

Cade felt confident Banks hadn't told his mother Cade was awake. It kind of bothered him that the kid had been so easily convinced. He wasn't used to people trusting him. He moved to the kitchen and checked out the window one more time. A man stood on the stoop of the restaurant. He pulled his hat down, hunched his shoulders against the cold, and started down the opposite side of the street. Cade noticed that the building next door to the café was the sheriff's office. It looked dark and deserted and there was no fire coming from the stovepipe. Strange, it seemed like the sheriff should have been over to check on him. Leah mentioned that her husband used to be the sheriff. Had they replaced him? Surely in four years' time they'd found a replacement. If so he would be here soon to question him about the shooting. It would be another thing to look out for. Another lie to add to his ever-growing list.

Dodger sat in the middle of the floor, with his head cocked to the side, and watched Cade as if he were trying to make up his mind about him. Cade opened the cabinet, shoved the shaving kit aside and removed the gun and holster. He popped the cylinder. It was empty and needed cleaning. He didn't have to look at the barrel to know it needed it too. It probably hadn't been touched since her husband died and she shoved it on the shelf and shut the door. He looped the belt around his waist. The cinch was well worn where it had hit her husband. He had to take it up another two notches. He removed it and checked the ammo slots. They were half full. He'd need more if he was going to leave. *When I leave* . . . Cade checked the shelf again by poking his hand into the back corner. He pulled forth a box of cartridges. *Yes! For once things are going my way.*

Another twinge of guilt hit him. He always said God mocked him and laughed at him. But the truth be told, God had watched out for him the past few days. Maybe meeting Timothy was what he needed to change his luck.

Not so lucky for Timothy . . .

That's just the way things were. The West was a dangerous place. If Timothy wasn't ready to take the risk, he should have stayed back in Ohio.

Or maybe you should have moved on and left him alone . . .

Cade checked out the window again. Still no sign of Leah, but another man stood on the porch with a big gray dog by his side. He looked toward the house and then walked into the restaurant.

If he was going to pass for Timothy, he'd better find out all he could about the man. Timothy's Bible was full of papers. Perhaps they would hold some answers. Cade shoved the gun and ammo back on the shelf and shut the cupboard door.

His stomach growled with hunger, but he'd been hungry before. Plenty of times. He wasn't strong enough to leave yet. He needed to wait until the weather broke and who knew when that would be? Cade went back to his room with Dodger on his heels.

Cade picked up the Bible and shook out the papers that he had stuffed back inside. Dodger lay down on the rug next to the bed. The kitten, attracted by the noise, timidly crept into the room while keeping a wary eye on Dodger. She finally made it to the bed and clawed her way up. Cade sorted the letters by stacking them into a pile, starting with the most recently dated. Ashes wiggled her behind and pounced on the stack of papers, scattering them across the bed. Her tail twitched and she pounced again.

Cade picked her up and she mewed in protest. He put her on his lap, rubbed her ears, and gathered the papers into order once more. Ashes chewed on his thumb as he picked up the oldest letter and began to read.

Dear Pastor Key . . .

ELEVEN

"Don't you bring that dog in here." Dusty yelled through the setup window as the cold wind reminded the dwindling group gathered in the Devil's Table why they were grateful to be out of the weather.

"Now Dusty, that's not a bit neighborly." Ward winked at Leah, grinned and walked right in with a big gray dog on his heels. "She's new in town and I told her this was the best place to eat. Don't you dare make a liar out of me." Wade sat down at his usual corner table with his back to the wall and the dog sat down next to him on the floor. She looked at the table with a hopeful eye.

"Tarnation!" Dusty yelled and went back to his cooking. Leah grinned. Dusty's bark was always worse than his bite. She dropped the dirty plates she'd just cleared from Zeke's breakfast into the dishpan and hustled over with a cup and the coffeepot.

"Morning Ward. Where did your friend come from?"

She poured his coffee and looked down into the friendly brown eyes of the dog.

Ward placed his hand on the dog's head. "She was curled up on the back stoop this morning, trying to stay warm."

She did seem friendly, as she paid no mind to Ward's hand. She was used to being touched. "And you decided to invite her for breakfast?"

"Seemed like the neighborly thing to do. Especially since I didn't have much to feed her. And she came right along when I asked." Ward's eyes twinkled with pleasure. Leah knew that for Ward the dog was a welcome change to the everyday monotony of drinking, playing cards and the bad weather.

Dusty clanged some pots together in the back to let the world know he was aggravated. That was nothing new as far as Dusty was concerned. Ward peered around Leah toward the noise and raised his coffee cup in an acknowledgment. Dusty chose to ignore him.

"So, eggs and bacon for two?"

"Sounds great." Ward sipped his coffee. "And then you can tell me how the preacher's fairing."

Leah hoped the cringe in her spine didn't show as she walked back to turn in Ward's order. Of all the people in Angel's End, Ward Phillips had a way of knowing what you were really thinking. She could say the preacher was fine and dandy but Ward would know there was something else going on. That's probably why he was so good at cards; he knew when you were bluffing. Leah went on into the kitchen just in case Ward could see what she was thinking.

The whole town was busting to meet Pastor Timothy. Everyone who came in today had asked about him, even Zeke Preston, the assayer, who didn't give a fig about anyone. All she could say was he's doing fine, still recovering, and she'd let them know when he was ready for company. Margy Ashburn was especially interested, since Pastor Key was unmarried. As she mentioned the fact several times.

Apparently Pris had shared her opinion of the pastor's good looks with the schoolteacher. Leah felt protective of Pastor Timothy in the face of Margy's questions and wasn't sure why. Margy was a kind and gentle soul. She deserved some happiness. Leah just couldn't see her finding it with Pastor Key. They didn't mesh in her mind, but stranger things had happened, especially when two people were lonely.

What about me? She couldn't deny that she was attracted to the man. Leah quickly pushed the thought down into the dark corners of her mind. It felt like she was being unfaithful . . . *to a dead man?* She'd never felt that way when she was with Jake. Could it be because Jake had never spoken to her heart like Pastor Key did last night?

Leah didn't mention to anyone who asked after Pastor Key that he couldn't recall what happened. There were things about his injury that didn't quite make sense. Like why his shirt had a bullet hole in the back, but his frock coat and overcoat didn't. Whoever shot him had to have been pretty close at the time for the bullet to pass all the way through his body, so that ruled out it being an accident. And he must have had both his coats off at the time and then put them back on after he was shot. Why couldn't he remember any of those details?

Then there was the way he spoke to her. It didn't quite fit with her idea of how a minister should talk. Leah shook her head at her foolishness. Did she expect the man to go about spouting Bible verses all the time? A verse for every situation? A homily for every statement?

"Gol-durn shyster thinks he can do whatever he wants . . ." Dusty's muttering was accented with pops of bacon grease as he attacked the skillet with his spatula.

"I thought you liked dogs, Dusty," Leah said. "You're always giving Dodger treats."

"I never invite him in and set him at the table."

"She's not hurting anything or anybody." Leah looked

through the setup window at the dog, now lying beside Ward, patiently awaiting her meal. "I wonder where she came from."

"You mark my words; he'll be bringing her in here every morning from now on, setting her at the table, and spoon-feeding her breakfast."

"Maybe she belongs to someone. Maybe her owner got lost in the snowstorm."

Dusty stopped his fussing and looked at the dog. He scratched his grizzled chin as he studied the animal. "It does seem strange, a dog showing up like this, in the middle of a blizzard. She sure don't belong to anybody I know."

"The Martins had a cat show up in their barn before the storm. With seven kittens."

"Seven you say? Tarnation. You think they'd want to give one away? I think we got mice."

"I'm betting they would." Leah smiled as she pulled a pan of biscuits from the stove. The tops were golden brown perfection and she dropped a dab of butter on each one and watched them melt over the crusty tops. Dusty was over his huff at Ward and on to something else. "We got one," she continued. "Banks named her Ashes. She's real pretty."

"Shoot, a cat don't have to be pretty to catch a mouse. Tell 'em I want a boy cat. Last thing I need underfoot is a bunch of kittens." Dusty slid the eggs onto the plates and then grabbed two biscuits and juggled them as they were still hot. Luckily they landed on the plates.

"I'm sure they have one to spare." Leah picked up the plates and carried them out to Ward. He wasted no time in feeding the dog who made short work of the entire meal.

"Looks like I'm going to need some more." Ward seemed proud of her appetite.

"Poor thing must not have eaten since before the storm."

"More than likely." Ward turned his dark eyes on Leah. "How's the food holding out at your house?"

"Just fine." Leah bent and picked up the tongue-washed plate. There wasn't a crumb left behind. "I heard Jake went home the night of the blizzard," she said, neatly changing the subject before Ward could ask any more questions about her patient. "Do you think he made it all right?"

"Why. Are you suddenly concerned?"

"As I would be for anyone who was out traveling in that storm."

"I'm certain he's fine." Ward leaned back in his chair and studied her. "You know Jake. He's too stubborn to die."

"How about if I start saving the table scraps?"

"Nah, you need those for Dodger. I can pay for this lady to eat," Ward said. He scratched between the dog's ears. "I think I just came up with a name for her." He grinned at Leah. "Lady."

"It suits her. I guess you're planning on keeping her?"

"Might as well. Unless someone shows up to claim her."

The door opened at that exact moment with a swirl of the wind. Ward and Leah both looked up, startled, as if it were an omen or an angel of providence announcing its presence. Instead, a man and two boys came in, the three of them bent and shuffling with weariness. They walked right by Lady without giving her a second glance and took a table in the corner. The sour smell of sickness and unwashed bodies mingled with the familiar scents of bacon and hot coffee. Lady looked at them curiously, let out a slight whine, and then lay down with a sigh. She moved with elegant grace, slowly closing her eyes as she rested her head on her crossed legs.

"Put their meal on my tab." Ward spoke quietly. "They look like they've had a hard road."

"I'll take care of it," Leah assured him. Ward had a good soul, even though he tried to hide it. He'd be mad as the dickens at her if she told anyone he'd paid for someone else's meal.

The smell was much worse as she got closer to the table. Leah stopped to grab a coffeepot and cup before she took their order. Dusty stared at the new arrivals through the window and raised a questioning eyebrow in Leah's direction. She shrugged and went to the table.

The boys looked to be around Banks's age. One older and one younger. Their clothes were threadbare and large on their frames. They both wore coats that would better fit an adult and boots that were too large for their feet. They kept their heads bent as if they were too weak to hold themselves upright. The top knobs of their spine and the tendons of their necks stood out beneath skin stretched tight above their collars. Dirty, stringy hair stuck out beneath their knitted woolen caps and red scabs peppered the skin that showed. Leah was certain she saw lice crawling among the strands of hair beneath their caps and she repressed a shiver. The poor things needed a hot meal, a thorough bathing and to be tucked into a warm bed. The smaller one sniffed and rubbed his nose on his sleeve.

"Welcome to the Devil's Table," Leah piped cheerfully. Dusty's name for the place usually got a laugh or at least a comment from the customers. She sat the cup down before the man and poured it full of steaming hot coffee. "What can I get for you?"

"Whatever you got that's hot and filling." The man wrapped his hands around the cup to soak in the warmth and then took a deep gulp. "And be quick about it. We want to be down the mountain before the next storm breaks." He spoke in short clipped tones, impatient and rude. "We'll take whatever you got that you can wrap up too." He pulled a small bag of gold dust from inside his coat and dropped it on the table. "I can pay for it." He looked up at Leah with darkly shadowed eyes in a hollow and gaunt face.

"Are you from the mining camp?" Miners came and went through Angel's End. A lot of them had their own claims and would come in every few weeks to cash in with Zeke and spend the night in town, most of them spending everything they'd worked weeks for in a few short hours at Heaven's Gate. She'd heard rumors from them of a small community of families who had gone in together on a claim and kept to themselves, even to the point where they'd shoot at anyone who came around.

"None of your damn business," he barked.

The Devil's Table was mostly empty. Ward, and a couple of cowboys who had ridden out the storm in town, and weren't too anxious to get back to work, were the only customers. They all looked up at the words. Ward sat back in his chair with one hand on the table, the other on his gun.

Leah shook her head at Ward. The man was tired and worn was all. More than likely he always spoke that way. If he didn't want conversation then that was fine. She was more worried about the state of the boys than how friendly the father was.

"What was that all about?" Dusty asked when she went back to the window.

"Man just wants to eat is all." Leah quickly glanced over her shoulder at the boys. "Poor things, they are done in. He's taking them out of here before the next storm. I'm not sure if they'll make it."

"Well it's his own business, whatever it is. Just as long as he don't do no more shoutin' in here."

"He said he'd take whatever is ready and any leftovers we can send with him."

"Dang fool." Dusty's judgment was quick as usual and right on target as far as Leah was concerned.

"There's no need for the boys to suffer for it," Leah said. "I'm going to do what I can for them."

"Be careful," Dusty warned. "Give them some of that milk I got warming, and give them some biscuits while I scramble these eggs."

Leah took the kettle from the stove and poured some water into a bowl. She tempered it with some cold water and grabbed a clean cloth. She added two mugs of milk to her tray, a half dozen biscuits and a jar of Nonnie's jam.

"That sure was a good breakfast," one of the cowboys said. "Nothing like a good hearty meal before you start the workday." Their eyes darted between Leah and the family, questioning and wondering.

The workday was nearly half gone for them and Leah was certain they'd hear about it when they finally made it back to their jobs. She smiled at them, reassuring them with her look that everything would be fine and they could be on their way. "I'm glad you liked it," she said. "Dusty? Can you settle up their bill?"

Dusty stomped out from the kitchen while the cowboys bundled up in their coats, scarves and gloves. They tipped their hats at Leah and nodded to Wade as they walked out the door.

Leah sat her tray down on the table. "How about if you boys wash up a bit before you eat?" She didn't look at the father; instead she knelt beside the boys with the cloth which was warm from the water. Leah glanced at Ward who kept a steady eye on the group. There was no doubt in her mind that even if the father protested, he wouldn't do anything to hurt her. Not while Ward was watching.

Leah picked up the trembling hand of the smallest boy and wiped away the grime. There was a huge scab on his wrist and it broke away when she swiped the cloth over it. Both boys kept their eyes down and were deathly quiet as she quickly did what she could for their hands and then went to work on their faces. The littlest one's nose kept running and was covered with crust but Leah kept at it until she was satisfied with the results.

"There now," she said. "You can drink your milk. It should be cooled off enough so it won't burn your mouths."

"Thank you ma'am," the oldest one said and quickly grabbed his mug.

The littlest one turned his pinched little face to Leah. "Our momma died," he said in a quiet voice.

The father hissed and the boy jumped. His eyes were wide with fear, the whites showing all around. She wanted nothing more than to gather him up in her arms and comfort him, but she didn't want to risk bringing down the father's vengeance after they were gone.

"I'm sorry to hear that," she said. "Now drink your milk and I'll bring you some more with your meal." The father nodded and the boy grabbed the mug.

Dusty stomped over with three full plates. Eggs, bacon, sausage, gravy and more biscuits. "Eat up," he said as he dropped them on the table with a distinct thud. He stood by the table with his arms crossed, and dared the man to say a word about anything.

Leah knew he didn't want her talking to the man anymore. She'd done all she could for the boys. Some people valued their pride before their children and this man was one of those. She knew, well enough, that when it came to Banks, no sacrifice was too great and she would gladly do whatever it took to keep him safe even if it meant crawling naked through the dirt. She left Dusty to take care of them and went to refill Ward's coffee.

"The mother died," she said quietly to Ward's questioning look.

"Where did they come from?" Ward asked. "How did she die?"

Leah shrugged. "They didn't say and the father isn't talking." She was suddenly very, very tired. She looked out the window by Ward's usual table. The street was deserted except for two horses hitched to the rail, both laden down with baggage. They must belong to the sorry little family. The wind, whistling down from the mountain, carved a narrow path right down the middle of the road. Smoke rose steadily from all the chimneys in sight except her own. She'd have to build the fires back up when she finished her shift.

School was in session. Margy, desperate to get in a full day while the weather was clear, had put out the word to all those who lived in town. The children from the ranches and farms would be excused. Banks should be in school. He was good at getting there on his own, although he usually came over for a bite of breakfast before he went. She missed seeing him this morning. He was supposed to tell her when Pastor Key woke up. The man must have been asleep when he left for school. *He sleeps all day and prowls around at night . . .*

"Have you been getting any rest?" Ward studied her.

"About what you'd expect." Leah wiped a few crumbs from the table. "The pastor was pretty sick from that wound. There were a few times when I didn't think he was going to make it." She looked at the table with the boys to keep Ward from looking into her eyes. "Now that his fever has broken, things should get back to normal."

"Maybe it's time for me to pay him a visit." Ward finished his coffee and put his napkin on the table. "Welcome him to town."

"He's probably still asleep." Leah stacked Ward's dishes.

"From what Jim said, it sounds like he pursues sleeping like it's his job." Ward stood and stretched a bit. Lady watched him carefully and followed him to the door. Ward clamped his hat down firmly on his head and buttoned the top button on his overcoat. "Usually preachers like to eat."

"And you would be an authority on that?"

Ward left her with a cryptic smile and Lady by his side. Leah watched him as he walked across the street to her house and went right in without knocking. *Time for you to wake up Pastor Key.*

Dusty poked his head through the setup window and

motioned her over. "He done paid." He handed her a burlap bag full of food. "Give him this so he can be on his way."

"Ward said to put it on his tab."

"He wouldn't have it."

Leah looked at the boys. "It might be all the money he had."

"Let it go, Leah. You can't save the world. Sometimes it takes every bit of what you got just to save yourself. That don't make it right or wrong, it just makes it the way it is."

"I guess you're right."

"I know I am." Dusty picked up a pan and went to work, scraping bits of egg from the sides. "Don't waste any more of your time on them. You got your own to worry about. Let them be on their way."

Leah passed the food on to the man. The family left as silently as they came in, without speaking another word. Leah grabbed her shawl, walked out on the stoop and watched as they rode down the street, with the wind pushing them all the way. As they faded from sight, long thin clouds trailed across the sky, like tattered banners left on a battlefield after the dead had been collected.

Leah pulled her shawl tight against the wind. More snow was coming. All she could do now was pray that the little family would find shelter before it hit.

TWELVE

The creak of the door brought Dodger to his feet. He growled and padded the hallway. The footsteps were too heavy to be Leah's. Cade's first instinct was to grab a gun and take cover. That wasn't something a preacher would do. A preacher would have nothing to hide. He on the other hand . . . Cade swept the letters beneath the blankets and placed the open Bible in his lap. Ashes perked her ears to the noise, poised to run and hide if necessary. Dodger sniffed the air and wagged his tail.

Cade set his face in what he hoped was a ministerial pose. It felt like the same face he made when he took a draught of bad cider. He huffed out his breath and tried again. It was too late to back out now. The cards had been dealt and he'd already bid. He couldn't just fess up now and say he was confused from being shot. There'd be too many questions, too many what-ifs, and all of them would start with how and why he had Timothy's things in his possession.

From what he'd read in the letters, no one in Angel's End had met Timothy face-to-face. Since he had met him, Cade knew he could pass for him on description alone, although he was a bit taller and much slimmer than the preacher.

A man and a dog appeared in the doorway. Ashes hissed indignantly, backed up to the headboard in close proximity to Cade and growled low in her throat. The stranger smiled at the kitten's antics. Dodger and the dog by the man's side went through the customary greeting ritual when meeting someone new. They sniffed each other.

"I reckon she already thinks she's the boss." The man walked into the room and scratched his finger at the end of the bed to tempt the kitten.

Cade smiled pleasantly at the man. He'd played this game before, many times. Jasper had taught him well the craft of running a scam, in the years he'd spent with him. Even though his visitor's face was open and friendly, the dark eyes had already sized him up, taking in his physical strength and the severity of his wound. You always watch the mark's eyes. That was where you'd find the answers. That was how you'd know the con was working. The lips may say plenty, but the eyes don't lie.

"I don't believe we've met," Cade said. He would remember if they had. This man wasn't one to be easily fooled. Cade would have to watch his step around him.

"I'm Ward Phillips." He extended his hand and the men shook. The grip was strong and easy. Cade knew his was weaker but it suited him at the moment. There was no need to give anything away. The man's name wasn't on the list of the search committee so why was he here? "I own the saloon." His tone was open and friendly as he crouched by the dogs and gave Dodger a good rub.

"The saloon?" Cade grinned. "Isn't that contrary to my purpose here?" He'd love to visit a good saloon.

Ward pulled the chair from the corner and sat down. "The Heaven's Gate."

Cade laughed. "Beware all ye who enter." Heaven's Gate Saloon and the Devil's Table café. Angel's End was turning out to be an interesting place.

Ward shook his head. "I believe in everything in moderation," he said with a lazy smile. "And to each his own." He nodded his head toward Cade's wound. "How you feeling?"

"Sore." Cade touched his hand to his side. He'd put his shirt on, since the house was cold. The fires were low. He should have fed them but he'd been concentrating on the letters instead. "I think I've got a couple of busted ribs. The bullet must have cracked them when it passed through."

"You were lucky it did pass through," Ward said. Cade waited for the inevitable. The questions about what happened. He'd decided the best course was to say he couldn't remember. The less lies he told, the less he'd have to keep track of. Keep it simple.

"God's providence," Cade said. "For which I am eternally grateful." He felt somewhat satisfied. He'd actually spoken the truth, or at least the truth according to Timothy. Cade knew God would have a punch line in there somewhere. He'd just have to wait for it, and hope he was long gone when it came. God would have the last laugh. It was just up to Cade to make sure he would survive it.

"Jim Martin said you didn't recall what happened."

"You're the first person I've talked to, besides Leah."

"You'd be dead now, if not for her. She's the one who found you in the middle of the blizzard. Right in front of the statue."

"Statue?" Cade tried to recall all the details that had been in the letters compared to what Leah had mentioned in conversation. "The angel statue? The one the town's named after?"

"That's it."

"The Lord does work in mysterious ways." Cade put his hand on his side again. Sitting around talking to the saloon owner wasn't helping him form a plan to get out of town. "I'm sorry to say it might be awhile before I'm able to take on my duties. I'm as weak as this kitten."

"There's no rush," Ward said. "We really didn't expect you to show up before springtime anyway. The snow makes it hard for people to come into town for church. We're lucky if we have one service a month in the winter. Of course those of us that live in town . . ." Ward leaned back in his chair. "Let's just say we're a real friendly bunch. Everyone will want to meet you and get to know you, have you over for supper, you know, the usual things."

That was exactly what Cade was afraid of. "Hopefully I'll be on the mend soon." The more people he talked to, the better the chance that they'd see through his lies. Cade flipped the pages of the Bible as if he'd been looking for a passage to disguise the fact that he was studying Ward. He definitely didn't want him sniffing around too much.

"So why is it a saloon owner decided to pay me a visit?" He looked at the Bible as if he'd found the passage he was looking for.

God has foreseen something better for us . . .

He noticed he was in Hebrews before he shut the Bible and put it aside. Ashes decided that the threat at the end of the bed was minimal and butted his hand with her forehead so he'd pet her. Cade picked her up and put her in his lap and rubbed her chin. Her purr rumbled deep in her throat, a big sound for such a tiny creature.

"You got some sins you're trying to atone for?" He gave Ward a charming smile.

Ward's eyes narrowed for a moment, and then he smiled right back at Cade.

"I imagine we've all backslid a time or two. And since I own the saloon, which is the center for all the hedonistic pleasures in town, I reckon I've done more than my fair share." He stopped for a few seconds, put his hand to his chin as if he were deep in thought and laughed. "Yep, more than my fair share."

"Nobody is keeping score." Cade shrugged. "And as you said, everything in moderation."

"Even Jesus drank wine?"

"Exactly." Cade touched his side again and added a wince.

"I'll let you get your rest."

"I'd appreciate it." Cade yawned and politely covered it with his hand. His mother may have been dead for decades but he still well recalled how to act in polite society, despite the company he'd been keeping of late. "And if you don't mind, tell everyone that I'm just not up to a lot of visitors quite yet. I want to be at my best when I finally do meet them all."

"Oh I'm sure everyone will . . ."

Cade stuck out his hand in dismissal. "Thank you for understanding."

Ward paused for a moment, and then took it. Cade was glad to see the man recognized when he'd been beat. If that meant he'd leave him alone for a while longer, then he'd take it and be grateful for it.

"Nice-looking dog," he added.

"Lady?" Ward tapped his leg and the dog came to him. "Why we just met this morning," he said. "As you can see, I'm a real charmer with the ladies, another one of my sins. Why just trying to save my soul is going to be a full-time job." Ward's smile was something Cade had seen in the mirror a time or two himself.

"Which is why I need to get my strength back up." Cade gave him an answering smile to let him know that he was onto Ward's little game.

Ward paused at the door. "Leah will take real good care of you."

Something happened at the mention of her name. Something strange, a notion that he had to share her, and he didn't want to, that the people in town knew her better and were closer to her. He didn't like it. He didn't like the notion, nor did he like the feeling. It was dangerous.

"She has," he said simply.

"You should have seen her with these boys that came into the diner." Ward leaned against the doorway, ready to talk more. Cade needed him to leave. The more time they spent talking the better the chance the saloon owner would see through his façade. As if in answer to his unspoken prayer, the door creaked open. Ward turned and looked, and a big grin spread across his face. "Speak of the devil," he said.

Cade recognized the soft sound of her footsteps. Ward left him with a tip of his hat and the big dog on his heels. Dodger bounded joyfully to greet her, and the noise of his greeting made it sound as if she'd been gone for days instead of mere hours. Good-byes were said between Leah and Ward. Cade listened carefully to the exchange. Was there something between them?

Did she remember last night? Or did he remember it wrong. Surely he didn't imagine it. Could it be that it was just another part of his fevered dreams? Was he imagining something that wasn't really there?

Cade listened as she talked to Dodger. She told him how wonderful he was, what a good job he did watching the house, and how much she missed him. Had anyone ever voiced the same words to him? Not in his adult life. Not since he was taken from the orphanage. *Never . . .*

Ashes chewed on his thumb. Her teeth were sharp and insistent. "Are you as hungry as I am?" The kitten stared up at him with huge green eyes. They reminded him of Leah's.

Cade heard the hesitancy in Leah's footsteps. What was she doing out there?

He kept hold of the kitten and watched the doorway. Finally she appeared. It was as if the sun broke through the clouds. *Get a grip . . .*

Her eyes quickly dashed over him and an odd smile quirked her lips when she saw Ashes on his lap. "Oh my goodness, I hope she hasn't bothered you too much."

"Nope." Cade grinned. "Actually she's been keeping me company."

She was nervous. He could tell by the way her eyes darted about, as if she needed something to look at besides him. "Are you hungry?" she finally asked.

"Starving." Cade kicked the sheets and blankets back and moved to the side of the bed. The pain in his ribs grabbed him and he flinched, bent over in agony as his entire body screamed in protest.

She was at his side in an instant. "I'm so sorry. I didn't wrap your ribs last night . . ." Her face turned scarlet and she turned away.

Cade fought to get his breath back. At first the pain had taken it, but then Leah's proximity, her welcoming scent, had left him breathless. Finally he recovered his good senses and was able to take a deep breath. Leah began to move away. He grabbed her hand.

Before he could think, he stood, willed his ribs to stop screaming and pulled her back. Her eyes widened in shock. He watched as those lovely gold flecks danced around in the green. Her lips parted as she slammed against him when he pulled one more time, stronger and harder than he meant to. Or maybe it wasn't. He wanted her close. He wanted to feel every inch of her against him. *I am going straight to hell but first I want to taste heaven.*

Cade buried his hand in her hair to grasp the back of her head and he kissed her. He felt her sharp and sudden intake of breath against his lips and he covered them with his mouth. Her hands fluttered against his shirt, then her fingers spread and she wrapped the fabric within them. She yielded, just a bit, but enough to let him taste her.

God, how he tasted her. He lost himself within her. Time ceased. He kissed her until he couldn't breathe and his ribs ached, as his lungs fought for air.

They broke apart, suddenly, when Dodger's sharp bark rang in their ears. Leah stared up at him, panting and threw her palms against her cheeks, shocked at either his behavior or hers, or possibly both. A sudden wicked, most unminister-like thought crossed his mind and he reached for her again.

"Yoo-hoo!"

"Bettina!" Leah gasped and whirled away, leaving Cade aching in more places than one.

THIRTEEN

Chocolate cake. Cade could not recall the last time he'd had chocolate cake. Maybe he'd never had it, just dreamed about it at sometime or other. It was the best thing he'd ever tasted, except for Leah.

It hadn't taken him long to figure Bettina Swanson out. She'd walked into Leah's house as if she owned it, all dressed up in her fancy duds and a coat with a fur collar and a hat that had him questioning the sanity of whoever made it, or sold it for that matter. She carried a fresh baked chocolate cake in a box tied up with a piece of ribbon and was determined to meet him. Since she was already in, Leah sat her down in the parlor and informed him he had a visitor. Then she'd given him a pair of slippers that were too short for his feet and politely shown him in. Bettina Swanson considered herself the first lady of Angel's End and she was here to show him she was so.

"Would you like another piece?" Bettina asked.

"Don't mind if I do." Cade placed his plate on the small table in the parlor where they sat. Just that small bit of movement was enough to make him wince with pain. It took every bit of his concentration to keep the small, pleasant smile on his face. His side was killing him. He desperately needed his ribs wrapped but he wasn't about to say anything in front of Bettina. He knew her type. She'd jump on Leah's care of him like a rat on a piece of cheese and use it as a juicy piece of gossip with everyone who walked into her store. Nope, he could suffer through until they were alone again. Then he'd get Leah to wrap his side again. She'd stayed away since they were interrupted, keeping busy around the house while he entertained his visitor.

Bettina pretended to be embarrassed by his unspoken compliment of her baking, sliced two more pieces, and served them both. She crossed her ankles beneath her fancy dress and lifted her pinkie as she took a sip of tea.

"So why don't you tell me about the townsfolk, so I'll have a finer appreciation of them when I finally do get to meet them." Cade gave Bettina a wink that let her know that he knew she was the one to talk to. He also knew, from experience, that the less he said the better off he'd be in the long run.

It was also quite obvious that Bettina loved the sound of her own voice. She leaned in close, conspiratorially, and was off, talking about people and giving him every minute detail she could think of, while shoveling cake into her mouth. It was a sight to behold.

She started with the assayer, Zeke Preston. Apparently the man had gotten on her bad side when he first came to town and she hadn't forgiven him. Or maybe it was that Zeke didn't give a hoot what she thought of him. Anyway, he bore watching in Bettina's mind and was probably robbing those poor miners blind. That led to a long commentary on the miners that went from calling them poor pathetic creatures that needed prayer and much ministering, to the fact that she had to watch them every minute when they came into the store because they'd steal anything that wasn't nailed down.

She went on and on. Cade ate his cake and casually watched Leah. She'd fixed them a pot of hot tea, and then gone to the back of the house. She walked to the kitchen with the sheets from his bed, and then made several trips back and forth with the bucket.

I should fix that pump . . .

"I believe we need more tea," Bettina exclaimed as she tipped the pot up to drain out the last drop. It was a good thing her husband owned the general store. The woman sure could eat and drink. He spared a glance at the floorboards of the parlor. Hopefully there were stout posts beneath it. He'd sat down in the rocking chair next to the fireplace as soon as he came into the parlor. He was certain Leah's worn sofa wouldn't hold both of them.

"Yoo-hoo," Bettina called out. "Leah dear, we need more tea."

"I'm fine, Mrs. Swanson," Cade said. If Leah brought another pot of tea he'd be stuck with this woman forever. "And I am feeling a bit tired."

"Oh you poor dear," Bettina exclaimed. "I know just what you need. You take a nice nap and then I'll send Margy over to read to you."

Cade's cup rattled against the saucer. "Margy?"

"Margy Ashburn, our schoolteacher. She's quite nice." Bettina smiled sweetly over her cup. "And single"—she leaned over the table and whispered loudly as if she didn't want Leah to hear.

Cade choked on the sip of tea he'd just taken. The convulsion felt like the kick of a mule. He couldn't help but grab his side as hot tea shot out his nose. He quickly grabbed one of the napkins Leah had brought in on the tea tray.

"Oh dear, are you all right?"

Cade wiped his mouth and face and once again was grateful for the lessons on propriety his mother had taught him when he was a boy. She'd been right; they had served him well as an adult. He removed the napkin to find Leah standing in the doorway, watching him with her lovely green eyes.

"Yes," he sputtered. "I'm fine. I just need some rest."

"I changed your sheets," Leah said.

"Thank you." Cade slowly stood. "Thank you so much for your visit, Mrs. Swanson." Cade extended his hand. "And the cake."

"Well." She stood and took Cade's hand. She looked around as if she'd forgotten something and settled on the cake. "I'll leave this for later. So you don't have to do so much dear," she said to Leah.

"You are always so thoughtful." Leah's voice sounded strangled as she walked Bettina to the door. Was it because of the kiss or because of the company?

The kiss. He shouldn't have kissed her. Why had he done it? He knew why. *Because she's beautiful and kind and I've never met anyone quite like her.* If he was going to survive he'd need to do a better job of thinking things through. Quit letting his cock do the thinking for him. She was a decent woman and he'd taken advantage of her. Kissing her would lead to more things that he couldn't and wouldn't let happen. He didn't want her close. He didn't want anyone close. He had to leave before they started asking questions he couldn't answer. They thought he was a preacher. They'd want him to preach a sermon. They'd even expect him to pray. Lord help them all when that day came about.

Just another one of God's jokes . . . And now the town gossip thought she could set him up with the schoolteacher. Of course she did. A single pastor and a single schoolteacher. It was a match made in heaven. Timothy more than likely would have loved it.

Not after he met Leah . . . Cade put his hand to his side. This predicament was worse than getting shot. Almost.

"Come into the kitchen and I'll wrap your ribs." The look Leah gave him was full of apology.

He would have sighed in relief but it would hurt too much. Instead he followed her to the kitchen. His sheets were soaking in the sink. She had been busy during Bettina's visit. All this effort because of him. Cade watched her as she gathered the things she needed to wrap his ribs. She'd already worked at the diner today and now here she was, taking care of him.

"When I'm feeling better I'll see about fixing your pump." He would do it before he left. It was the least he could do.

"That's nothing for you to worry about," she said.

"You shouldn't have to work so hard just to have water, not when there's a pump already here." Cade eased his body into a chair and unbuttoned his shirt.

Leah picked up a roll of bandage. "I know they hurt," she said. "Why didn't you say anything? You didn't have to suffer through that visit with Bettina just because I didn't take proper care of you."

"I didn't want her to know."

She tilted her head as if it helped her to see him. "Why?"

Cade shrugged. "It wasn't any of her business."

She looked shocked. Of course she did. He wasn't supposed to say things like that. Ministers weren't supposed to pass judgment on people, at least not while eating cake in parlors. That was for Sunday morning service, and it was supposed to be done in a kind and general way, so that it didn't exactly point a finger at anyone. That way people like Bettina could sit in the front row and feel smug.

He could be wrong. Maybe Timothy was one of those fire-and-brimstone type preachers Jasper had posed as a time or two. Scared the people into emptying their pockets into the collection plate before taking off in the middle of the night with their tithes.

No, Timothy wasn't one of those preachers. And Timothy never would have said those words. Of course Timothy never would have found himself in the same situation. If not for Cade, Timothy would be fine and dandy and eating chocolate cake like there was no tomorrow.

Not only do you have to think like Timothy, you have to think like Jasper.

Cade rubbed his forehead. "I'm sorry. I shouldn't have said that." He looked at Leah. "It's just that you've been so kind to me and I've seen people like Mrs. Swanson before. They do love to talk."

She studied him. Her forehead wrinkled with the intensity of her thoughts. Thoughts that could be dangerous for both of them. Especially for her.

"I shouldn't have kissed you." *No matter how bad I wanted to . . .*

Leah opened her mouth to speak, then changed her mind and clamped it shut in a firm line. Guilt, a common enough companion that he usually ignored it, gave him a sharp poke. He couldn't look at her. Shouldn't, because he'd just kiss her again.

"This will be easier if you take off your shirt and stand up." Her tone was all business, as if she were talking to Banks and telling him to do his chores. Cade did as she told and held perfectly still as she padded his wounds and wrapped the bandage tightly around his ribs. He kept his eyes on the cabinet that held the gun. Tonight, while she slept, he'd get it out, give it a good cleaning, then sneak out and get the lay of the land. He might not be strong enough to leave yet, but there was no harm in planning ahead.

She smelled like roses. Her hair was right beneath his face and he could smell it. Each time she moved the scent drifted upward and tempted him to bury his head in her neck and breathe deep. How could someone smell like roses in the middle of winter?

"Is that too tight?" She backed away, afraid to be close, even though he'd apologized.

Cade put his hand to his side. The bandage was so tight he could barely breathe. That was the way it should be. It would keep him from moving too fast. From doing anything stupid.

If only everything else could be that easy.

FOURTEEN

There was no way Leah could live with that man in her house. The town would just have to make other arrangements for the new preacher. She'd ask Jim to tell the search committee that it was more work than she thought, that she didn't need the money . . .

That you want to kiss him again and do some other things that are on the "thou shalt not" list. She shouldn't be thinking such thoughts about a minister. But just because he was a minister didn't make him less than a man. Maybe that was the problem. Was she looking at him as a minister or as a man? Why couldn't he be both? A very desirable man who happened to be a minister. Just like Nate was a sheriff and Jake was a rancher and Ward a saloon owner.

And what was so wrong about thinking that way? Did she really want to spend the rest of her time on this earth alone? Was it wrong for her to want to love again? Just because she didn't have any feelings for Jake didn't mean she couldn't have feelings. It was just so unexpected. He was at least a dozen years older than her—not that he looked it. And he definitely didn't act it.

Leah huffed in frustration as she crossed the street to the diner. She kissed him! He probably thought she was the biggest whore in Colorado. Lord have mercy, what had she been thinking?

He kissed you first . . . Yes, but I threw myself at him. Didn't I? And now Bettina wants to set him up with Margy. *Why not me? Why shouldn't I have him?*

"Will you get a hold of yourself and just think for a minute?" Leah chastised herself as she stopped on the stoop in front of the diner. She grabbed on to the post and put her cheek against it. Her face felt hot and the wood, nearly as chilly as the winter air, helped cool her skin. Pastor Key surely had an effect on her.

Leah looked up at the heavy clouds gathering in the sky and wondered if it was right to ask God for help in such a situation. It seemed to her as if the devil was more involved at the moment than God. The truth of the matter was she couldn't blame her feelings for Timothy on the devil as it was all her. He had awakened something inside of her that she'd thought she'd buried with Nate.

She needed to talk to someone. If she kept thinking about it she'd drive herself crazy. Leah set off again, back across the street to the Martins'. She heard the steady ping-ping of Jim's hammer and breathed a sigh of relief that he was at work. This was not something she wanted to talk about in front of Jim.

"Come in," Gretchen called out when she knocked on the door. Leah followed the sound of her friend's voice to the back porch where she found Gretchen washing clothes. Even though the air was frigid, Gretchen's red hair was plastered to her head with sweat from the hard work and the hot water that steamed the air.

"I'm hoping to get this load done before the next storm hits," Gretchen said by way of greeting. "Of course with this brood that's an impossible task."

"Don't stop on my account," Leah said. "I don't know how you do it," she confessed. "Just taking care of Banks wears me out."

Gretchen looked up from the washtub. "Taking care of Banks wears you out or taking care of Pastor Key?" It didn't take Gretchen long to get to the heart of the matter. "He wasn't quite what you expected, was he?" she asked with a teasing grin.

"I don't think he's what anyone expected," Leah said.

"What do you mean?" Gretchen wrung out a shirt and tossed it over a line strung between the porch posts.

Leah chewed on her lip, not sure of how much she should say. "Where's Nonnie?"

"She walked out to the stable with Dusty. He came to get a kitten." Gretchen gave her a look; much like the one she gave her children when they were disobedient. "What happened?"

Leah glanced around to make sure there wasn't anyone to hear. "He kissed me?"

"What?" Gretchen looked up from the washtub. "Really?"

"Yes, but then he said he shouldn't have."

"Well of course he shouldn't have. But he did." Gretchen grinned. "How was it?"

"Um . . . it was nice, I guess."

"What do you mean 'I guess'?"

"I mean it was nice when he kissed me, but then when he apologized it made me feel . . . I don't know . . . cheap? I would rather he hadn't kissed me at all, if he was going to apologize after."

"He's confused," Gretchen advised. "Just like you are. He feels like he's overstepped the boundaries. And he's probably weak because of his illness."

"That does make sense," Leah agreed. "But . . ."

"But what?"

Leah wasn't sure if she should tell Gretchen more. That she felt like there were things about Pastor Key that didn't fit. The pieces were all there but something wasn't quite right. He kissed her like there was no tomorrow and then he apologized. He gave vague answers. He said he didn't remember getting shot. How could you not remember something like that? And he didn't seem to want anyone to pursue his attacker. She needed time to figure it all out. She wasn't ready to pass judgment on him. It wasn't her place.

"Did something else happen?" Gretchen asked.

"No," Leah answered honestly. "He just eats a lot."

"What minister doesn't?" Gretchen laughed. "But be honest. Are you uncomfortable having him there? Do you need him to go someplace else?"

This was her chance. Did she want him gone? If she asked someone else to take him there'd be talk. People would want to know why. It was a small town with a long hard winter that was just now getting started. Everyone would gnaw on the news like a dog with a bone, and more than likely what they came up with would be far worse than what had actually happened.

"No. There's no need for him to go. But do you think you could ask Jim to get my doors finished?"

"Should he put locks on them too?"

"No," Leah laughed. "It's not that drastic. It'll just keep things from getting uncomfortable if . . ." Her voice trailed off, as she wasn't sure what she wanted to say.

"I will." Gretchen quickly assured her as she wrung out one of Jim's shirts and plopped it on the line. She dried her hands on her apron and wiped the sweat from her face with the back of her hand. "If you answer one question for me."

Leah wasn't sure she wanted to hear the question. But there was no going back now. "I'll try," she said.

"Would it be a bad thing if something did happen between you and the pastor?"

"Oh no, I don't want . . ."

"Why not?" Gretchen interrupted. "It's been four years since Nate passed. Do you really want to be alone for the rest of your life?"

"I'm not ready," Leah insisted. Or was she?

"Will you just think about it?" Gretchen put another pile of clothing in the washtub. "There must be something there or it wouldn't have bothered you so much."

Leah had to admit the older woman was right. But she wasn't exactly sure how she felt, and she didn't think anything else was going to happen. Not after Timothy regretted kissing her. "Thanks for listening. I'll think it all over. Now I'd best get back to work."

"Good luck!" Gretchen called after her.

Leah took a deep breath as she headed back to the diner. Talking to Gretchen hadn't solved her problem but she did feel better. It was almost as if she'd gone to Gretchen seeking permission. For what exactly she couldn't put her finger on.

Smoke poured from the chimney of the white steepled building at the northern end of the street. The paint on it was still so new that it matched the fresh coating of snow piled up around it. The people of Angel's End had all donated to the building of it, all participated in its construction, even Banks and the Martin kids had driven nails and painted the walls. The building had been built to serve a double purpose. It was the church and the schoolhouse. Banks was there now, working away at his lessons. He was her first and only concern. She couldn't, and she wouldn't, expose him to anything unseemly. Timothy's apology led her to believe that nothing else would happen between them. She would take him at his word and let things be for now.

And he did offer to repair the pump. She hadn't dared ask anyone else to fix it because then there would be comments about her not making it on her own. They'd all predicted she couldn't survive on her own when Nate died. Everyone thought she was crazy for not marrying Jake. Sometimes pride was a horrible companion. It sure didn't do much to keep you warm on a cold winter's night. *That's what Dodger is for* . . .

Leah smiled at her foolishness. The answer to her dilemma was quite simple actually. All she needed to do was keep things formal between her and the pastor. It should be easy now that he was healing up. She wouldn't have to get close to him. Wouldn't be tempted. And hopefully Jim would have her doors done soon, especially since Gretchen knew why they needed to be finished sooner rather than later. Until then she could hang a drape over the openings to the bedrooms.

Once he was better and about his job she'd probably not see much of him. Everyone would be eager to have him over for supper, and Dusty was supposed to take care of the rest of his meals. It would be easy to stay busy at the diner so she wouldn't have to talk to him much. She would just make sure to be out the door before he got up in the mornings.

Maybe he and Margy would hit it off. They could get married and the town would build them a little house by the church where they could live happily ever after. Just like she'd planned with Nate.

He pushed me away . . . Leah had to admit her ego was crushed in no uncertain terms. She was humiliated and embarrassed. She felt like a fool. But he was the one who kissed her. She'd only gone where he led her. The man was confusing with the kissing and the spouting of Bible verses and the way he looked at her. She shouldn't let her feelings cloud her judgment. The problem was she couldn't figure out exactly what her feelings were at the moment.

"You gonna stand out there all day?" Dusty interrupted her musings. "It's colder than a nun's teat out here."

Leah grinned at Dusty's colorful language. He could be creative when the need called for it. And sometimes when it didn't. "It actually feels kind of nice. I've been cooped up way too long."

"Maybe it's just because some tasks are more trying than others." Dusty gave a deliberate look at her house. It was no secret that Dusty didn't want a preacher in town. He said his business was between him and God and he didn't need no preacher running interference for him.

Leah refrained from rolling her eyes. She heard a faint mew and raised an eyebrow questioningly. Dusty grinned and opened his jacket. An orange kitten popped its head out. "Gretchen told me to take one before the youngins got home from school. What do you think?"

Leah touched the head of the orange kitten that peeped out of Dusty's coat. "I think you got a winner. You picked out a name yet?"

"Peaches." Dusty grinned from ear to ear. "He looks just like a fuzzy new peach, don't you think?"

"I sure do."

Dusty rubbed the kitten's head with his forefinger while he looked up and down the deserted streets. Smoke poured from all the chimneys and the faint sound of Ward playing the piano drifted out of the saloon. "Kind of strange, all these critters suddenly showing up." He cocked his head to one side, thinking hard on his statement.

"Yes, it's been a week for strays. Momma cat, a dog and a preacher, all in the space of five days."

"Speaking of strays, here comes Jake." Leah looked north, beyond the schoolhouse, and sure enough Jake was riding in and looked to be in a hurry. His horse was lathered and blowing hard when he pulled up in front of the diner.

"What's got you in such a hurry?" Dusty asked.

"You know that mining camp up on Rattlesnake Creek?" Jake swung out of the saddle and smacked his horse on the rump. The animal, well trained, took off for Martins' livery where it knew a warm stall and a rubdown awaited him.

"I've heard of it. They're the ones that'd just as soon shoot you as look at you."

"I had a donkey show up on my front porch this morning, making a horrible racket. When I tried to catch it, it ran off. So I saddled up to trail it, thinking someone must be hurt or dead and it led me straight up the canyon to the camp. The entire camp was dead, wiped out by measles from the looks of it."

"The entire camp?" A chill chased down Leah's spine. Measles was a horrible way to die.

"Someone must have survived. A few of them were buried before the snow but the rest . . ." Jake shook his head. "We're going to have to go back up there and burn the bodies."

The chill she felt worsened. "Those boys . . ." Leah looked at Dusty as words failed her.

"We had a man with two boys in early this morning," Dusty explained to Jake. "And he was in a big hurry to get out of town before the weather hit."

"Did either of you touch them? Get close?"

Leah was shivering now. She wrapped her shawl tighter around her body. "I gave the boys a good washing."

"Damn it, Leah!" Jake exploded. "Every person that happens to walk by doesn't need to be taken care of. Most people just want to be left alone. Who else have you been around?"

Leah shook her head, shocked by Jake's outburst and the fact that she had been exposed to such a deadly disease. "Pastor Key. Bettina came by . . . and I talked to Ward some. Dusty here, and I just left Gretchen. But as far as touching anyone . . ." Leah flushed as the memory of the kiss came rushing back. "Just Pastor Key. I changed his bandage when I went home," she hastily added.

Jake took off his hat. Ran his hand through his hair. Looked around the empty streets. "We're going to have to quarantine you. Until we know for sure. And him too I guess."

Locked in the house . . . with Timothy Key . . . "Banks, oh my goodness, Banks . . ."

"We'll make sure Banks is taken care of." For a moment there she thought Jake was going to touch her. Pull her to him. Tell her everything was going to be all right. Instead he turned away and looked down the street toward Heaven's Gate. "Leah, go on home and tell the pastor what's happened."

"Jake, don't you think you're overreacting?" Leah asked. His tone with her had her feeling mutinous. Did he really expect her to jump at his command like that?

Jake whirled around to face her. "I'm not overreacting." His jaw was clenched and his voice tight. "You didn't see them. You don't ever want to see what I just witnessed up there. Now go home and stay there, please, for all our sakes."

"All right." The look on Jake's face was frightening. "I'll go." Leah stepped into the street. Jake was already walking away. "I fixed Bettina some tea. You might want to watch her also."

"Don't you worry none," Dusty assured her. "We'll make sure she stays put until we know what's going on."

Jake stopped and turned around, his face now livid. "Damn it, Leah! You always got to be taking care of people."

Leah straightened her spine. She refused to cry. She knew Jake was frustrated. His anger wouldn't help. It wouldn't change a thing. "They were boys Jake. Little boys who needed some care."

Dusty, for once the peacemaker, put a hand on Jake's arm. "Go on home, Leah," he said. "We'll check in on you in a bit."

What if I have the measles? What if I die? Who would dare come to help her if she got sick? At least she knew the town would care for Banks. Leah went into her house. It felt cold. So very cold. Dodger, always faithful, always waiting, greeted her at the door. Leah dropped to her knees and wrapped her arms around the dog.

"Please God, let it be all right."

FIFTEEN

Leah was crying. Why was she crying? Cade hadn't expected her to be back for hours. He quickly slid the gun beneath the mattress. Ashes meowed sleepily at the interruption and went back to her nap. Cade went into the hall. Leah crouched before the door with her arms around Dodger and her face buried in his fur. She looked small and helpless, not at all like the woman who had cared for him the past few days.

It must be her son . . .

Logical thought left him. What was it about her that made him so weak? Cade went to her, knelt beside her and touched her arm. His ribs screamed their protest but he ignored them. "Is it Banks? Did something happen? Is he hurt?" A sudden cold fear gripped him deep in his gut. He wanted to wrap his arms around her, hold her, soothe her, tell her everything would be all right, but how could he? He didn't know what had happened. He didn't trust himself around her.

Go, while you can . . .

"Wha—Banks? No it's not Banks." Leah covered her mouth and looked up at him. Tears hung to her dark lashes like tiny pieces of stars. She quickly wiped them away. "It's nothing, I'm just being silly is all."

Cade pulled her up. "Tell me, what happened?" He peered out the window, searching the street for answers. All he saw was a donkey, running down the middle of town and hee-hawing as if its life depended on it. Leah turned at the noise and let out a laugh at the sight that sounded alarmingly close to hysteria.

"What happened?" he asked her again.

"We're quarantined."

Cade swallowed . . . hard. Quarantined sounded an awful lot like prison. He looked out the window again. No men with guns stood about keeping guard. There was no one to say you have to stay. Instead he saw a group of men walking from the saloon across to the livery.

"Why?"

"A family came into the diner today. We think they were from the mining camp. Jake Reece was up there this morning and said everyone was dead. He thinks it's measles."

"You were that close to them?"

Leah nodded. "It was two little boys, about Banks's age. I washed their faces and hands before I served them."

"And then I kissed you." Should he tell her he had measles when he was just a boy? That he caught it from the Cheyenne when his father took them west? That once you were infected the chances that you would catch it again were very slim?

Leah nodded, her face apologetic. "I'm so sorry." She rushed on, clearly not wanting to dwell on the kiss. At least she was thinking logically. It was more than he had done where she was concerned. "They said for us to stay inside until we know for sure . . ."

It made sense. Not that he planned on doing what *they* said. Still, sticking around would be what Timothy would do. He was fairly certain he couldn't catch the disease again. And however irrational it was, he wanted to stay with Leah. "It could be worse you know."

"How could it possibly be worse?"

"Mrs. Swanson was exposed also. They could lock her in here with us."

Leah laughed. She laughed good and long and hard. Cade watched her with his own amusement as she doubled over, her arms wrapped about her stomach as if she were in pain. Dodger whined, concern and confusion obvious in his dark and loving eyes. She was very close to losing control.

Cade guided Leah into the kitchen and helped her find a seat. Dodger followed along and lay down next to the table with a great huff of disgust. Leah finally was able to stop laughing and picked up a towel to wipe her eyes.

Cade sat down across from her and took her hand. *What are you doing?* His conscience screamed at him. He couldn't seem to stop touching her. She looked at him from beneath her lashes, clearly embarrassed at her loss of control. Not that he could blame her. Measles was a horrible disease. *I kissed her . . .* If he did happen to get sick; wouldn't that give all the fine people of Angel's End something to think about? How close were Mrs. Findley and the preacher? And once they found out he wasn't really who they thought he was. She'd be ruined.

"How about a piece of cake."

"What?"

The cake was sitting on the table, right beside their intertwined hands. "I find that life generally looks better after a piece of cake."

Leah shook her head. "You are the strangest minister I've ever met."

"Have you met that many?"

"No." She shook her head. "You're just not what we, or maybe just I, expected."

He couldn't argue with that. At least she still believed he was a minister and if they were going to be stuck together in this house for a while he needed to make sure she kept on believing it. "So tell me, what did you expect?" He released her hand so she could retrieve the plates and forks from the side of the sink where she'd left them to dry earlier.

Leah placed a piece of cake before him and sat down with one of her own. She looked at him shyly, as if she were afraid he might bite her. Or maybe kiss her again.

"I expected someone older," she said. "It seems like you're more my age than thirty-seven."

"That comes from clean living," he said with a grin. "What did you expect? Should I be walking with a cane? Have gray hair and a beard down to here?" He slashed his hand across his waist. Be deaf as a fence post?" He put his hand to his ear and made a face. "What was that you say?" he said in a squeaky voice.

Leah giggled. "No," she said. "Although that sounds a lot like the minister who married Nate and me."

"Had one foot in the grave did he?" Cade teased. "And obviously setting a bad example for the rest of us."

Leah nodded in agreement. "I guess he was a young man at sometime. Although . . ." Her voice trailed off.

"What?"

"I'm just trying to imagine him . . ." She blushed as she shook her head. She wiggled her nose as if she smelled something bad. "And you're not a bit shy about . . ." She pulled her lower lip between her front teeth.

"Walking around without my shirt on?" Cade supplied.

Leah blushed again, sweetly this time, and her lovely green eyes darted away for a quick moment before settling on him again.

"I was going to say kissing me."

"Oh . . ." He couldn't lie. Not when she looked at him like that. "I was overcome?" He shrugged. "You're a beautiful woman Leah. And I'm a very weak man."

She seemed pleased with his answer so he took a bite of cake and watched as she took one too. A crumb caught on her lip and she caught it with her tongue. Then she smiled, blissfully, at the taste of the chocolate.

"My momma used to say that something that tasted this good was a sin," she said.

Cade could not stop staring at her mouth. Remembering how she tasted. "Mine used to say that God made things taste good because he loves us. He created us and he created the way things taste." Even though he had plenty of cake in front of him, Cade stole a bite from her plate. He grinned at her. "So therefore, we should enjoy it and be thankful for it."

A sweet smile lit her face. "Your mother must be very special."

He hadn't mentioned his mother to anyone. Not since he was fifteen years old. Whatever possessed him to mention her now? "She was," he said. What would Leah say if he told her how his mother died?

"How old were you when she died?" Leah asked.

It was easy enough to spare her the details. "Ten," he said simply.

"Old enough to really miss her," she said. "I don't remember my parents. I was only two when they drowned." She took another bite of cake. "At least you had your father."

Cade caught himself before he voiced the bitter words about his father's abandonment. Instead he said, "My brother and I grew really close." He didn't realize how much saying those words would make him miss Brody.

"Are you still close?" Leah asked.

Cade could be truthful here. "I haven't seen him in years," he admitted.

"Is his name Brody?"

"Yes . . . How did you know that?"

"You said his name when you were sick with fever."

Before he could wonder what else he might have given away during his illness they heard someone knocking on the front door. Leah went immediately to answer it. Cade waited at the entry to the kitchen, curious to see who had come.

It was a woman with bright red hair. Leah introduced her as Gretchen Martin. He well remembered the chicken stew she made. He couldn't see her clearly as she stood back on the edge of Leah's porch.

"We'll take care of Banks," she said.

"Thank you." Leah leaned against the door frame in obvious relief. "I don't know what to tell him. I want to see him because I'm sure he'll be scared but I don't want to make him sick." Her voice broke on the last word. Cade took the two steps necessary to stand behind her. Making sure the woman on the porch could not see what he was doing, he put his hand on Leah's shoulder which was hidden behind the angle of the door. He gave it a gentle squeeze.

"I'll bring him by and you can talk through the window," Gretchen suggested.

"Yes. Thank you." Leah wiped at her eyes. "Tell everyone I'm sorry."

Gretchen took a step forward, thought better of it and stopped. "You've got nothing to be sorry for Leah. And Jake's an idiot who is worried about you. You did what any loving Christian person would do." She crossed her arms as if she needed protection. "The men are on their way up there now. To burn the bodies. I just hope they get back before the snow starts." She looked off to the north. Cade ducked his head, the better to see the sky and saw the heavy clouds that had gathered and were waiting to dump their heavy load. Gretchen moved again so she could see him through the open door. "Pastor Key they thought maybe you could go up and say a word after . . . when you're feeling better."

Cade nodded. "Sure I will." Little did they know he hoped to be long gone before the ashes got cold.

"If you need anything . . ." Her voice trailed off.

"Thank you Gretchen," Leah said. "For everything."

Gretchen nodded, paused for a moment, looked at Leah, opened her mouth as if she wanted to say something, then changed her mind and left. Leah watched until her friend disappeared into the house by the livery then she stepped back inside and shut the door with a heavy finality.

"Don't worry," she said with a smile. "We'll be fine. They're being cautious is all."

Now if he could only remember to do the same.

SIXTEEN

Leah walked into the parlor and stood before the window. She could see the school plainly from here as the parlor side of the house was even with the porch. She needed some time to gather her thoughts. Sitting at the table and eating cake with Pastor Key had made her forget that they really were to be quarantined. Gretchen's offer to take care of Banks made her realize that the threat of the measles really was serious.

Our momma died . . . The poor little boys from the diner, who lost their mother to such a horrid death. Did they have to watch her die? Shrivel up upon herself as she wasted away? Were her last thoughts of her sons and what would happen to them? She put her head against the pane of glass, between the lace panels that she'd scrimped and saved for when Nate first built the house. It felt cool against her forehead. She sensed Pastor Key watching her. The muscles of her shoulders clenched with the force of it.

Timothy . . . you kissed him, you might as well call him by his given name. She heard his footsteps as he finally walked away with Dodger following. She heard the back door open and close. It was nice that he saw to Dodger's needs.

What to do . . . She could either stand around and see if she was going to get sick, or she could make sure her house was in order. Leah chose the latter.

The sheets she'd washed earlier still needed drying. She could hurry the task up by ironing them. But first she'd make some bread and start something for dinner. As she worked she heard a steady chip-chip sound. Someone was digging in the ice. Leah looked out the window. The streets were deserted, everyone safely behind their doors, all waiting for the coming snow and dreading the possibility of disease arriving with it.

A flash of color caught her eye. It was Gretchen, on her way to the schoolhouse to gather up the children. Leah picked up Ashes and went to the kitchen window and anxiously waited for her to return with Banks. Snow began to fall, big fat flakes that quickly coated the hitching rail across at the Devil's Table and joined the inches that covered everything else. Ashes put out a paw as if she could catch the flakes that reflected back against the pane of glass.

In a matter of moments Gretchen returned with the children. Banks came to the window and Gretchen stayed back with the youngest set of twins. The rest of the children hurried on by, their shoulders hunched against the cold wind that blew against their backs. Leah opened the window, just a crack, enough so she could hear him and talk to him, but not so she could touch him.

"Hey Momma!" Banks seemed excited. Gretchen must have told him he was just spending the night again. Ashes poked her head at the crack and swatted a paw at Banks.

"Hey sweetheart." She took a deep breath. Now was not

the time to get scared. She needed to be strong for Banks's sake. "Make sure you mind Gretchen and Jim. And do your reading for Gretchen."

"I will."

"And eat all your supper and go to bed when you're told."

Banks stuck a finger beneath the sill and Ashes batted it. "Can I take Ashes?"

"No." Leah put the kitten on the floor. "Gretchen wanted Ashes to live with us, remember? It wouldn't be fair to take her back to her brothers and sisters and then make her have to leave again."

"But . . ."

"Go on now, before the snow gets so deep you can't get to the Martins'."

"All right." He turned to leave.

"Banks!" Her voice cracked. Leah swallowed and quickly wiped away a tear before he turned around with a questioning look on his face. "I love you."

"I love you too."

Leah blinked back the tears while they trudged away. She was a weakling where he was concerned. As long as Banks was safe she could be strong. The snow, long coming, was already clinging to Gretchen and the twins' backs. Gretchen put up her hand in farewell and Leah closed the window.

Ashes swatting at her skirt hem and the steady chip-chip sound drug her back from her morbid thoughts. Who was digging in the ice?

Since Timothy hadn't come back inside yet, it had to be him. What could he possibly be doing? She opened the door and found him wrestling her washtub from beneath the snow and ice. He wasn't wearing a coat but had put his boots on instead of the slippers she'd loaned him earlier in the day. His back was wet from the snow and his damp, dark hair curled wildly from his exertion. He stopped his digging and put his hand to his ribs as he braced himself on the slope of frozen snow. Around him were chunks of ice where he'd flung away pieces as he dug. Dodger watched from the corner of the porch, well away from the shovel and the heavy, wet snow that floated down from the sky.

"Have you lost your mind?"

"I'm beginning to think so." He leaned heavily on the shovel. "I didn't think it would be that hard when I started." He touched his wound again. "Little did I know."

"You're going to start bleeding again if you're not careful."

"I've just about got it." He bent over and grabbed the handle of the tub. "Just one more tug."

"Let me help." Leah moved to his side and grabbed hold. The tub was loose and moved a bit, but was still caught on something beneath the snow.

"On the count of three." She nodded and he counted. On three they both pulled. The tub screeched and then turned loose suddenly. They both lost their balance and with arms flying out, they fell. There was a loud clanging noise and Timothy said something, something that didn't quite make sense to her addled mind as she fought for balance. Leah landed on the drift that led up to the porch and slid down it on her back with her skirt rucked up around her waist.

The fall knocked the air from her. She lay on the snow, stared up into the darkening sky and watched the snowflakes spin above her. They settled on her face and stuck to her lashes. A cold chill seeped into her bones yet she could not seem to move. Dodger came to her side and whined. He poked his nose into her side.

He cursed. It had been vile, something that a minister would never say. And then he said it again. She heard another clang and realized he'd thrown the washtub. It must have landed on him when they fell. Her breath came back and she quickly sat up.

"Are you hurt?" she asked.

He waved a hand over the drift that separated them. It had blood on it. Leah felt a momentary panic until he spoke once more. "That goddamned washtub hit me in the head."

Definitely not the words of a minister. Of course being hit in the head by a washtub might give one a valid reason to curse. Leah managed to find her feet and scrambled over the snow to where he'd landed. He was on his hands and knees and trying to rise.

"This was not one of my better ideas," he admitted. Blood trickled down from a cut on his temple. "I just thought it might make your life easier."

"I can't fault you for that." Leah grabbed on to a porch post and held out her hand. "Can you stand?" He grasped her fingers and slowly climbed to his feet. He took a deep breath that obviously pained him and then he touched her face. He scraped some snow from her cheek with his thumb and pushed her hair back behind her ear. Was he going to kiss her again?

"Timothy?"

"Cade." He seemed fascinated with her hair. He smoothed his hand over it, drying off the snow with each pass.

"Cade?"

"It's my middle name. Kincaid actually." He slowly smiled. "It's what my mother called me."

"Cade," she said, trying it out. She liked it. It was what his mother called him. It seemed to fit him, much better than Timothy did. Did it mean something more, that he wanted her to call him by that name? Dodger whined, interrupting her musings. "We should go inside. You're bleeding."

He touched his temple and looked at the blood. "Yes, that's definitely blood." He shook his head sheepishly. Dodger, relieved that they were both unhurt celebrated by jumping around while they made their way back into the house. They went into the kitchen and once more he sat down in the chair and she cleaned his wound.

"It's not deep," she said as she peered intently at the cut. "You're soaked."

"As you are. Why didn't you at least put your coat on before you went out?"

"I didn't think it would take that long to dig it out. And I thought you needed to be alone. To talk to Banks and to . . ." He shrugged. "Think things over?"

"Most preachers would have had a prayer meeting." She dabbed at the cut once more and then put pressure on it.

"As I said before, I'm not your typical preacher."

"Amen to that." She didn't mention his cursing. He might not have realized he'd done it. "I think we both would have fared better if you'd worked on the pump."

"It's next on my list." He put his hand up to the cut. "I can take care of this. Why don't you go change before you get . . ." His voice trailed off as he looked at her intently with his dark brown eyes. Would he kiss her again? Did she want him to?

"Sick?" Leah shook her head. "I'm pretty sure that's in God's hands now."

She touched the bread, which had been rising for a while, deemed it ready and put it in the oven. "Dinner should be ready soon. I'll find you something dry to put on."

Leah went to her room. What was going on? He pushed her away one minute and kissed her the next. She took off her shirt and turned up the lamp before she looked in the mirror. She ran her fingers over her breastbone and studied her skin. No spots yet. She couldn't remember which came first. The rash or the fever.

What she did know was that measles could wipe out a town in no time. Jake was smart to quarantine her. If only the man with the boys from the mining camp had used the same common sense. The town would have helped him. They would have given them food. Yet Leah could understand how desperate he was. She'd do anything if it meant saving Banks's life. Lie, cheat, steal, maybe even kill. And stay away from him, even though it broke her heart to do so.

Leah pulled one of Nate's shirts from the trunk at the end of the bed. It wouldn't fit Timothy, who was several inches taller than Nate had been, but it would do until his dried. She found him in the kitchen, stripped of his shirt and examining the pump. Her eyes went to the bandage about his ribs to make sure he wasn't bleeding again. He wasn't. Then she could not help but watch the muscles of his back flex as he tried to work the pump.

"Do you have any tools?"

"In the shed," she said. "I'll get them."

"No, I'll get them," he interrupted. He put his hands on her shoulders and looked intently into her eyes. "Let me take care of things for a change."

"But your wou—"

He touched a finger to her lips. "Check your bread." He tilted his head toward the stove and grinned as she spun round to do as he asked. She opened the oven, afraid that it had burned, but found that it was fine, golden brown and crusty on the top. The stew she'd put together earlier bubbled on the stove top. Leah heard him whistle a tune as he pulled on Nate's shirt and went out the back door.

Leah set the table for two. Dodger watched for Cade to reappear from his bed in the corner. Ashes played under the table, pouncing upon imaginary mice that hid around the chair legs. If she closed her eyes and imagined, Leah could almost see Nate sitting at the table and Banks in his high chair. The footsteps coming back down the hall didn't belong to her dead husband, but the feeling of domestic rightness remained, even when Cade came back into the kitchen with the toolbox.

"It's coming down pretty hard now." He went through the tools with a frown until he found the one he wanted. "I bet there'll be another foot or two before morning."

"Welcome to a Colorado winter," Leah replied. "Dinner will be a few minutes yet." She opened some apples she'd canned in late summer and stirred them into a small pot with a touch of cinnamon and sugar.

"It seems like this is a nice town," he said, while he took apart the pump. "People looking out for each other . . ." He glanced over his shoulder as he wrestled with the part that went beneath the cabinet.

"It is. The people in this town genuinely care for each other."

He grinned and turned, holding the wrench in one hand and the pipe from the pump in the other. "So why hasn't anyone fixed your pump?"

Leah blushed. The eyebrow he cocked in her direction seemed mischievous, almost devilish.

"No one knew it was broken," she said quietly and turned back to the apples.

"Hmm." He poked a long screwdriver into the pipe and held it up to the light.

"What about Jake?" He moved the lamp from the table to the sink and peered down into the pipe.

"Jake?"

"The idiot who is worried about you?" There it was again. That devilish quirk of the eyebrow. "Why did your friend feel the need to apologize for him?"

"Because he was angry with me."

"I see." He jerked the pipe back and forth and then stopped to put his hand on his side.

"You really shouldn't . . ." Leah began.

He held up his finger to silence her and then knelt on the floor, and opened the cabinet. He removed the contents carefully. "Hold the lamp for me please." He gingerly turned over on his back and slid inside.

Leah obliged, after navigating around his long legs. Nate's shirt was too short, as she knew it would be, and hiked up around the bandage which left the area above his once again sagging pants exposed. Her skirt brushed against it as she moved into place and he gave a small jerk.

"So is this Jake person sweet on you?"

"Jake Reece," she reminded him. "From the search committee."

"He must have had ulterior motives for finding a preacher."

"What do you mean ulterior motives?"

"A wedding?" There was a lot of rattling and clanking going on beneath the sink.

She peered down into the space where the pipe was. "Nope. No wedding."

"Can't see," he said. Leah moved her head and returned the lamp. "Why no wedding? Is he mean? Doesn't have a job? Doesn't like kids?"

"He owns a ranch outside of town. He raises cattle. And he's very nice to Banks."

"Sounds like a great prospect for marriage."

"Except I don't love him."

The clanging stopped. "Can you pour some water inside the pipe?" Leah did as he said. "Aha! Found it." The clanging started again. "Does that matter so much?"

"Does what matter?"

"Loving him."

"Yes, it matters very much."

"Ouch, damn it!"

"You sure do curse a lot for a preacher." There was complete silence. Leah peered down in the hole again. He had his thumb in his mouth. "But maybe there are times when it's called for?"

He took his thumb from his mouth and once more gave her that devilish look that looked all the more so, as his face was mostly in shadow.

"Should I have blessed my curse first?"

"What do you mean, bless it?"

"Put God's name before it."

"Wouldn't that be taking the Lord's name in vain?"

"So you're a stickler for the Commandments?"

"No." Leah laughed. "I mean I try, but usually fail."

"Don't we all. Watch out." The pipe came up through the hole. "Hold this while I reattach it."

It wasn't a command, or even a request. It felt more like a casual intimacy. Well, they had kissed . . . Leah took a firm hold on the pipe and felt tiny jerking motions as he connected it.

"I guess I could say *holy* first. Like holy hell?"

"I wouldn't recommend saying anything like that outside these walls."

"Would that offend?"

"Certain folks would find it offensive."

"I'll keep that in mind."

The man was peculiar. It got quiet. No noise from below the sink at all. Leah couldn't see down the hole anymore as the pipe was attached. She let go and it didn't wobble. She moved to look beneath the cabinet. He was very still. "Are you all right?"

"I think you're going to have to help me up."

"I knew you shouldn't be doing all this stuff so soon."

"Well it's done now." He stuck out his arm and Leah took it. He pulled on her for leverage until he was able to slide out from under the cabinet. He sat up and hit the top of his head on the overhang.

"Holy . . ." His voice trailed off and he grinned at Leah. She shook her head and went back to the stove. The apples were ready so she placed them in a bowl and put the food on the table while he connected the pipes. He dipped some water from the pot on the stove and poured it down the pipe to prime the pump before attaching the final piece, and with a few quick pumps water flowed forth.

"Thank you so much." Leah didn't waste any time filling a pot with water and putting it on the stove to warm for the dishes. They sat down to eat and he quickly filled his plate and started in.

Leah watched him for a moment. He didn't say grace . . .

"Is something wrong?" he asked.

"No. Nothing is wrong." She smiled at him. "Nothing at all."

The fire had melted the surrounding snow. It burned so high and so hot that the ice pellets that poured from the sky dissolved long before they hit the ground. Ward felt sweat running down his neck beneath the kerchief he wore over the lower half of his face to protect him from any contagion. Seventeen bodies had gone into the fire. Men, women and a few children. It was heartbreaking, yet it had to be done. They didn't know their names, nor could they go through their things to find out. Everything was burned. Every piece of clothing, every blanket, every tent, even the pots and pans were thrown into the fire. The smell was horrible, as if hell itself had opened up and spewed forth its rot.

Who had started the epidemic? It must have been a traveler, someone moving through the area. Had that person perished here or left, not knowing that he or she carried death with them? Ward tried to think of any strangers who'd been through recently; most stopped at the Heaven's Gate and nearly all ate at the Devil's Table. And now Leah had been exposed and would most likely catch it. And if she did, would anyone else in town? She'd poured his coffee this morning, right after she touched those children. Ward sighed heavily. He wasn't ready to die. Was anyone ever ready for that? At least now they had a minister to prepare them for the afterlife.

But Leah dying . . . *I'll take care of Banks . . . it's the least I can do* . . . Ward couldn't help but cringe as he replayed the night when Nate died. He should have done something . . . he should have stopped him.

Gus Swanson rode up beside him. The man's face was ghastly pale. Ward knew he'd puked his guts out at the sights and the smells. Gus was not hardened by war like he'd been at a young age. Gus wiped at his sweaty face with his kerchief. Jake and Jim, who'd circled the camp one last time, joined them by the fire.

"Gretchen asked the preacher if he'd come up here later and say a prayer over them," Jim said as they watched the flames leap against the darkening sky.

"Poor bastards," Jake said. There was nothing left for the men to do, so they turned and started the hard journey back to town.

The wind pushed against them and tiny ice pellets stung the parts of their skin that were exposed to the elements. It was a miserable ride. Jake fell in beside him when they exited Rattlesnake Canyon and the road widened enough for them to ride side by side. The only thing on Ward's mind was staying warm beneath his heavy coat and the shot of whiskey he'd have as soon as he got back. And Lady. It was funny how he'd taken to that dog so quick.

"I reckon this is where she came from," he said to Jake as he came up.

"Who?"

"The dog. Lady." Jake looked at him in confusion. Ward was so used to having Jake around that he'd forgotten that he didn't know about the arrival of his newest friend. Although she'd been right by his side when Jake stormed into Heaven's Gate and told him about the devastation at the mining camp.

"A dog turned up on my stoop this morning," he explained. "And the Martins had a momma cat with a bunch of kittens show up in their barn."

"And I got the donkey," Jake said.

"If you're claiming it then I'll send you the bill for its feed," Jim called out.

Jake shook his head. "The last thing I want is a donkey. Keep it and sell it for all I care."

"Fine with me," Jim called back.

"So I hear you finally met the preacher," Jake said.

"Yep."

"And?"

"And what?"

"You're the only person who's talked to him. Besides Leah."

"Gus's wife talked to him. Said he ate half a cake."

Jake shook his head. "What do you think?"

Ward couldn't help but enjoy himself at Jake's expense. "About what?"

Jake let out a heavy sigh. The truth of the matter was, Ward didn't know what to think. The few minutes he'd spent with the man hadn't been helpful. Ward usually knew when he was being played, but this guy . . . this preacher . . . Ward needed more time and more conversation to figure him out. Dodger seemed to like the man, which went a long way in Ward's opinion, but still, there was something about him that just didn't set right.

"If you're so interested in the man why don't you go talk to him?"

"Going to be kind of hard if he's got the measles."

"Well at least he and Leah will both be in the same place and we can isolate it if they do get sick."

"Yeah," Jake muttered. "They're both locked up together."

Ward laughed. "So that's what's got you so twisted up. You're afraid Leah is going to go sweet on the preacher."

"Won't do them any good if they both wind up dead," Jake growled.

Ward put a hand on Jake's arm. "Look, I know you're

worried about her. Hell, we all are. But there's nothing we can do about it now. If she gets sick then she gets sick and we'll do what we can for her and Banks."

"So basically you're saying it's in God's hands?"

"I reckon I am."

"Somehow that doesn't make me feel any better."

Ward shook his head. "Me either."

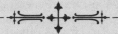

SEVENTEEN

I can't believe I told her my name. It wasn't as if he lied. Kincaid was his middle name. Matthew Kincaid Gentry, Kincaid after his mother's family. Cade stood in the hallway, silent, and watched Leah as she slept with the kitten curled up against her back. The wind rattled the window above her head. He hoped in his heart that she would forgive him someday.

You're turning soft . . .

Dodger stood watching him with his head cocked to one side. Cade wore Timothy's heavy overcoat. Beneath it Leah's dead husband's gun was strapped to his side. Leah had fallen quickly asleep after dinner and he'd made good use of the time.

"Go to sleep boy," Cade quietly urged the dog. Dodger followed him to the back door. "Be quiet now." Dodger made to follow him but Cade quickly latched the door in his face.

The thick wet snow made it a miserable night to be out

and that suited Cade just fine. Several inches of snow had fallen in the hours since it started, which was a good thing. It would cover his tracks. Cade walked out to the opposite side of Leah's shed and looked back toward town. Heavy, fat flakes covered his coat in a matter of seconds. All he could see was the faint outline of the buildings and the occasional dim glow of turned-down lamps behind windows closed securely against the weather. Behind him was nothing but darkness and a swirling mass of snow. He knew there was a stream, and beyond that a heavy forest of pines that led up into the mountains that sheltered the valley.

If not for the snow he'd move that way. Lose himself in the mountains. Maybe head for California. He'd always wanted to see the ocean. This time of year it would be suicide. Especially in the shape he was in. But he couldn't afford to get stuck here all winter. The town might not have a sheriff but he was pretty certain it had a jail. They'd lock him up for sure if they knew he was impersonating Timothy. And more than likely accuse him of his murder.

Cade moved on. The livery was a few houses down. There was a corral behind it that went all the way down to the stream. Smart move on Martin's part. The water was right there for the horses. Beyond it he saw the glow from the forge. It was sheltered under a roof that was open on three sides. Another smart move. Less risk of fire but cold work this time of year.

The corral was empty. Cade looked behind at his trail and was happy to see his tracks had already filled with snow. By morning no one would be able to tell what had passed through here, only that something did.

A wolf howl sounded. Long, sharp and mournful, it froze him in place. It carried into town, drifting through like a silent wraith. A dog, not Dodger thank God, barked from behind the stout walls of his house, heroic because he knew he was safe inside. The wolf was close, come down from his mountain into the valley to hunt. More would follow. Coming up against a pack of hungry wolves was a battle he'd rather not fight. Not until he was much stronger at least.

Cade gingerly climbed between the bars of the corral. His ribs were killing him. Just the thought of mounting up and riding out was painful, more proof that he was in no shape to go. Digging the washtub out had taken nearly all of his strength. Yet here he was prowling about town when he should be resting up for when he could go. But he couldn't help himself. He wanted to get a lay of the land for future reference.

Two wide doors from the stable opened into the corral. They weren't locked, not that a lock had ever stopped him if he wanted what was inside. Thankfully he didn't have to mess with it as it was so cold his fingers would be practically useless if he took off his gloves. He opened the doors enough to enable him to quickly slide inside.

Cade paused a moment to give his eyes a chance to adjust to the darkness that engulfed him. The only light was on the opposite end, from a lamp turned so low it was barely more than a pinpoint. The wind rattled through the doors and windows, finding the weakness of the stable's defense against the weather. A low grumbling growl sounded and the horses sheltered within tossed their heads in ghostly apprehension. Cade stood, silent, while they shifted around in their stalls. A ghostly white head appeared at the one closest to him. Cade recognized the horse that had carried him through the blizzard.

He rubbed the long nose. "Hey there boy. I never had a chance to thank you for saving my life."

The horse snorted in response and snuffed against Cade's gloved palm.

"I reckon they're taking good care of you here." The horse dropped its head and nibbled delicately at the straw beneath its feet.

A cat stood in the middle of the stable when he turned. She studied him for a moment with eyes that glowed like coals and her tail twitching before she stalked off, confident that he was no threat to her domain. There were a few more horses that stared at him curiously as he walked through. The gear was stashed in a small room close to the street side door. Saddles lined up on a rail and the bridles hung neatly from hooks. A donkey was penned across from it. The creature stared up at him and stretched its lips out as if he wanted to say something. A feed bag sat on a barrel outside the tack room. Cade flung a handful at the donkey's feet and then checked the street by offsetting the doors.

The saloon was directly across from where he stood. It was difficult to see if anyone was inside with the heavy snow falling down. Or maybe it was because there was something in the middle of the street. The statue? Cade moved to a window.

He'd expected the saloon to be open. It was late, but not that late. He suddenly realized he had no idea what day it was. Hopefully a Monday so he could be good and gone before Sunday got here. The doors were barred and the only light shone from a room up above. Still it'd be best if he went out the back of the stable. If anyone was up and watching they'd surely notice someone walking down the middle of the street.

Cade went out the way he'd come in. Quietly he circled the town, moving slowly, so that he was nothing more than a shadow covered with snow. He tested the locks at the back of the general store and the assayer's office. Cade moved on and came to the end of the line of buildings. He wandered down the trail a bit before crossing to the other side. He skirted the back of the buildings on the opposite side of the street, making sure to stay well away from the saloon. When he came to the back of the sheriff's office he placed his hand against the wooden building. It was as cold as ice and no smoke came from the stovepipe. He cautiously looked in the window and confirmed his suspicions. Angel's End wasn't only lacking a preacher; it was also without a sheriff. The last building on the south side of the street was the diner. It was locked up tight.

Cade walked between the diner and the deserted sheriff's office next to it. He stood there for a moment, lost in the shadows and the snow and stared at Leah's house. The quiet settled over him like the flakes of snow that obliterated his body from view until he was no more than an extension of the building he leaned against. Yes, he was cold and yes he hurt like hell, but he ignored it, as he'd had to so many times in his life.

Leah... Of all the times in his life to meet someone like her. If things were different, if he wasn't on the run, if the past had been different. If he was a different man. If he was good and honest and she knew him as what he could be with her.

"All those blows to the head must have rattled your brain," he said to the empty streets. Thinking that way would get him killed. He had the wound to prove it. Thinking that way was what got him in this predicament in the first place. It was another one of God's jokes. The one time he tried to do good he paid for it. The smartest and the safest thing to do was get out of town as fast as he could. Maybe in a few days he'd be feeling better. In his present condition there was no way he could survive the elements.

Cade looked to the north. The church stood there, the steeple taller than any other structure in town. He felt as if the church stared down at him with expectation. He'd felt the same thing when Timothy looked at him. Cade shook his head at his foolishness. He should skirt around the diner, cross behind the church, and return to Leah's.

As was the case lately, he did exactly the opposite of what he should do. Instead he stepped out of the shadows and walked straight to the statue. It stood in the middle of the street like a sentinel that never wavered from its appointed task. He couldn't make out the base as the snow was piled around it. It had to be standing on something because it was close to nine feet tall. The outstretched wings were at least five feet wide. Snow covered the peaks and valleys of the wings and the shoulders and the carved indentations of the robes.

Someone hauled this thing west and left it here? They must have been crazy.

Crazy to bring it west with them. Desperate when they abandoned it after carrying it for hundreds, possibly even thousands of miles. Cade walked around to the front. The angel faced south with her arms outstretched and palms facing upward. Why? Was she supposed to be welcoming? Waiting? Praying? He stood in the snow and looked up into the carved face that had been beaten by the elements.

An image flashed before him. One from his feverish dreams. The angel, bringing him water, bringing him relief, bringing him momentary peace.

Leah . . .

His longing for her made no more sense than the fact that he was wandering around the middle of town during a blizzard. He should get back before someone caught him and started asking questions. Cade looked once more behind him to make sure there was no sign of his passing. The heavily falling snow quickly filled his tracks. It was as if he'd never gone out. Never existed.

He dusted his coat off before he entered the house. Dodger lay in the hallway, right outside Leah's room, keeping watch on both her and the door. Cade knelt down and let Dodger have a sniff.

"Nate?"

She must be dreaming. Nate was her dead husband's name. Still it would be difficult to explain to her why he was out and armed in the middle of the night. He moved on silent feet to the door of her room. She moved restlessly beneath the blankets. A pillow hung off the side of the bed and the kitten stood on the far corner washing a paw. Had he disturbed her or was she caught in a dream?

She coughed, a dry hacking sound that grated hard in her throat. He stepped into her room and looked at her closely. A fine sheen of sweat covered her face. Her mouth moved, silent words spoken to the ghosts who visited her dreams. Cade slowly reached out his hand and touched her face. She was burning up with fever. The measles had struck.

Thank God he hadn't been stupid enough to leave town. She needed him now. The prospect didn't scare him as much as he thought it would.

EIGHTEEN

"What are you doing?" Cade leaned casually against the kitchen doorjamb with his arms crossed.

"I'm going to fix breakfast." Leah coughed and rubbed at her watery eyes. She felt like she'd slept in a stagecoach. Her body ached all over and her eyes were swollen and watery. The light, what little bit there was, hurt and she blinked against it. The realization that she was once more talking to Pastor Key . . . no, Timothy . . . no, he said to call him Cade . . . wearing nothing but her gown hit her, but for the life of her she couldn't summon up the strength to care.

Dodger lay in the hallway with his legs before him and his head tilted to the side as he looked at her. "Where is Banks?" she asked. "Did he go to school?"

"He stayed with his friends last night. Remember?"

Ashes swatted at the hem of her gown. Leah pushed her fingers to her forehead. She had a pounding headache and felt confused. She wasn't really sure what day it was. And this man, this preacher who didn't talk like a preacher, was standing in her house and leaning against the door frame like he owned it.

"I've already fixed breakfast," he said. "Why don't you try to eat something before you go back to bed?"

"Why would I go back to bed?" Why was he arguing with her? Why was he even here? Why didn't he go away and leave her alone. "I've got to go to work."

"No. You've got the measles. You're going back to bed."

Leah sputtered. A pair of strong arms circled her and suddenly she was lifted into the air. "What are you doing? Put me down this instant."

"You are one stubborn woman." He carried her into her room and in a surprisingly gentle motion, placed her on her bed. "Stay here." He pushed her back with one strong finger to the middle of her breastbone and pulled the blankets over her legs.

"I'll bring you something to eat."

"Wait!" He turned, crossed his arms and quirked an eyebrow at her. There was no doubt in her mind that if she tried to get out of the bed he'd chase her down in a heartbeat. Leah put her hands to her face, then before her, turning them up and down to look. "Do I have spots?"

"Not yet." His grin was cheeky as he left. She wanted to slap him but instead flopped back onto her pillow. She heard him moving about in the kitchen. He was probably making a huge mess that she would have to clean up.

"I don't want to be sick," she moaned as Ashes clawed her way onto the bed. She wiped her nose on her sleeve. "This is not good . . . not good at all." She coughed. What was going to happen to her? No one would be able to come and help—it would put the entire town at risk being exposed to the deadly disease. How did it happen so fast? It was only yesterday that she helped the two little boys.

But now that she thought on it . . . there was a tinker who

came through a few weeks ago. He'd been friendly and talk-
ative. He'd also coughed a lot and was moist with sweat.
He'd blamed it on the unseasonably warm weather they'd
experienced that week and kept wiping his face with a napkin. Leah recalled it being soaking wet when she cleaned
off the table after he left.

"I bet he's the one who gave it to the miners." The poor
man. He was more than likely dead now, caught up in the
blizzard or else he'd spread it on to another unsuspecting
town. Thank goodness Jake had followed that crazy donkey
back to the camp.

If she'd been exposed a few weeks ago did that mean that
she'd passed it on unwittingly in the time since? Or was she
only contagious once her symptoms started? *We really need
to have a doctor in town . . .*

What if Banks gets sick and needs me? What am I going
to do? Leah smoothed down the blanket on either side of
her. She didn't know what to do with herself. She just
couldn't be sick. She had to be well so she could take care
of her son. She threw the blankets back and moved to rise.
She didn't recall it being this difficult earlier this morning.
Or maybe it was. Slowly she stood. The room spun around
her. She heard a crash just as the world went black.

Cade had a choice between the breakfast tray or Leah. Much
to Dodger's delight, he chose Leah. He caught her right before
she hit the floor. Her head hung limply as he arranged her in
his arms to put her back in bed. Her cheeks were bright red
with fever, yet the rest of her skin was pale and shiny with
moisture. He placed her carefully on the bed and touched her
cheek with the back of his hand. She was burning up.

"Like I said. Stubborn. You know what you get when
you're stubborn? You get to live with a busted pump." He
pulled the blanket over her and tucked it in around her arms.

Dodger looked up expectantly from his unexpected treat. Cade squatted beside him and picked up the broken pieces of her dishes and mopped up the spilt coffee with the napkin. "Hope she's not mad at me when she finds out I broke her dishes."

Dodger nosed the floorboards for missed crumbs and followed Cade to the kitchen. He'd made a big mess while cooking her breakfast but he'd been proud of the outcome. Dodger seemed to have enjoyed it. He placed the unbroken things in the sink. A small crock sat on the sill and he opened it. The scent of roses filled his senses.

"So that's where it comes from." He inhaled deeply, smiled, and put the crock back where he found it.

Cade peered out the window. The snow had let up since dawn and streaks of blue appeared in the cloud-strewn sky. It looked as if the weather was going to take it easy on them for a while. Remind them of what a beautiful winter's day looked like before hitting them again with another punch. That meant the townsfolk would be out and about. Wanting to visit, wanting to get to know him. But that would be impossible since the house was quarantined.

He'd already shoveled out a path to the outhouse, fed the chickens and collected the eggs. Leah's little rooster had been indignant at his invasion and pecked at his ankles until he left. He'd done it all before dawn lit the sky.

With the exception of Leah's bedroom he'd also been over every inch of her house, including the loft. It wasn't that he was looking for anything in particular, he was just looking. He'd only caught a few hours of sleep after his exploration of the town. He was tired and his ribs ached painfully. It would take forever for them to mend. He needed to sleep. He needed time to heal.

Cade walked back to her room. Leah had already torn the blankets away with her restless jerking. The fever was heavy upon her. What should he do?

His memory of having the measles was cloudy, either from time, or the fever that came with the disease. He was only seven when it struck the Cheyenne village they lived in.

He remembered the stink of the dying and the mass grave his father prayed over.

He was immune. He could take care of Leah with no risk of catching it. He could get her through and the town and her son wouldn't be exposed. It was the least he could do. He owed it to her for taking care of him.

He owed it to Timothy.

Dodger barked with the pounding on the door. Someone had come to check on her. He opened the door to a man he'd never seen before, but he knew the type. The cut of the man's coat was similar to Fitch's.

"You must be Jake Reece," he said.

"I am. Where's Leah?"

Cade could not resist. "In bed." He didn't even try. He'd read a book about Proverbs one time that said, "The road to hell is paved with good intentions." He couldn't say the same about his path to hell. His was paved with deliberate actions that he knew, good and well, were wrong.

Cade arched an eyebrow at the rancher as he walked into the house and straight back to Leah's room. Jake stopped at the doorway as if he was afraid to go in when he saw her fretful tossing and turning on the bed.

"Have you had the measles?" Cade joined him.

"No." The rancher looked him up and down. Sized him up. "You?"

"Yes. When I was seven. Once you have them you can't catch them again. I'm immune."

"Someone needs to take care of her."

There it was. The challenge. The summons. God's pay-back. Cade crossed his arms. If he stayed then he'd be caught in his lie sure as he was standing here. There would be hell to pay. Wasn't there always, where he was concerned?

Wasn't that how he wound up in this predicament in the first place?

Cade looked at Leah. Her braid had come loose from her movements and tendrils of it stuck to her face. He should wipe her skin for her. Cool her down as she had him. *I thirst . . .* "I will." He felt the noose tighten around his neck. He was neatly trapped. He could practically hear God laughing at him.

Jake's sigh of relief was audible. "I'll tell the Martins to keep Banks until it's over."

"You don't think she's going to make it?"

"If you'd seen what I saw up at that camp . . ." Jake turned to look at him. His eyes were a steely gray. Piercing. He was a man used to having his own way. A lot like Fitch, except without the inherent meanness. "You're not what I expected."

Cade knew he shouldn't meet him eye to eye. Knew there was a chance the rancher would see him for what he was. But the alternative was looking away and then Jake Reece would know for sure he wasn't who he claimed to be. Instead he fell back on one of Jasper's tricks. Just as he'd done with Ward he put Jake on the defensive. "You can tell that much about a man in five minutes' time?"

"Out here you have to." Jake met his challenge head-on. "Five minutes can mean the difference between life and death."

Something Cade knew well enough. That direct attack didn't work with the rancher so he went with distraction. "You have feelings for her."

Jake's eyes narrowed with something. Possession? Fear? Jealousy perhaps? "That's between me and Leah," he said.

Cade already knew the answer to his question. Leah admitted Jake had feelings for her the night before and her reasons for not reciprocating. He thought her foolish when she said she didn't love Jake Reece. He didn't say, because it wasn't any of his business, but he thought she should marry the man. She'd be provided for. She'd have a home and a pump that worked and she wouldn't have to worry or work. And her son would have a decent father. That was more than most had.

But she didn't love Jake Reece. And Cade didn't feel like analyzing why that made him so happy.

"I'll be back to check on her later." Jake turned to go. "Do you need anything? I can have food left for you."

"That would be helpful." He walked Jake to the door. The rancher stood for a minute as if he didn't know what to do.

"I reckon you've seen how special Leah is," he finally said.

"I reckon I have," Cade replied. He stood for a moment, considering things. Things he didn't know, things he had no business knowing. "What happened to her husband?"

"He died four years ago." The answer was vague and cryptic and something Cade already knew. Jake really didn't want to share any part of her. Cade pushed onward, suddenly desperate to know.

"She told me that much. I want to know how he died. How she wound up here alone."

Jake looked at him for a moment, and then walked into the parlor. Cade had been negligent and let the fire burn low. He wanted to conserve her wood. Winter had just begun and she'd been going through it at a fast pace. Jake went to the window behind the worn sofa, pulled the lace panels aside and looked out to the street.

"Nate Findley was our sheriff. He showed up with Leah eight years ago. They were young, Leah was fresh off the farm and still glowing from the wedding. Nate was from Kansas. His father was a U.S. marshal and had fought in the border wars."

"That was some bad times," Cade said. While the rest of the nation was fighting a war, his family had been with the

Cheyenne. His mother and sister died in 1864 at Sand Creek. Dead at the hands of the U.S. Army. Meanwhile Kansas and Missouri were having their own problems, which became more violent during the Civil War.

"He answered an advertisement, just like you did. Showed up all full of himself, ready to bring law to our little town. I think he was kind of disappointed that the only thing we needed him for was to round up the boys when they got especially rowdy on a Saturday night. Sometimes they'd get into it with the miners. We just needed him to keep the peace." Jake dropped the panel and turned to face Cade who stood up after feeding the fire.

"He built this house." Jake pounded his palm against the wall next to the window. "He sure knew what he was doing when he built it. Then Banks was born and things were going pretty good around here. The town was growing."

Ashes poked her head up from the mending basket beside the fireplace and noisily yawned at the interruption to her nap. Jake smiled and shook his head at the kitten's obvious disdain at being awakened. Dodger, who was watching the two men closely stuck his nose in the basket and snuffed loudly. Ashes, over her earlier disdain for the dog, rolled over and swatted playfully at his nose. "Nate got Dodger from a family that settled here. He made sure he met everyone who came through town. Always made the rounds, checking on the ranches and the mining camps."

And then came home to his beautiful wife and baby boy. Cade looked at the rocking chair. Imagined Leah sitting in it, holding Banks in her arms, and waiting for her husband to walk through the door. Having dinner prepared and putting the baby to bed and then opening her arms . . . Such things he could only imagine. Jake must have imagined it also. He walked over to the chair and pushed it gently so that it rocked. Ashes left the basket and curiously watched the rocker move back and forth.

"One day this kid rode into town. He was a cocky little son of a bitch. Fast with a gun. Had a couple of kills notched on his belt. Trying to make a name for himself." Jake ran a finger over his upper lip. "There are a lot of those types out here."

Cade couldn't admit that he knew the type. That he was running from a man who sounded exactly like the one Jake described.

"Ward spent most of his time searching for the bottom of a whiskey bottle at the time. So he wasn't much use when this guy beat Janie within an inch of her life."

"Janie?" Cade asked.

"She was the . . . soiled dove at the Heaven's Gate." There were things ministers were supposed to turn a blind eye to in towns such as Angel's End. Prostitutes were one of them.

"It was late at night. I wasn't here, but there was talk that you could hear her screaming. Someone came and told Nate and he went to call him out." Jake shrugged. "Guy just up and shot Nate before he could even think about drawing his gun, and then he lit out. Nate was gut shot . . . bad. It took him awhile to die. A good long while." Jake knelt down and took Dodger's head in his hands. "Dodger howled like he was being skinned alive when Nate passed. I've never heard anything like it. I hope never to hear anything like it again."

Cade shook his head at the story. He'd probably heard hundreds like it. Knew men on both ends of it. "He died here?"

Jake nodded. "Leah attempted to take out the bullet, but she couldn't. Nate tried his best to bear it but he was in agony. We don't have a doctor here, or a sheriff since Nate."

Or a pastor . . . It must have been hell for Leah.

Jake stood and stretched as if he'd just awakened from a deep sleep. "Leah won't abide a gun now. She hates them. Won't let anyone even mention anything about shooting in front of Banks. Going to be hard on that kid when he gets older." He stood before Cade now with his gray eyes boring into him. "I'm all for peace and goodwill but you've got to know that things are different in the west than they are in Ohio. There are men who would just as soon shoot you as look at you, and they'll do it in a heartbeat."

He waited, for what Cade didn't know. What was he supposed to say? Jake wasn't telling him anything he didn't already know. But then again, Jake thought he was talking to a minister. What would Timothy say? That he'd be praying for them? No help there. The last thing he wanted was for God to play one of his jokes on Leah. "I'll keep that in mind."

Jake must have liked his answer. He nodded as if in agreement. "I'll tell the Martins what's going on." He went to the door. "Someone will bring food and check in on you later."

Cade shut the door behind him. Dodger whined and lay down in the middle of the hall. "What?" Cade asked. The dog stared at him with those dark eyes that saw everything. It was probably a good thing that dogs couldn't talk.

NINETEEN

"Drink." Leah felt Cade's hand behind her back, felt him lift her, easily until she was almost upright. Why shouldn't it be easy? She was boneless. There was nothing within her body to support her. She weighed nothing more than a feather, yet she felt as if she were nailed to the earth. That had to be why she ached so much.

"You need to drink more," he said.

Why didn't he just leave her alone? She pushed at his hands and the cup, but he was persistent. He was stronger than she was and more stubborn, if that was possible. Anything was possible yet nothing could be done. She was powerless to stop Cade and yet grateful when cool water trickled down her throat. It gave her such wonderful relief even though swallowing was so very painful. Leah had to concentrate with all her might to open her eyes, and immediately regretted the effort. The lamp on the table by her bed glowed as brightly as the sun and her eyes teared up with the pain.

"Banks?" Her voice sounded strange, deep and harsh, as if it didn't belong to her. It hurt to speak. Everything hurt.

"He's fine." The strong arms gently lowered her to the mattress and caring hands pulled the blankets over her. "He's at the Martins'."

She immediately pushed the blankets away. She was hot. So very hot. "Why are you here?"

"I'm taking care of you."

"Why you?" Leah shook her head. She felt petulant. Like a child. Something in her world wasn't right beyond the fact that she was sick. "I don't know you."

"Leah. You know me." His voice sounded different now, so she opened her eyes to see if he were still there. He'd turned the lamp down to a soft glow and she was grateful. He sat on the edge of her bed but his face was lost in the shadows. He shouldn't be that close. It wasn't right. Yet she'd done the same for him, and more, when he was sick. Hadn't she? Or did she dream it? If it was a dream before, was it a dream now?

"I think you know me better than anyone has for a long, long time."

Why did he sound so sad? Was it because she was dying? She could be. Lots of people died from the measles. Especially adults. Maybe he was sad because he was dying. He shouldn't die because of her. "But you'll catch it too," she told him, confident that he would leave. But then she'd be alone. She didn't want to be alone. Yet she didn't want anyone else to get sick.

"I've already had the measles. When I was a boy."

"No . . . it doesn't make sense." Not the measles. She understood that. He didn't make sense. Her world had been strange since he came. Different. Off kilter. She pushed his hands away as he tried to cover her once more with the blankets. "You're not him."

"I'm not who?"

"The preacher. You can't be him."

"Leah you're confused." He won the war of the blankets when he tucked them in around her arms. "Because of the fever."

Leah tried to think. It seemed like she was confused before she got sick. The trouble was she couldn't recall not being sick because the ache and the burning was so *present*. If only she could clear her mind of the hot fog that enveloped it she might find the answers. It seemed like they were right there, so very close, yet hidden. She could almost see them. If only her head didn't hurt so much. If only everything didn't hurt so much. *Please God make it stop.*

And just like that she knew why he wasn't who he claimed to be. She opened her eyes once more and looked at him. His face was closer now and his dark sad eyes watched her closely. Behind his head the light shimmered and burned which made it painful for her to look. As if she were gazing upon something she should not see. One of God's warrior angels. Michael, Gabriel, Raphael. That was what always went through her mind when she looked at him.

"You didn't pray." She watched his face, even though it hurt to keep her eyes open, in hopes that an answer would show, but it didn't. All she saw was the sadness that seemed so much a part of him.

He wiped her face with a wet cloth. It cooled her burning skin and she could not help but think he also used the snow to bring her comfort just as she had done with him. He quoted scripture to her before, when he was sick. Was that the same as praying? Maybe she was wrong. Maybe she shouldn't think about it so much. Maybe she should just not think at all.

"Try to rest," he said and she closed her eyes without thought, so glad that the burning stopped when she did. She heard his footsteps as he left. She didn't want him to leave. She had questions. Questions that desperately needed answers.

* * *

Cade used the time until dark to thoroughly search Leah's shed. He considered himself lucky when he found a set of saddlebags. Her rooster protested mightily at the injustice of his intrusion, but decided to let it slide when Cade threw some feed at him and his brood of hens, who clucked in satisfaction. Why shouldn't they be satisfied? They were warm and well fed. Apparently no one had used the saddlebags for quite a while because they were dusty and the leather stiff. They had more than likely hung there since her husband's death.

He put some things in it he would need when the time came to go. Some coffee, flour, and beans. Socks and a knitted sweater that was her husband's. Things he would need. For now he wasn't worried. As long as she was sick no one would come, no one would expect him to act like a minister. All he had to concentrate on now was taking care of Leah. He hated that she was sick, but at least it gave him the time he needed to heal. Cade stuffed the saddlebags up into the ropes beneath his mattress and checked on Leah again.

Her motions were jerky and her breathing raspy. If only she could rest. There wasn't anything more he could do. She had to beat this. If she didn't, if heaven forbid she died . . .

He refused to even consider it. Cade went back to his room and retrieved the revolver. He strapped it to his hip and went out the back door. Dodger quickly jumped up from his place in the hall with a huff and followed him out. Cade's restlessness was rubbing off on Dodger.

Cade stood on the back porch and watched Dodger run around the yard with his nose to the ground, sucking up the scents buried beneath the snow. In the distance a wolf howled, a signal to his pack to start the hunt. It was quickly followed by the yipping of coyotes. Cade tested the revolver on his hip over and over again, to make sure it slid easily from the holster, instead of catching on the frost.

If and when he left, would anyone follow him? Surely not. Wouldn't they just think he lit out, overwhelmed by the weather and his wound and the responsibility of ministering to the people of Angel's End. Surely they'd curse his name and call themselves every kind of fool for trusting him.

Curse Timothy's name . . . Timothy certainly didn't deserve that.

Leah knows I'm not Timothy . . .

Maybe it was better that she did know he wasn't Timothy Key. She could say she had her suspicions when everyone talked about it. And there would be talk. Not enough for anyone to go looking, but enough that if and when Fitch caught up to him, they could send him on his way. No harm done.

No harm at all.

He should check on her again.

"Come on Dodger," he called out. "Let's get back inside where it's warm."

Dodger turned from his smells and took two steps before a howl stopped him in his tracks. The dog stood by the shed and tested the air with his nose. A low growl rumbled in his throat and the ruff around his neck stood straight up. Cade stepped into knee-deep snow and cut a path to where the dog stood watching the darkness on the opposite bank of the stream.

Dodger growled again. Cade saw a movement, nothing more than a shadow in the darkness. Dodger saw it also and crouched low. Suddenly there was an explosion of snow. A rabbit took off, moving this way, then that, twisting back and forth along his hasty path. On its trail were six coyotes. Cade buried his hand in the fur behind Dodger's neck.

"Not tonight boy."

Dodger whined.

"I know. They're close. Too close." Cade tugged on the dog. "Come on, boy. Let's go inside where it's warm." They heard the death scream of the rabbit as they stepped onto the porch. Cade pushed Dodger through the door, and then turned to watch and listen. The wolves had heard it too. Their howls sounded over the selfish snarls of the coyotes as they ripped apart their kill. The coyotes would be done and gone before the wolves got there.

There was nothing lonelier in this world than the mournful sound of a wolf, especially when you were out on the trail on a cold winter's night on your own. Cade had spent many a lonely night listening to the howls, and many more nights with company that made the wolves seem generous in comparison. Alone was better to his way of thinking. Unless . . . Cade shook his head. He was crazy to even think such things. To think that he could have some kind of life with Leah.

"Don't go."

Cade turned to find Leah standing in the hall. Her hair, loosened from its braid, hung in damp disarray around her face. The buttons on the front of her gown were open and it hung precariously off one shoulder, nearly baring a breast. Her face was lost in the shadows but he saw the heat of the fever glistening on her skin. He shut the door firmly behind him. He shouldn't have left it open. The chill was likely what woke her.

"I'm not going anywhere," he lied.

"You've got your gun on, Nate. If you go out there he'll kill you." Cade looked at his hip where her dead husband's gun hung and then back at Leah. She took a step toward him with her hand outstretched. Her eyes shone eerily in the dim light. "Don't go. We need you."

She was reliving the night that her husband died.

"I hate guns. I hate them," she said. "I wish you'd never got one. I wish you'd never put one on. I wish we'd never come here. I wish . . ." She put her hand to her forehead. She screwed her eyes up tight and then put the heels of her hands to her eyes.

"It hurts." She opened her eyes again and looked at him. "Make it stop."

He picked her up and felt the heat off her feverish skin through his shirt. She was burning up with it. Leah clung to him. She tucked her head beneath his neck and grabbed on to his shirt. "Don't go," she said again. As if she could read his mind. As if she knew, inside, what he wanted more than anything.

"I won't," he said, and he realized he wanted to stay here with her forever. If only it were possible. If only she wanted him too, but she thought he was her dead husband. "It's so hot," she murmured against his throat.

Cade put her down on the bed and untangled her fingers from his shirt so he could straighten up. What to do now?

Cade went back out. The washtub hung safely on a hook on the porch wall. He took it down, sat it in the hallway and with the door open, shoveled snow into it until it was full. It was heavy when he was done and his ribs screamed in protest as he half carried and half drug it to her room. Once there, he wrapped Leah up in her robe, sat her in the tub and piled snow around her. He braced her neck with a towel rolled up behind it and folded her arms over her stomach. Her feet hung over the end, and he pulled her thick woolen socks off.

Dodger whined.

"I'm trying to help," he said to the dog.

She coughed, hard and croupy, deep in her throat. "What are you doing?" Her voice was hoarse and cracked. She barely opened her eyes, just enough to take in her surroundings.

"Cooling you down."

"Leave me alone," she protested weakly.

"Make up your mind," he teased gently. "You said to make it stop."

She shook her head and muttered something so low that

he could not hear it. Cade crouched by the tub, wrapped a handful of snow in a towel and ran it over her face.

"You are the darnedest woman I've ever met," he said. "Taking in wounded men and stray cats and helping little boys with the measles." He picked up a slim arm and ran the icy towel down the length of it. "Stubborn too." He held her fingers in his palm and cooled them with the snow. "Won't tell anyone your pump is broken. Would rather melt snow and haul bucketfuls of water from a stream than ask for help."

Ashes clawed her way onto the bed and watched the tub with curious eyes and a twitching tail.

"And you've got me so twisted up inside I don't know which end is up." He turned her hand over and rubbed the palm. "One minute I'm imagining what I'll do when I leave and the next I'm daydreaming about a life with you." He started on the other arm. "Mostly I just want to kiss you senseless."

A fleeting smile lit her face.

Cade touched her cheek and pushed her hair back. Sick as she was, he wanted to kiss her again. What was wrong with him? She was sick!

He could only hope that the snow cooled her fever. But now what was he supposed to do with her? Her robe and gown were soaked and her bed was wet from her fever. Cade grunted as he lifted her from the tub and carried her across the hall to his room where the sheets were fresh and clean. His ribs were never going to heal at this rate.

He took off her robe and gown. "I'm doing this for her own good, not mine," he reminded God and the devil, whichever one was listening. He caught a glimpse of plump breasts and the curve of her hip as he pulled the blankets over her. He touched her face and was relieved to find it felt somewhat cooler.

He went into her room and stripped the sheets. Even

though it was late, he made use of the snow. He carried the tub into the kitchen, heaved it to the stove top so that it would melt. He stoked up the fire to warm the water and dropped her sheets and gown in to soak. He hung her robe close by the stove to dry and searched the shelves until he found what he hoped was soap flakes. As he dropped them in the water the smell of roses wafted into the air. At least he knew he'd never forget her. Every time he saw a rosebush he'd think of her. Luckily he didn't see that many in his travels.

You'd be better off to forget her . . .

Cade went to her room to get one of her gowns. He really should put something on her. She'd more than likely be put out with him when she realized he'd seen her naked. A delicious grin lit his face at the thought, along with the realization that she more than likely had looked her fill when he was sick. "Yes, I am definitely going to hell."

A high bureau with a mirror sat on the wall opposite the doorway and, as he made to open the top drawer, he caught sight of his reflection.

How long had it been since he really looked at himself? He saw the man in the mirror; saw the lines and angles of his face beneath the three-day growth of beard. He saw the dark hair that badly needed a cut. He saw the deep brow and the dark eyes, shadowed beneath and filled with shame.

He saw his father as he had last seen him. The face looking back at him was younger, not as time worn, not as creased with grief, but the look, the image, the soul that looked back with the same dark brown eyes was an exact replica. He saw the same incrimination staring back at him that he felt every time he thought of how his father abandoned him and Brody. When had he turned into the very thing he despised?

"Banks!"

Cade grabbed a gown and ran to Leah's side.

*   *   *

Banks. She had to find him. It wasn't safe. She could not leave this horrible place until he was safe. The cabin was on fire and she ran through the rooms and battled the flames as she called out his name. She could hear him, in the distance, calling for her, but she couldn't see him. Everywhere she turned, the flames burned high, blocking her view and blocking her escape. If only she wasn't so hot. Lost. Confused. If only someone would help her.

You are alone . . . you have been since Nate died . . . She didn't want to be alone. Alone was such a sad thing to be. She'd seen that same sadness in Cade, she'd seen it in his eyes. Cade . . . Leah, trapped in the flames, wept because of the sadness and the loneliness, and because she could not find Banks. Without Banks there was no reason to care. There was no reason to go on. Without Banks she would just give in to the flames and let them burn her up until she was nothing but ash and could float away on the wind.

She didn't ask for the strong arms that gathered her up and held her close. She didn't tell him to wipe her brow and pour cool water down her throat. Yet somehow he knew. He knew she was lost. He knew she needed help. Leah opened her eyes.

"Cade?"

"Yes." She saw his smile. Saw the creases it made in his face and the way his eyes crinkled up at the corners. "I'm Cade."

There it was again. The confusion. The unsettling feeling that something wasn't right. "That's a strange name for a preacher."

"I'm not a preacher Leah. I'm not what you think at all. Now get some rest."

She didn't want to rest. Every time he told her to rest the

flames came back and she was lost. She had to find her son. "Banks?"

"He's fine. He's at the Martins'. He wants you to rest so you will get better."

She couldn't rest. She could never rest because it was all up to her. He was her responsibility. There was no one else. Yet Cade was here. "Why are you here?"

He smiled at her again. His smile was so nice. It completely transformed his face. Yet there was still the sadness in his eyes that gave her an ache, deep in her heart. "Because I have no place else to be right now. No place else at all."

"I'm glad you're here." She put her hand on his cheek. It felt so very cool against the heat of her palm. She wished his sadness would go away. He should be happy. Everyone should be happy at some time in their lives. Shouldn't they?

"Don't leave me."

He smiled at her. But his eyes were still sad. "Get some rest."

TWENTY

Ward looked up from the table as the door opened with a blast of cold air. He was surprised to see Jim Martin walk through the door. It wasn't because Jim was against drinking; it was just usually an issue of time. Between the livery and six kids underfoot, the man had little time for anything beyond work and sleep. What was stranger was the fact that it was so late at night when Jim stepped through the door.

"Any news?" Jake asked.

"Not unless you count coyotes as news," Jim replied. He nodded when Ward waved the whiskey bottle in his direction. Ward poured him a shot. Jim took off his coat and hung it on the back of the chair before he joined the men at the table. "I found one snooping around the edge of the corral. I didn't have my gun with me or I'd have taken a shot at it."

"Everything's gone to ground with the cold," Jake said. "How's Banks?"

"He's all right," Jim said. "He's been too busy playing to miss his mom, although he did ask about her when he went to bed."

"Has Gretchen been back?"

"She took some food up. Leah was asleep and the preacher was out back. She didn't hang around."

"I don't blame her," Ward said. The sight of the dead bodies and the smell from the fire was still fresh in his mind.

"She said it looked like he was doing a good job taking care of her, although the kitchen was a bit of a mess. Leah was clean."

Ward watched Jake. As he expected the man flushed at the thought of the preacher keeping Leah clean.

"We'll look in on them in the morning," Jim added, and Jake nodded. Jim took a sip of his whiskey. "So what do you think of him?"

"You haven't talked to him?" Jake asked.

"The one time I tried he was asleep. I know Bettina has but all she can think about is when she can get Margy down there. I think she wants the woman out of her house more than she wants to fix her up with the preacher."

"You talked to him," Ward reminded Jake. "What did you come away with? He must have said something to impress you, or else you wouldn't have left Leah there with him, even if he is immune to the measles."

Jake shrugged. "I don't know. There's something about him. He's not what I expected for a minister but when he said he'd take care of Leah, I couldn't help but believe that he would, to the best of his ability."

Ward looked down at Lady, who'd quickly taken to his schedule. She lay on the floor by his chair with her head turned toward the door so she could see whoever came in. He rubbed the top of her head. Dang if he hadn't gotten attached to her real quick. "You know what I think?"

The other two looked at him expectantly. "Dodger seems to like him, and you know how protective he is of Leah and Banks. If Dodger has no problem with him, then he must be all right."

"I think I'll reserve judgment until I hear him preach a sermon," Jake said.

"Well since we know the chances of me setting foot inside the church to hear him are slim, I'll just have to go along with Dodger," Ward replied.

It was like fighting a losing battle, but so was everything else he put his mind to. And he approached it with the same stubborn tenacity that had kept him alive so far. Cade spent what seemed like hours cooling Leah down and then she'd get hot again. Her fever was sneaky, waiting until the few moments that he walked away to attack again. As long as he kept after her with the snow, wiping and cooling her skin, she was fine. But as soon as he stopped, because he was afraid of giving her frostbite, it would shoot back up, crawling higher and higher each time, until he was afraid she would burst into flames when he touched her skin.

"Come on now, Leah." Cade sat in the chair by the bed and wiped her face with snow. "You're stubborn. You've got to fight this."

She muttered something, but he couldn't understand the words. She was lost in a dream with ghosts from her past. Still, she was talking and Cade took it as a good sign, so he kept on.

"I thought you were an angel the first time I saw you. I reckon I had you mixed up with that dang statue sitting out in the middle of the street."

She shook her head, jerking it back and forth on the pillow, as if she were arguing with someone. Dodger put his paws on the edge of the bed and rose up to look at Leah. Cade rubbed his head, and the dog whined before he lay down on the floor beside his chair.

"It makes sense when you think about it. You're a lot like that stone angel, standing there with its arms all stretched out, ready to welcome everyone into the fold." He started on her arms again, wiping the length of them, and each delicate finger. "You took me in and saved my life." Cade laughed. "Of course, if you'd known who I really was, you probably would have left me out in that blizzard to die."

He bathed her neck, pushing her hair out of the way as he did so. "But here's the thing. I believe in angels. It's not that I've come across that many of them, but I know they're out there. They have to be, because there are so many demons around. If you've got demons then there have to be angels. It's the only way to keep balance. There's winter and there's summer, there's spring and there's fall. We've got the desert and the forests, the plains and the mountains, the land and the sea. There's good and there's bad and there are angels and demons. In case you didn't realize it, I'm kind of an authority on demons. I reckon I've spent enough time with a bunch of them."

Leah tossed her head and muttered again.

"It's funny you know." Cade talked to her as he'd never dared talk to anyone before. "I never really thought about it much. I just thought that this . . . my life . . . was the way it was. That there could never be anything different. But now . . ." He pushed her hair back from her brow. "Now I wish for things I never knew existed."

Leah turned her face into his hand and sighed.

"A very wise man told me we have no way of knowing where God's path will lead us. God only knows that I've had no purpose in my path. I can't help but wonder if I was supposed to wind up here. I can't imagine why. I can't imagine how my being here can be of any use to anyone, unless it's just because I'm able to take care of you while you're sick."

He had not realized his ramblings would turn into such introspection. He only thought to keep her focused. To keep her from slipping away. "It surely wasn't of any use to Timothy."

Leah mumbled again. Cade bent closer to the bed. "Prayers . . ." she sighed.

Cade shook his head. "God doesn't want my prayers," he said.

"No, no, no . . ." She was out of her head with the fever and he was a fool to ramble on the way he had. Cade stood and stretched from the long hours he'd spent in the chair. He needed to clear his head of the nonsense he'd dredged up from deep inside. He'd spoken of things he'd never given voice to before. Things he should never voice.

He felt so helpless against Leah's fever. Admitting it was frightening, especially since with it came the realization that he now knew what it had been like for his father. He'd been unable to stop the horrific murder of his wife and daughter. He'd blamed himself for their deaths and his guilt had been so strong, he could no longer care for his sons. And what about Leah? Had she felt the same hopelessness when they carried her husband in, and she had to watch him die?

Cade went out back. The creaking of the door shutting behind him startled something beside the shed. He heard the rustle of Leah's chickens and their panicked clucks. He saw a coyote racing across the snow toward the stream. The pickings must be slim for one to come so close to town. He'd better make sure his gun was handy next time. Just in case.

The sky to the east, over the mountains, was streaked with pale grays, pinks and purples that announced the coming of dawn. Another night gone, another day closer to someone discovering his deception. Was it worth it? Only time would tell.

The cold was vicious and intense. Maybe he should bring Leah outside and pack her in snow. No . . . that would be too much. It was so cold that he shivered, he who usually ignored it. It would kill her and that he would not allow.

He heard the click of Dodger's toenails on the wood floor and his scratch at the door. He let him out. The dog whined and nudged Cade's hand with his nose. "Go on," he said, thinking the dog just needed to go. Dodger didn't move, instead he gave Cade another nudge.

"Leah?" Cade returned to his room. She lay still, very still, where before she'd been fretful. Cade touched her forehead. She was burning up, hotter than ever. What should he do? What else could he do?

"LEAH?" Cade shook her. She didn't move. Cade dropped to his knees by the bed and laid his head on her breast, with his ear over her heart. Her breathing was shallow and he could hear the flutter of her heart in her chest. It was going too fast as it tried its best to fight the fever which held her in its grip.

She's dying . . .

"Please God . . . not this."

Timothy's Bible still lay on the table beside the bed. Cade picked it up and flipped the pages to Hebrews. He knew exactly where to find it. His father taught him to recite the books of the Bible soon after he learned his ABCs. He trailed his finger down the pages, skimming until a verse caught his eye.

> *Let us then with confidence draw near to the throne of grace, that we may receive mercy and find grace to help in time of need.*

"That we may receive mercy . . ." Could he receive mercy? Was it possible? If he asked, could it be given to

Leah? She was so very still, so very quiet, so very lost in her battle.

Cade folded his hands and dropped his forehead to rest on them. He sighed deeply, searching inside for the words to begin.

"God I haven't asked you for anything in years. But I'm asking you now, Lord . . . no, I'm begging you. Don't take this woman. She's good and she's kind, and she saved my life when I didn't deserve it." He wiped his forehead across his folded hands, to press his mind for the correct words, words that would convey the need right before him.

"She's got a boy. A boy that she loves with her whole life. A boy that needs her. A boy shouldn't lose his mother . . ." Cade spoke from experience. He could easily say his life fell apart when his father took them west, but he knew it was the horrid death of his mother that destroyed them all.

"If you let her live, God, I'll go on my way. I'll leave and never look back, even though there's nothing I want more than to stay here and try to build some sort of life. I think with Leah in my life I could be good. I could do something besides waste my life and the time you've given me."

He took a deep breath. What else could he say? What else could he offer in trade for her life? "Lord, I know I'm not worth saving, but Leah is. I'll never ask for anything else for the rest of my life. Please Lord, just let her live." Cade dropped his head to the bed and took Leah's hand in his. It was so hot and felt so frail. "Please Lord, just let her live . . ."

Exhaustion finally overtook him and Cade dozed, still gripping Leah's hand as he was caught in that half world between dreams and reality. Something finally awakened him and he realized it was the bed shaking that brought him back. He looked up to find Leah shivering violently.

"Please . . . I'm so co-co-cold." Her teeth chattered so hard that he thought they might break. "Hel-help me."

Cade wrapped the blankets around her and scooped her out of the bed.

"Wha-what arrre you doing?"

"Taking you someplace warm," he explained. He'd let the fires die down overnight to help cool her fever. Cade took her into the parlor and laid her on the sofa. Leah clutched weakly at the blankets as she shook so hard that she nearly slid into the floor. Cade threw kindling into the fireplace, and then stacked log after log onto the fire as it flared to life. When the heat rolled forth, he picked her up again. With one foot he scooted the rocking chair around until it faced the hearth then he sat down and bundled Leah onto his lap.

She huddled against him. Her arms curled against her breasts as she continued to shake. "What's wr-wrong with m-me?"

Cade pulled the blankets up tighter around her. Tucked the corners in. Folded her into his arms and placed her head up under his chin. "Don't worry, it's a good thing," he said. "The shaking is your body's way of staying warm."

Dodger padded into the parlor and sat down on the rug beside the chair. Ashes peeped up from the mending basket where she'd been sleeping and squeaked out a yawn. Cade pushed at the hearth with his feet and the chair rocked gently back and forth. The fire popped and cracked and the bird popped out of the clock in the hall and chimed the hour. Eventually the shaking subsided, until Cade, with Leah still safely on his lap, leaned forward and tossed another log on the fire.

"How long has it been?" she asked.

"Two days."

"It feels like forever."

Cade rubbed his cheek against the top of her head. "Yes it does."

"And you've taken care of me all this time?"

"It's the same you did for me."

"Thank you Cade," she said, and sighed.

Even though every one of his instincts told him to let go, to run, to leave town this very minute, Cade continued to rock the chair and held her even tighter against him.

TWENTY-ONE

"When did you have the measles?" Leah finally felt warm. She felt safe. She was exhausted, yet she felt content. She didn't want to move from her place in his arms so she watched the fire as the flames licked at the logs and pressed her head against his chest with the rumble of his words.

"When I was a boy. I was seven."

"Tell me about it."

Cade tilted his head to look down at her. He looked tired and worn, but a smile quirked the corner of his mouth. "You really want to know?"

She smiled back. "I really want to know."

"We were living with the Cheyenne."

"The Cheyenne? Why?"

"My father was a minister. And according to my father, God wanted him to minister to the Cheyenne. They were his chosen flock as he called it. He took our family west when I was six. Soon after we arrived at the village, there was a measles outbreak. My brother and I both got sick, and my mother nursed us inside of a hide tent, as we were living as they lived. She'd had the measles when she was a girl, so she was immune like I am now." He shook his head at the memory. "We had to sleep on pallets. I remember hating it, as the ground was cold and hard and I ached all over. The entire time I wished that I was back at home and in my bed."

Leah listened with fascination to the way his voice rumbled deep inside his chest as he spoke. His hold on her felt so solid, so strong and so comforting. She had no desire to move. She wanted to stay this way, safe and secure, until sleep overtook her once more, yet she felt sorry for the boy he must have been, far away from home, living with strangers and so very sick. It must have been horrible for his mother to be in a strange place and worried over the lives of her children. She wanted to know more. This glimpse into his childhood was unexpected and seemed so private.

"It must have been frightening for your mother."

Cade suddenly went quiet and Leah turned from her perusal of the fire to look at his face. He must not have taken the time to shave in the past few days, not since she did it for him that night that seemed like ages ago. The dark stubble of his beard trailed down beneath his chin to the soft and smooth skin on his lower neck where his breastbone lay. The indentation above seemed very vulnerable when he swallowed.

"If she was frightened, she never showed it," he finally said. "I just remember her singing to us. Smiling a lot and telling us everything would be all right."

"She sounds like a very good mother." She wanted her to be, just as she wanted to be. She wanted Banks to look back when he was grown and know that even though they didn't have much, he was loved and cared for. She hoped that Cade had the same memories of his mother.

She wanted the sadness to be gone from his eyes.

"She was."

"What happened to her?"

"She died during the massacre at Sand Creek." His voice did not change in timbre when he spoke and she looked up to see his eyes were focused on the fire as if he were far, far away.

Leah swallowed her gasp of shock. She watched his face carefully. "Were you there?"

He stared into the fire and the rocking of the chair was steady. "Yes. I was. I saw it happen. The soldiers raped her and then stabbed her with their bayonets. They bashed my baby sister's head in with their rifle butts. My father held me back because I tried to run to her. He wouldn't let me save her."

"You were just a boy. How could you save her?"

His eyes, so sad, darted down to her face, then quickly moved back to the fire. Did he see her death once more? "I could have made them realize she was white. Her hair was light brown, not black. It was a bit darker than yours. Her eyes were blue. How could they not see that she wasn't Cheyenne? Not that it should make a difference. She was a woman. They shouldn't have hurt her, no matter what tribe she belonged to."

"I'm so sorry . . ."

He stopped rocking abruptly and looked down at her. His dark eyes searched her face. Was that why he was so sad? Because he'd seen his mother murdered? And even though he'd seen such a bad thing happen, he'd still gone on to be a minister, like his father. It spoke volumes about his heart.

And he'd nursed her. Taken care of her in her time of need. Where would she be if he hadn't been here? Would someone else have taken such good care of her? She gave him a tremulous smile.

"You're the first person who's ever said that," he remarked.

"Said what?"

"That you were sorry. About my mother."

What a strange thing to say. And a stranger thing to happen. Why had no one comforted the small boy who lost his mother?

"What happened to you then? Did your father bring you back east?"

His eyes left her face and he once more stared into the fire. "My father dropped me and my brother in an orphanage and we never saw him again." The words were bitter and venomous. Full of hatred for the man who abandoned him. Yet he became a minister . . .

The rocking stopped and he shifted in the chair. Leah realized he was done speaking, that he was done sharing. She waited, expectantly, for him to move, to release her, to tell her to rest, or to eat, or something, but he didn't. He just shut his eyes, as if the things he saw in the fire were too painful. She watched him, watched his face for some movement, some sign. He swallowed, once, and she watched the movement with quiet fascination, and then her eyes, so very heavy because she was so achingly weary, closed into sleep.

If he let her go, he would have to leave. When he let her go . . . After all, he'd promised God that he would leave. Cade looked down at Leah as she snuggled deep within the blankets, safe and sound in his arms. The fever was gone. She slept, exhausted from her fight. Cade smiled at his next thought. She'd be covered in spots soon. He was certain she wouldn't like that a bit.

Why had he told her about his past? It wasn't as if he

forgot he was supposed to be Timothy, it was more like he just didn't care. He wanted her to know about his past. He wanted her to know his secrets. Since he was leaving, it didn't matter. She would know he was a liar soon enough. But despite that he wanted her to know something true about him. He wanted her to know there were reasons he left.

Cade closed his eyes and fell asleep with Leah still safely in his arms.

The smells woke him. Warm smells that drifted from the kitchen and made his stomach grumble in anticipation. How long had it been since he ate? Yesterday? The day before? His arms felt numb and his legs cramped. Leah was still asleep in his arms. Dodger was gone from his place by the chair and there was no sign of Ashes. Cade heard the creak of a floorboard and turned his head to the door. An old woman stared back at him with a knowing smile on her face. Cade arched an eyebrow in her direction.

She dipped her head in his direction. "I'm Nonnie," she said. Her English was heavily accented. She was from somewhere in Europe. Germany? Austria?

"The apple strudel?" Leah had mentioned her. She went with the Martins. Jim and Gretchen and the passel of kids. Banks's friends.

"Yah." She bobbed her head. "Leah is better now?"

"Her fever broke this morning." He flexed his cramped muscles carefully, so as not to disturb her. She made a small sound, similar to the one he'd heard Ashes make in her sleep, and he could not help but smile.

"That is good." Nonnie came closer. She approached him as if she were afraid he might hurt her. "May I?" She touched the blanket close to Leah's shoulder.

"Sure," Cade said. The woman wanted to see for herself if Leah was still alive. He couldn't blame her for that.

Nonnie pulled the blanket away. "Ach! She has the spots. See?"

Cade grinned as he looked at the rash that covered Leah's breastbone. He wasn't leaving quite yet. After all she was still contagious which meant he might be too.

I will leave . . . as soon as she is better.

TWENTY-TWO

"What's the total today? A thousand? Two?" Cade put Ashes on the floor and leaned in her doorway with his arms crossed. He looked infuriatingly handsome and agonizingly spot free. He must have shaved while she napped after breakfast, and from the fresh clean smell that drifted her way it seemed he'd washed up too. His hair, still shaggy, shone from a good brushing and his smile shone as bright as the sun.

"I don't think either one of us can count that high," Leah replied. The spots were aggravating, but at least they didn't itch after Nonnie had helped her bathe in oatmeal and smoothed her special rose ointment on her skin. All after hanging a sheet over her doorway, and promising to make Jim get her doors done. Her fever had returned but it wasn't near as bad as it was before, and just left her feeling very tired. She wore a clean gown and her hair in a braid that fell over her shoulder. She was tired of lying about, but unfortunately didn't have the energy to do much of anything except sew. She put his frock coat aside where she'd been stitching a new collar on with some scraps of velvet.

He took a few steps into the room and stopped well away from the foot of her bed as if he were afraid of getting too close. Funny that, since he'd been so close before, when she was so sick. Close enough to touch her, to bathe her, to hold her in his arms. Leah recalled how she'd studied him when he was sick. Had he done the same with her? Had he seen every part of her, just as she had with him? The idea made her think of things she shouldn't, made her want things she couldn't have. Could she?

Maybe not, as he didn't seem inclined to come any closer. Yet he did study her, as if contemplating something . . . Dodger's tail thumped on the rug beside her bed. Her heart beat a steady accompaniment. What a pair they were. Both of them falling for the man.

"It appears to me that we'd only have to count to one, as it looks like they've all grown together." He was teasing her wasn't he? Was that a glint in his eye? A hint of happiness? Or was it just a trick of the morning light, like the dust motes that Ashes determinedly stalked around the floor.

"Actually I think they're fading," she said as she rubbed a hand over her arm. His eyes followed her hand, watching her every movement. It was strange, yet thrilling, when he watched her like that. As if he wanted to touch her instead. *I have got to stop letting my imagination run away with me . . . It must be because I've been sick . . . because I almost died, that I've got such fanciful thoughts in my mind.*

"What are you working on?" he asked.

She held up his coat. "I replaced your collar. It looked as if it was burned."

"Hmm," he said.

"You still don't remember what happened to you?"

He shrugged. "I got shot, remember?"

Leah shook her head. "The question is how and possibly who."

He moved to the foot of the bed and sat down on the edge, close enough that she could stretch out her feet and touch him if she wanted. Which she wanted to very much. Without thought she flexed her foot and he put his hand on it, over the blanket, in a casual and intimate pose. He tapped his foot and Ashes wiggled her behind and pounced on the toe of his boot.

"Does it matter?"

What was that supposed to mean? Did he not know how lucky he was not to have died in the middle of nowhere all alone? "Yes it does, someone is out there shooting innocent people, and probably robbing them too. You could have died."

"But I didn't. Because of you."

"What would have happened to you if your horse hadn't brought you into town?"

"But he did." He continued to play with Ashes who repeatedly stalked and pounced on his foot. Dodger raised his head from the rug and watched for a moment before resuming his nap.

"Is this supposed to be a sermon on forgiveness?" she asked.

He studied her once more. What exactly was he looking for when he watched her that way? "Are you the forgiving sort?"

Leah shook her head at his whimsy. "I'm not the one who got shot."

He nodded his head in agreement. "Well"—he squeezed her foot and stood—"do you want something to eat?"

"The way you keep setting food in front of me I'm going to be as big as Bet—as big as one of Jake's cows, in no time." Leah felt her skin burn at her almost slip. It really was hard to do good all the time. At least he wouldn't be able to tell she was flushed with embarrassment. Not with all the spots on her skin.

He shook his head. "I don't think that will happen. At least not anytime soon. You'll be up and back to work in no time. Just like before . . ." He looked off beyond her, out the window. First he was pensive, and now he was restless. Maybe he felt like he should be about his work. He was healed now. She hadn't seen him favor his ribs for the past several days. She was better too, except for the rash, which made her want to hide until the spots were completely gone. That didn't mean he couldn't go out. There was no reason at all for him to hang around the house. Yet he stayed close by, as if there was no place else he'd rather be.

Leah arranged the sheet over her quilt. She folded the hem evenly and smoothed it with her hand. "You don't have to wait on me anymore," she said. "I'm able to move about."

"I know." He tilted his head to study her again. Leah felt suddenly more self-conscious than she had before. The thought that he'd seen her naked as the day she was born was not comforting at the moment. "I'm afraid I have some bad news for you."

Leah's heart leapt into her throat. Was it Banks? Was he sick too? She blinked at the sudden rush of tears that threatened at just the thought of something being wrong with her son. "What is it?"

"A coyote got one of your hens last night."

Leah put her hand to her heart and let out the breath she had not even realized she'd been holding. "At least it was only one," she said. "Are you sure it was a hen and not Roscoe?"

"Roscoe?"

"My rooster. I named him after this man that lived in the same town as my grandmother and I. He wasn't more than five feet tall in his stocking feet and wore his Sunday clothes every day of the week. He carried a cane with a shiny silver handle and always bowed and tipped his hat to the ladies when he passed them on the street. His name was Roscoe Peabody. His hair was long and very shiny and black.

"Like the feathers on the rooster," Cade said with a grin. "I'm glad to know his name now. It will make it easier for me to threaten him the next time he comes after my ankles."

"I don't think he'd have a chance of getting at them with those boots you wear."

Cade looked down at his feet. A shadow crossed over his face, a realization of some sort that made him seem suddenly off-kilter. Or did she just imagine it?

"He can thank my boots for keeping him out of the stew pot then," he said and grinned once more, as if all was well. Wasn't it? He walked to her bureau and touched the brush that lay there. He turned, and she saw that sadness in his eyes again. Ever since she'd awakened from her fever she hadn't noticed it so much. She'd thought perhaps he had purged it when he told her about his past, about his mother's death and his father's abandonment.

A pounding on the door interrupted whatever it was he was about to say. "Company again." He grinned, shook his head, and went to the door with Dodger on his heels, as usual. It was funny how fast Dodger had taken to him. As if he now felt responsible for him after saving his life.

Now that she was past the fever and the worst of the spots, people had come by. There had been a steady stream of visitors since she'd come out of the fever. Mostly Gretchen and Nonnie, who helped her wash up, and Dusty, who carried something over for them to eat every day and then would stay and talk about Peaches as if he was the smartest kitten ever born.

Jim had brought Banks by one day after school. It had been a week since she'd seen him. He stood in the doorway, because she wouldn't let him come any closer, and talked to her. She missed her son so terribly much.

"Hello!" Leah recognized the voice. "I'm Margy. I'm the schoolteacher." She must be here to discuss Banks's schoolwork. Leah hoped he wasn't using her illness as an excuse to fall behind. She wanted so much for her son. Something more than living and dying by the gun.

"Pleased to meet you," Cade said. "I'll tell Leah you're here."

"Oh no, I wouldn't want to disturb Leah," Margy trilled. "I'm sure she needs her rest." She giggled. Leah's mouth dropped open as she listened to the exchange. *She's giggling. Like an idiot!* "I thought perhaps you could use a break?" Margy continued. "Maybe get out of the house for a bit? We could go over to Dusty's and have some coffee if you'd like."

Would he go? Leave her here alone after so carefully watching after her all of these days. Leah listened carefully for his answer as she silently cursed Bettina for finally getting her way. Margy was here to catch herself a man.

Ward stood on the porch of Heaven's Gate and watched to see if Margy and the preacher came out again. As soon as he'd seen Margy walk down the street he knew she was going to see the preacher and not Leah. Bettina's work no doubt, as Margy was the shy type.

"Looks like the preacher has a suitor," Ward remarked to Lady who sat by his side and watched the goings-on with her soft brown eyes. If he didn't know any better he'd think spring was in the air, instead of Christmas fixing to sneak up on them. Thanksgiving would be here next week and the council was planning a big celebration to welcome the preacher, and of course give thanks that both he and Leah had survived their calamities.

The weather was even smiling on them for a while. The skies were clear and the air mild enough to melt some of the snow. The street was passable and hopefully would remain so instead of dissolving into a quagmire of muck and mud, as was the case most times when the spring thaw was upon them. Swanson's mercantile was busy and Ward knew his place would be hopping tonight, as it was Saturday and the miners and cowboys would be heading into town after suffering through the past few weeks with cabin fever. Pris certainly hoped so. He could hear her, upstairs, singing to herself as she washed her hair, so she'd be especially pretty to garner extra tips tonight.

The arrival of Jake made things pretty much perfect. Not that Jake had been much company lately, what with his worry over the preacher moving in on his territory. Since Margy had thrown herself into the mix things might get interesting though.

"Howdy," Ward said as Jake rode up.

"Howdy, yourself."

Yup, Jake was still in a mood.

"What brings you to town so early on a Saturday?"

"Gus wants the search committee to meet. We're supposed to go visit with Pastor Key as one. Tell him it's time to go to work."

"Looks to me like Margy went ahead without you."

"Huh?"

"She just went down to Leah's. And I'm pretty sure it wasn't to check on the patient."

Jake looked up the street toward Leah's house and grinned. "Well isn't that an interesting turn of events."

"You mean to tell me you didn't know that was Bettina's intent as soon as she found out Pastor Key was young and single?"

Jake scoffed. "I never pay attention to Bettina."

"Well that explains a lot then," Ward said dryly.

Jake shook his head and Ward laughed, which made Jake look at him in confusion. "For as smart as you are, you sure are dumb sometimes," Ward said.

"What the hell is that supposed to mean?"

Ward looked out over the street. "Not a dang thing." Jake's dismissal of Bettina was a big mistake on his part. The woman might be hard to take but she was smart and she was sly. If Jake had had enough sense to enlist the aid of Bettina in the first place, he might have Leah now instead of just pouting about it. It wasn't as if Bettina hadn't thought of it herself, but she wasn't about to help him, since he didn't put up with her nonsense.

People were foolish sometimes, putting their pride above everything else. Pride was a sorry companion when you were alone. His life was a living testament to that.

Gus came out of the store, buttoning his coat as he went and Jim exited his stable at the same time. "Maybe I'll tag along to this committee meeting," Ward said. "Might be that I'll be interested in attending church one of these days."

Jake scraped some snow off the step with his boot. "I'd say hell was freezing over but since there's a bit of a thaw going on . . ."

"Come on, Lady," Ward said and the three of them joined up with Gus and Jim on the street.

He never should have let her in, but dang it, he didn't know the schoolmarm was there to see him, he just figured she'd come to talk with Leah about Banks's schoolwork or something. Now he was stuck in the parlor and the woman was preparing to read him a sonnet. A sonnet! Cade was trapped. She stood between him and the door arranging her cookies on a plate. She offered them up to Cade with a smile. She was actually kind of pretty with her blue eyes magnified behind her glasses. But she wasn't Leah.

"I can't believe you've been in town these few weeks and this is the first time we've met," she said.

"Well things have been a bit trying," Cade replied. "And

I'm just now getting back to normal." He looked at the plates of cookies in confusion. They looked like blobs of oats with some sugar sprinkled on top.

"It was my mother's recipe," Margy explained as she arranged her skirts before she primly sat on the edge of the sofa. "They don't need to be baked."

Well that explained why they looked the way they did. Margy opened her book and cleared her throat. She looked over her glasses at Cade with much the same look he imagined she gave her students, and he suddenly felt the need to sit down. He took a seat in the rocker and mentally prepared himself for what he was certain was going to be a painful experience.

At least I have some food to tide me over . . . Cade took a bite of the cookie and immediately choked. She looked at him with a hopeful smile and Cade gritted his teeth and swallowed.

Margy began to read. "'Wild nights, wild nights were I with thee, wild nights should be our luxury . . .'" She paused and looked at Cade. "Oh I just love Miss Dickinson, don't you?"

"Er." Had he misheard her? Something about wild nights. Seriously? "I believe this is the first time I've heard her . . ."

"Oh I hope you forgive me, I do not mean to offend," she said. "I find her no more titillating than the Song of Solomon."

"I wouldn't know," Cade admitted. He did know the Song of Solomon. Jasper used to recite it when he posed as a preacher. He'd used it to seduce women. Any mention of it usually made him cringe.

Margy resumed her reading.

Dodger sat in the hallway, his usual position when people were scattered throughout the house. Cade lowered his hand with the cookie to the opposite side of the chair from Margy and motioned with his finger for him to come. Dodger cocked his head.

"Come," Cade mouthed. Dodger slowly got to his feet and walked in the room. He stopped a few steps in. Cade motioned again. Dodger finally took the last steps that would bring him close to Cade. Cade dropped the cookie and Dodger sniffed it.

Come on . . . since when have you been so picky about what you eat? Dodger generally ate everything that was put in front of him. Finally he took it in his mouth and swallowed it with one gulp. He snuffed around the floor for crumbs then turned and went back to his place in the hall.

One problem solved. Now to get rid of the schoolteacher who seemed to be getting a bit titillated over her sonnets. If only Leah would need something . . . anything. If she'd call out then he could go, but she was silent. *She must be asleep . . .*

Chork! Margy stopped her reading and they both looked at Dodger. He stood, facing the parlor, and made another strange noise. His entire body cramped. They both watched in fascination as his body convulsed from his hind quarters all the way forward through his throat. He gagged again.

"Oh my," Margy said. She fanned her face with her book.

Cade covered his mouth with his hand to keep from laughing out loud and adopted a look of pure concern as Dodger finally yakked up a glob of oats. The dog smacked his lips a few times and sniffed at the mess, then walked into the kitchen and lapped at his water bowl.

Cade turned to Margy, thrilled that Dodger had given him an escape plan, even though he didn't let it show. She was deathly pale. She put her hand to her heart, then her forehead and then, in a fashion that would have impressed Letty Middleton during one of her cons, Margy swooned and crumpled dramatically onto the sofa.

"I see you swept her right off her feet," Leah said. She gingerly stepped around the mess Dodger left in the hall as she belted her robe.

He was happy at the sight of her. "Are you jealous?"

Leah rolled her eyes to the ceiling and shook her head. "Are you just going to leave her lying there like that?"

Cade ran a hand over his throat as he studied Margy, who was half on, half off, the sofa, more reclined than falling off. "She looks comfortable doesn't she?"

"Oh my goodness," Leah exclaimed. "You are no help at all."

Margy let out a soft moan.

"You take care of her," Cade said. "I'll clean up the mess." He chuckled as he walked by her. There was no way in hell he was going to fall into the schoolmarm's trap. He knew she wanted to get him in a compromising position. He was certain of it when he looked out the kitchen window and saw the four men who were headed for the house. Timing was everything in a con and Miss Ashburn thought she had hers all worked out.

So let the search committee find him on his hands and knees cleaning up dog puke and Leah with the schoolmarm. What could they say?

TWENTY-THREE

Dang that kitten. It seemed like Ashes just waited around for him to open the door so she could dash outside. He'd carried her in more times than he could count in the past few days. Maybe he should just let her go, but he'd hate to see her get taken by the coyotes. He kind of enjoyed having her underfoot. She'd taken to hiding under a bench that sat in the back hallway, and scampered past him when he carried the towels that he'd used to scoop up Dodger's mess outside. Dodger followed him out also and paused on the porch. Ashes went to the door to the root cellar, and sniffed at it.

He heard the knock on the door, heard Leah greet the men. He wasn't in any hurry to go back in, so he took his time. He washed the towels out in the snow and hung them over the clothesline to dry. He knelt down and called to Dodger who shuffled slowly to him with his head down.

Cade buried his hands in Dodger's ruff and rubbed the

sides of the dog's head. "I'm sorry about that, boy. I didn't think it would make *you* sick. Will you forgive me?" *Are you the forgiving sort?* Dodger licked at his face and Cade tolerated it because it was Dodger's way of saying "no harm done." He released him, and Dodger wandered to the back of the yard.

It was time to leave Angel's End. He'd put it off long enough. He'd used Leah's illness as an excuse. It was just that it was so easy and so good to be here with her. He loved teasing her and watching her get all aggravated before she realized that he was just teasing. It was something that he'd never even known he could do. With her it was just as natural as breathing. He also loved watching her, even if it was just to see her sleep as she had so often with her illness. He looked at it as storing up memories to take with him. Something to get him through the cold and lonely nights. *I love her* . . . He'd known it for days, but he refused to admit it until now. Admitting it would just make it that much harder when it was time to go. Admitting it didn't make the hurt go away, nor did it make it any easier to handle.

Cade took a deep breath. So where would he go? He had to keep clear of Fitch, so north, maybe, and west. California, to see the ocean? Oregon, or maybe just north toward Montana.

Brody . . . He hadn't thought of his brother in a long, long while. He used to wonder where he was, what had happened to him, if he was doing okay, or if his life had turned into the hell that his had. Had he survived it? Had the man whose name he did not know, the one who'd taken him, been as bad as the Middletons? Was there any possibility that he could find him? He had no idea where to start looking for his long-lost brother.

The truth was, he had no place to go and no desire to leave, except for the fact that staying here would be a huge mistake. Not only for him, but for Leah and her boy. So he had to go. If Fitch found him here, with her, there would be hell to pay for sure. Fitch lived by the code of an eye for an eye. He'd take Leah from him by any means possible, even it if meant killing her, just to see Cade suffer.

Cade would make sure things were taken care of before he left. First he'd shore up the shed so the chickens would stay safe from the coyotes. Since it was a nice day he went over and opened the door of the shed to let the chickens roam a bit. Ashes found a perch and settled down to watch them as they scattered about in the tromped-down snow.

It was funny how little things like chickens pecking around a yard made for simple pleasures. It gave him a sense of home, even if it was for just a few stolen moments.

"Cade?" Leah stood at the back door. She'd put on a dress and pinned her hair up. Her spots had even faded. She looked absolutely beautiful. "You've got company."

"I know," he said. "Give me a minute."

She walked out on the porch and shaded her eyes against the bright sunlight. "Are you all right?" The smell of roses drifted to him on the mild breeze.

Cade looked around the yard. Snow dripped from the eaves. It would more than likely freeze overnight and make the trip to the outhouse a bit hazardous in the morning. Dodger trotted up to Leah with his tail wagging, over his sudden upset stomach and back to normal. Ashes still watched the chickens and Roscoe strutted around, ready to take on the world.

"I'm fine," he assured her. But deep inside, he knew he wasn't fine at all. If only he could find a way to fix it.

They were all waiting on him. Jim Martin, Jake Reece and Gus Swanson. And Margy Ashburn of course. The search committee minus Bettina, who must be minding the store.

The saloon owner, Ward Phillips, was present also, though he stood in a corner with his arms crossed and the huge dog by his side.

"Sorry to keep you waiting," he explained when he walked into the parlor. "I was just taking care of some things out back."

"No problem," Gus said. "We appreciate how you've pitched in and taken care of Leah for us." Who would have cared for her if not for him? There hadn't been a long line of people stepping up.

He could hear Leah in the kitchen, fixing tea for the visitors. Margy's cookies still sat on the table. If he was going to hell, he might as well go in style. Cade picked up the plate and went around to everyone in the room. "Cookie? Miss Ashburn made them. They are wonderful."

Margy smiled in appreciation from her seat on the sofa. *Wonderful for making you sick.* Gus wisely abstained but Jim, Jake and Ward all took one. "Miss Ashburn?" He held the plate before her.

"Oh no," Margy said with a trill. "I'm watching my figure." Her hand fluttered to her bosom. It was as if she'd taken a class in seduction from Letty. Unfortunately, that was where it ended. He was certain that it was all for show. He noticed Ward grinning in the corner when he returned the plate to the table.

"So to what do I owe the pleasure of this visit?" Cade took up a stance before the fireplace and watched as the men took a bite of their cookie. Jim went into a coughing fit while Jake made a face and looked at his as if Cade had handed him a cow pie. Meanwhile Ward casually dropped his on the floor. Lady nosed at it before returning to her station beside her master.

Smart dog . . . Leah walked in with the tea tray. Jim quickly grabbed a cup and drank. Leah looked at Cade with a question in her eyes. He smiled back.

"You shouldn't be doing this." Jake took the tray and placed it on the table.

"Nonsense," Leah said. "I'm tired of lying about. Jim, I'm ready for Banks to come home too. I miss him."

Jim made a face and cleared his throat. His voice was raspy when he spoke. "Actually Jake and I are taking the boys out to the ranch to spend the night. They've all got cabin fever and well Gretchen is . . ."

Leah laughed, a happy sound that made Cade think of sunshine and summer days. "That's fine, Jim. Please take him out and show him a good time."

"I thought I'd get him on a horse tomorrow," Jake said. "If that's all right with you."

"I know you'll watch out for him Jake. And you're right, he needs to learn how to ride . . ."

I could teach him . . . Cade could almost see it. Banks before him on his horse, and Leah watching and laughing with light and love in her eyes . . .

"Just be sure to bring him home tomorrow night so things can get back to normal."

Normal . . . things would never be normal for him again. Cade hated normal. He wanted different. He wanted more.

"Speaking of things getting back to normal," Gus said. "We're glad to see you've recovered from your injuries, Pastor Key."

"I owe that all to Leah," he said. She was adding sugar to a cup of tea for Margy and glanced up at his words through her dark lashes. The bright sunlight of the day brought out the gold flecks in her eyes. She *was* feeling better.

"You still don't recall what happened?" Jim asked.

Cade shook his head. When had lying become so easy? Was it because he'd been doing it for so long? "I don't remember anything from the time I got on my horse until I woke up here." Actually that wasn't a lie. After he left

Timothy's body smoldering in the fire he didn't recall a thing. The sorry part was he would never forget anything that happened since. Would the ache in his heart go away with time? Would he wake up some morning after he was long gone and realize that the pain was no longer with him? How long would it take?

"It doesn't matter," Leah said. "What does matter is that he's here now, and he's fine. And he's anxious to be about his work." Her gaze on him was steady and was that hope he saw in her eyes? "Aren't you Cade?"

Everyone looked surprised when she called him Cade. Why shouldn't they. They knew him as Timothy Key. Maybe they wouldn't think it strange. The hope flared for an instant before he saw the narrowing of Ward Phillips's eyes and the confusion in Jake's.

"The Lord said to feed my sheep." Timothy had made it sound so easy. But he didn't dare try. He knew his limits. He knew there was a limit to what God would tolerate from him.

"Excellent," Gus replied. "We've planned a celebration for next Sunday so you've got a week to prepare. We'll celebrate Thanksgiving with a town potluck dinner at Dusty's after the service." Gus pumped his hand. "We've got a lot to be thankful for this year."

"Yes we do," Cade said, with his eyes upon Leah.

"Leah, I promise I'll get on those doors first thing next week," Jim said as they all turned to go.

"Doors?" Cade asked.

"I promised Leah I'd make doors for the bedrooms," Jim said. "Things have been a little hectic . . ."

"He was supposed to have them done before you showed up," Leah explained.

She did need doors. It made sense, considering the circumstances. "I'd love to help you," Cade volunteered. It was something else he could do for her. Something else to delay his departure. He had a week at the most. A week to build up some memories. A week to say good-bye.

The idea seemed to please Leah too. She had a big smile on her face as he left. Yes, he wanted to fix the doors for her. But he also wanted an excuse to be in the stable so when it came time to go, he'd be able to get in and get out in a hurry.

The sooner he left, the better; unfortunately, he was leaning toward later.

Ward was intrigued. The preacher certainly wasn't what he expected. Ward almost liked the man. And why did Leah call the preacher Cade? It seemed she liked the new preacher as well.

"Pastor?" Ward stopped him on the porch. Margy stood hesitantly on the step as if she were afraid to step onto the street. Gus and Jim had already left. Jake was lingering of course. He heard the way Leah said the man's name also.

"Goodness me, I'm afraid I might slip and fall in this dreadful snow," Margy said from the step. She hadn't given up on the pastor yet, even though it was quite obvious that there was something going on between him and Leah. You lock a man up with an attractive woman for a week and something was bound to happen eventually, even if one of them was a minister. Just because he wore a collar didn't mean he stopped being a man. Ward scratched his chin. Did he wear a collar? Not all preachers did.

"Dang Margy, you made it up here all right," Ward said with a grin. "And you haven't had any problem going to and from school every day that I've noticed."

"Humph," Margy said. "Some people should do something constructive with their time instead of sticking their noses in everyone else's business; don't you think so Pastor Key?"

"I think it's not up to us to judge," he replied calmly. Yes, the man was smart enough to know when a trap was being set for him. As if of one mind, they both paused and gave Margy time to get ahead of them. She stomped off with her nose in the air. The pastor took the opportunity to kneel down and make friends with Lady.

"She's a beautiful dog," he said. "Smart too. You can tell just by looking into her eyes."

"They say the eyes are the window to your soul," Ward remarked.

"If only it were that easy." The preacher stood and walked out into the street. Strange . . . he wore boots. Boots that were well broken in. What was a preacher from Ohio doing in a pair of boots like that? Boots that had been worn for so long they were like a second skin. They weren't something that you could buy, but they were something you could steal. Especially if the person who wore them was dead.

Ward followed with Lady on his heels. "I bet in your business it would be hard."

"If it were easy then there wouldn't be a need for ministers."

The man was inscrutable. Never a direct answer except when he volunteered to help with the doors. They walked a few more paces in silence. The preacher looked around, studying the buildings and the people who were out and about. A few waved and he raised a hand in greeting but didn't offer to go and talk to any of them. Something about that didn't set right with Ward.

But the dogs like him . . . In his experience, dogs were generally a better judge of character than a man. But a dog could love a man who was meaner than a snake, as long as he didn't abuse the dog.

"Leah called you Cade."

"It's my middle name." He didn't look at him, just kept on walking toward the livery.

"I reckon the two of you have gotten pretty close."

The preacher stopped. They were in front of the stable, directly across from Heaven's Gate and the statue. He studied the statue for a moment then looked at Ward. "I hold her in the highest regard," he said and walked into the stable to join Jim.

Ward believed him, still it didn't keep him from thinking there was something not quite right about the man. There were things that just didn't add up. Things he needed to think on. As he always did his best thinking when he played his piano, Ward returned to his saloon and soon the sweet melodic sounds of his music filled the street.

Later, when he'd stopped for a bit and walked out on the porch he noticed the preacher had his horse saddled. He talked to Jim for a moment, and then swung up in the saddle with an ease and grace that would have put Jake to shame. It was something else Ward added to his ever-increasing curiosity about Pastor Timothy *Cade* Key.

"I'm glad to see you're feeling better," Jake said.

"I am," Leah replied. "Much better." She felt so much better that her face hurt from smiling. It didn't hurt near as bad as the muscle aches from a few days back. It was definitely a pain she could live with.

"I was worried about you," he said.

"I appreciate it Jake, and everything you've done for Banks."

"He's a great kid."

"I know." Her pride was evident and more than likely a sin but she didn't care. She'd shout it from the mountaintops. "He is." She went about the parlor, picking up the odds and ends of the tea when she came across the remnants of a cookie sitting on her mantel. Leah picked it up and looked at it in confusion when she noticed another cookie lying on the floor in the corner where Ward had stood.

Leah looked at Jake who in turn looked at the ceiling as if there was something very interesting up there. She laughed. "He made all of you take one didn't he?"

"Well I should have known something was up when Gus passed." Jake grinned.

Leah laughed harder and Jake joined her. "I gotta say, I'm kind of anxious to hear his first sermon," Jake said.

"Me too." Leah smiled.

"You seem really happy, Leah."

She thought about it a minute, thought about all that had happened in the past few weeks. "You know, I am happy."

Jake leaned on the mantel and ran a hand through his close-cropped hair. "Is it because of him?"

"Nothing's happened Jake." *Nothing beyond a kiss . . .*

"I didn't say it had." He turned to look at her. "But you do have feelings for him, don't you?"

She thought on it again. Thought of the conversations with Cade, thought of how he kept her off balance, how he made her laugh, how he fixed her pump and talked to Dodger and played with Ashes and how he held her and cared for her when she was sick. There was still Banks. He'd yet to really spend any time with her son, but she knew a man who was good to her animals would be good to her son. There was something there. A spark . . . a potential . . . hope.

"Yes, I'm sorry Jake, but yes, I do have feelings for him. And I think maybe he has feelings for me."

"Dang it Leah, it's obvious he has feelings for you. All you got to do is see the way he looks at you, at the way you look at him . . ." Jake sighed. "I've never seen you look at me that way."

"You can't choose who to love, Jake. Sometimes it chooses you."

"Like fate?"

"Yeah . . . like fate."

"Well . . ."

She could tell he was upset. But what could she say? She'd never led him on, she'd always been honest with him and told him she didn't have feelings for him. Jake just didn't want to accept no as an answer. Would he make things harder for Cade now? Would he be an enemy instead of a friend?

"I'll make sure Banks is back before dark tomorrow," Jake finally continued.

"I'm sure he'll love spending time at the ranch."

"He could have it all someday if . . ."

Leah held up her hand. "Don't Jake. Just don't. It's not meant to be. Can't you accept that? Can't we continue on as friends?"

"Give me some time to get used to it."

"I can do that Jake. If you promise me that you won't make things hard on Cade if something does happen between us."

"Cade?"

"It's his middle name. Kincaid. He told me to call him that. He said that's what his mother called him."

"Sounds to me as if *something* already *has* happened."

"We'll see." She followed Jake to the door. "Take care of my son."

"You know I will. No matter what else happens, I'll always take care of him."

"You're a good man, Jake Reece."

Jake shook his head and walked out the door.

TWENTY-FOUR

Cade rode out of Angel's End to clear his head and to get the lay of the land. To escape the townsfolk who saw that he was out and about and wanted to welcome him to town. *Welcome Timothy* . . . He could not help but think, even though he barely knew the man, that Timothy would have loved Angel's End. He would have embraced the town and the people with open arms, just like the statue in the middle of the street.

Jim had showed him the wood he'd set aside for the doors. The pieces sat on sawhorses in his shed. The planks were already glued together and the wood had cured but they still needed to be planed and sanded and hinges attached. Cade had always been good with his hands, especially after Jasper had trained him to be a pickpocket. Later on it served him well when he learned to use a gun. Shooting, he discovered was something else he did well. Finishing the doors was a job he could do in a day's time, if the weather cooperated and *if* he was left alone. He knew better than to think the townsfolk would leave him in peace to work. He also knew that he should be able to handle their curiosity about him until next Saturday. He could pretend he was Timothy awhile longer, if it gave him a chance to stay with Leah.

The trails that peeled off from the main road to the north and west led to the mines. Men left their homes and families and came west to dig in the hard rock or pan in the streams in hope of finding treasure, yet for the majority of them, it was a dead end to riches and the loss of a dream. They wound up working harder and longer and most of them died alone. Still, there were the ones, like the man with the boys who came into the Devil's Table, who brought their families west to live in tents and hovels in search of a better life. These were the sheep Timothy wanted to feed, just as the Cheyenne were for his father. Timothy would have gone to the camps and dug right alongside these men while sharing the word.

Feed my sheep . . . Had Timothy really expected him to carry on his work when he spoke those last words? Or was it a reminder to God that he had a job he was supposed to do. What a shock it must have been to him when he realized he was not going to be able to carry out his calling. That he came so far and got so close and then he was killed, senselessly, all because he shared his fire with a man. Because he thought he was *supposed* to help Cade. Because Cade was *supposed* to stumble upon his camp. Because it was *all* part of God's plan. More like another one of God's jokes.

To the south and east, roads led off to ranches and farms. Signposts hammered to tree trunks pointed in different directions at each path that fed into the main trail. Cade stopped and looked at the one that said Reece. The brand beside it was a *J* laid back, like it had been tipped over. Either a lazy *J* or a rocking *J*. From what he knew of Jacob Reece, he'd say it was the latter.

Leah should marry the man . . . The thought of her with
another man felt like a punch in the gut. Just being away
from her was painful. He'd hoped that the ride would give
him a better perspective on his feelings for her. Big help that.
He couldn't wait to see her again. He turned his horse back
toward town and once more ignored the part of his mind that
said he should have been long gone from this place.

Cade had been gone a good long while. Leah was pleased
he was getting to know the townsfolk and learning about
his new home. He'd be excited about meeting them, more
than likely hungry when he returned, and ready to share his
thoughts with her, or so she hoped.

Leah had just about finished cleaning the kitchen and
started fixing dinner. Ashes, still excited from her adventure
outdoors, followed her around, swatting at her skirts every
chance she got while Dodger settled down onto his blanket
in the corner by the stove.

Since she wanted the meal to be hot when Cade got back
and she had no idea when that would be, Leah set the boiled
potatoes on the corner of the stove and put the ham steaks
in the iron skillet. They were well seasoned and she would
wait until Cade's arrival to fry them. Then she went to her
room. Ashes dashed ahead of her and slid beneath her bed.

"What's got you so rowdy tonight?" she asked the kitten.
The chiming of her grandmother's clock reminded Leah of
something the older woman always said. Animals sensed
when the weather was going to change. The more active
they were, the worse the weather coming in.

"We must be in for another storm," Leah said as Ashes
clawed her way onto the bed, then with tail twitching leapt
off the edge and scampered beneath the curtain that covered
the entrance to her room. Leah laughed at her antics and
moved to the bureau.

She turned the lamp up and unbuttoned her dress. She pulled the two sides open and looked carefully at her neck and the skin above her breasts. The rash seemed to be gone. Still her skin felt dry. She slipped out of her dress and unlaced her camisole. Nonnie's jar of salve sat on the bureau and she spread it over her skin to soothe the dryness. Since she was at it, she kicked off her shoes and socks and placed a leg on the side of the bed to better spread the salve. The scent of roses filled the room.

Leah heard the back door open, heard the snick of Dodger's nails on the wood floor as he went to welcome Cade, and then Cade's warm greeting to Dodger. She imagined him kneeling in the hall and rubbing Dodger's head as he always did. She heard the creak of the floor as he stood and knew he hung his coat on the hook. Another creak meant a step and then Ashes flew into her room. The curtain billowed out with her rush and the kitten turned around and attacked the monster that chased her. She sank her claws into the fabric and swung outward with the impetus of her charge. Leah laughed at the kitten. There was the sound of tearing, as the sheet used to cover the door was old and worn, and it gave way with the slight added weight of the kitten.

Both fell to the floor and Ashes panicked. Cade knelt and untangled her from the trap and stood with the kitten in his hands. Leah stood watching, wearing nothing but her camisole and petticoat. She didn't even realize it, she'd been so preoccupied with Ashes's antics until Cade looked at her and she felt the heat of his gaze on her skin. His eyes roamed over her like a caress and stripped away the few garments she wore. She could have picked up the quilt from the foot of the bed to cover herself, could have told him to leave, she could have screamed to the heavens, if she wanted.

All she could do was look at him, at his dark sad eyes, at his warrior angel's face and the pain that moved over it.

"You'd tempt a saint, Leah," he said, finally, after interminable seconds passed, each one counted off by the ticking of the clock.

"Are you a saint?" It was a risk to ask him. A risk she achingly wanted to take. She refused to think of him as a minister in this moment. She only saw him as a man, a man who she wanted very, very much. She knew it could backfire. Leah knew he could walk away and condemn her for her actions. She felt reckless for asking, and brave for standing there barely clothed, and she prayed desperately that of all the things that might come next, shame would not be one of them.

There was no going back. He could have turned away, he could have apologized, he could have made a joke of it and teased her if he wanted. He put Ashes gently down on the floor and pushed her toward the kitchen before he took the five steps that brought him to her.

No going back . . . She wanted to tempt him and knew he'd be tempted. But more, she wanted him, no, she needed him, to need her, to put everything aside for her, even his beliefs. Would he be tempted by her without the sanctity of marriage? He stood before her and looked into her eyes, searching for something. She felt her body lean, of its own accord toward him, yet he did not touch her and she was afraid, so afraid that if she touched him he'd turn away and call her a harlot. Leah saw the rise and fall of his chest as he inhaled the heady scent of roses that surrounded them.

"You don't want this Leah. You shouldn't want me."

"Don't I? Why shouldn't I? We're two lonely people, Cade." If he walked away now, she would die of shame, of embarrassment, of need. "God made us, made man and woman, for each other, to love each other. Why can't we love each other?"

His face filled with pain. "I'm not who you think I am."

"Aren't you?" Leah grabbed his forearms and he pulled

his hands into fists beneath hers. "You're a man. With wants and needs and desires. It doesn't matter what you do for a living. God gave us life. God gave us this"—she squeezed his forearms—"to enjoy. There's no reason for either one of us to be lonely."

Cade looked down at where her hands wrapped around his arms. He felt the pressure of her grip as his muscles and tendons expanded as he clenched his hands into fists. It was the only way he could keep himself from touching her. He had to warn her. He had to stop her before she made the biggest mistake of her life.

"Be careful what you say Leah," he warned her. "Be careful what you ask for."

"Why?" He thought she'd be worried, instead she was determined. She was stubborn. It was one of the things that made him love her. One of many. "Because it's a sin to make love without the benefit of marriage? How can something so good, something so wonderful be a sin?"

Cade shook his head. She didn't know what she was saying. If she knew who and what he really was . . . *If you love her you'll walk away . . .*

"I want you Cade. I want all of you." She closed the distance between them and pressed her body against his. She wrapped her arms around his waist and pressed her cheek to his heart. The lamp shining behind her illuminated her hair and cast a golden hue around her. *Like an angel . . .* Her body was all smooth soft curves and it beckoned to him, showing him his weaknesses. He knew the devil was laughing at him, knew he was making a list, to check off his sins when he condemned him to hell.

If he was going to be condemned, then he'd have no regrets. And neither would she. When it came out, when all was said and done, and he was gone, and they talked about what a bastard he was, she would not be ashamed. She would know that he loved her.

God . . . he loved her.

Cade buried his hands in her hair, and scattered the pins that held it in place until the strands fell down around his arms and her shoulders. He bent and took her mouth beneath his. She opened to his kiss and he plundered her with his tongue, possessing her. He would not let go now. It would kill him to let go. He held her face between his hands and kissed her until he could not breathe, yet he could not stop. Leah sobbed deep in her throat, wrapped her arms around his neck and pressed closer, if that was possible.

He couldn't stop kissing her. His blood pounded in his ears as his mouth slashed across her face and down her neck. He buried his face, right where her shoulder joined her neck and inhaled the scent.

Roses. Forever he would remember her because of the roses. She sobbed again. Her hands fumbled with his shirt, searching for the buttons. She tore it open, in frustration, finally. The buttons flew to the floor and she moved her hands across his chest, spreading the cloth wide. Her mouth followed the trail of her hands, spreading soft kisses across his skin.

He would burn in hell for eternity and he didn't care. Cade picked her up and carried her the two steps to the bed. He gently placed her on it and put one knee beside her. She pulled him down and he felt himself falling . . . falling . . . falling into Leah.

Leah . . . This was where his wandering had brought him. To this place, this time, this night, this woman. He knew he couldn't keep her. He couldn't stay. But he could pretend for one night that their relationship could be true. He would treasure it. He would remember it, even when he was in hell, burning for all his sins.

It was just a matter of pulling a ribbon to loosen her camisole to spread it wide so he could look upon her. God . . . she was so beautiful. And he was not . . . he shouldn't touch her, but he did. He felt the calluses on his fingers as he cupped her smooth breast.

She gasped as his thumb grazed her peak. Cade looked into her lovely gold-flecked eyes and saw the mix of emotions. Was he that easy to read where she was concerned? Was it obvious to everyone in town that he was in love with her? With just the one look, he knew what she wanted, what she needed, what he must say, to let her know that this wasn't wrong, even though he was so very wrong for her.

He needed it too. He needed the words. He needed to say them to absolve the small bit of his conscience that tried to reason with him. "No matter what happens," he said. "Don't ever forget this night and this one truth."

Confusion dashed across her lovely face. Her green eyes, heavy with passion, studied his face as he stopped his caress for one short moment.

"I love you, Leah."

"Really?" She laughed and he knew that was what heaven would sound like, even though he'd never see it. "You love me?"

"I do. It's the one truth." He had to make her understand. "It's the only thing that is important."

"I love you too," she said with a sigh. He lowered his head to kiss her again, and then he let his mouth trail down her jaw and to the place where her neck met her shoulder. Leah gasped as he kissed her there and twisted her fingers into his hair.

He wanted to take his time. He wanted to enjoy every second of this exquisite moment so he could play it over and over again in his mind. He slid the strap of her camisole down her arm, slowly, while his mouth trailed over her shoulder, and then he did the same on the other side.

Leah's palms pressed into his head. Her body trembled as he placed his hand on her breastbone and spread it wide with his forearm between the soft mounds of her breasts.

His skin was so very dark against the paleness of hers. He felt her heart pounding beneath his palm and her dark eyelashes fluttered against her cheeks as his eyes drank his fill of her soft beauty, like an angel had come down from heaven just for him.

He'd never done this before. Never experienced this quiet worship of another's body, never given of himself so that all he wanted was her pleasure. He carefully watched the emotions run across her face as he cupped her breast and found joy in her small gasp of pleasure, before he lowered his head to caress her with his mouth.

She moaned and arched her back as Cade placed his hand over her other breast before trailing his fingers down the smooth rose-scented skin of her stomach to the waist of her petticoat. He trailed a finger beneath the fabric and the muscles in her stomach quivered in anticipation.

Leah moved her hands from his hair to his shoulders. She pushed his shirt down and Cade flung first one arm and then the other out so she could remove it. Just those seconds it took, when he couldn't touch her, was pure torture. When the shirt was gone she ran the tips of her nails down his spine and heat spread across his skin from her touch. Her hands stroked across his lower back and then came around to the front.

Cade groaned and kissed her again as her fingers fumbled with the buttons of his fly. She was driving him insane with her urgency. Heat roared through his veins, like the flames of hell. He wanted nothing more than to bury himself deep inside her, yet he wanted to make it last, he wanted to savor each moment and watch the wave of emotion wash over her face.

Leah finally wrestled his fly open and she pushed his pants wide and down over his hips. They caught on the curve of his buttocks and her arms weren't long enough to push them any farther.

Her hands came back around to his waist and the trail of her fingers nearly unmanned him. Cade took a deep breath and dropped his forehead against hers. He breathed in the scent of her. Roses. Crisp pine-scented air. A mix of seasonings from the kitchen. Fresh bread. Leah.

"What?" Leah asked beneath him as he fought for control.

"I want to make this last," he said huskily. "For as long as we can."

"I can't wait," she said. "I want you now"—she touched him—"inside me." She wrapped her hand around his shaft. "Please fill me Cade. Fill up the empty place that's inside of me."

He was afraid to move, afraid if he did, he'd lose control. His pants were in the way as was her petticoat. He had to move to get both out of the way, yet not touching her was agonizing. He raised his hips and Leah wiggled beneath him, sliding down so she could tug at his pants. He finally was able to toe them off and then she raised her hips and untied her petticoat and he jerked it off in one fluid motion and pitched it at the foot of the bed.

Cade slowly and gently stretched out on top of her. Her breasts cushioned his chest and she spread her legs and wrapped them around his hips as he settled his body against her. All he had to do now was slide inside her. But he couldn't, not yet. Not until he was sure it was good for Leah. He touched her, in the place where he knew it would give her pleasure. She gasped and her eyes gazed up at him in wonder.

"I've got you," Cade said tenderly. "Just let go. I'll take care of you."

Leah closed her eyes and she moaned deep in her throat as his fingers moved inside her. She shuddered, from the top of her head to the tips of her toes and then she gasped again. Her head moved back and forth on her pillow and then she grabbed Cade's shoulders as she arched up off the bed. Cade watched her face as she shook with her pleasure.

"Please," she said when she could talk again. "I need you." She sobbed in anticipation as he slowly pushed into her. She was tight but she was wet and he felt her warmth surrounding him as he settled into her body. She tilted her hips back to accept him and then she sighed.

Cade swept her hair back from her face. He cupped her jaw within his hands. She looked up at him with her lovely green eyes and a smile played at the corners of her mouth. He dipped his head to kiss her again, and then he moved, slowly, because he wanted the memory of this moment to last for the rest of his life. Still he couldn't help but pray before he lost all thought beyond his purpose, that if there was any way possible: *Lord, can I stay, can I have this with her for the rest of my life?*

TWENTY-FIVE

Early morning light streamed through the window and washed across Leah's face. Cade had spent the morning hours watching Leah sleep. He lay beside her, propped on his side and soaked in every detail of her lovely face. He was conscious of every soft breath that she took. Even with her eyes closed in an exhausted sleep, and the kitten curled up against her side, she was beautiful. Cade ran a finger between Ashes's ears and she let out a soft mew.

Had he taken too much from Leah? Nothing more than what she willingly gave. And willing she was. He'd never experienced anything like it, because he'd never experienced love; after Letty's sadistic urges, all he'd ever sought was release. Now that he had experienced love, would he be able to walk away?

I have to . . . He'd made a big mistake in his escape. He'd forgotten about his boots. Leah noticed them and he was fairly certain Ward Phillips had also. It didn't make sense that a preacher would wear boots such as his. Only cowboys wore them, men who spent hours in the saddle. Timothy Key would have no use for them. Cade closed his eyes for a moment to recall the preacher's shoes. They were stout and sensible. If people around here noticed his boots then Fitch would notice the lack of them on Timothy's burned body. He'd know it was a ruse and he'd keep on the trail. Fitch was a bastard that way. If he wanted you dead he'd move heaven and hell to make sure it happened.

And Cade just so happened to be sitting in that exact place, between heaven and hell. Heaven was the woman sleeping peacefully beside him. Hell was what waited for him. And he could only put it off for so long. The devil was good about taking his due, and Cade had sold his soul for these few precious moments with Leah. Moments that were slipping away. Would it be so bad if he woke her?

Dodger did it for him. He stood and shook off his dreams with a noisy ear flapping that woke both Leah and Ashes.

Her lovely green eyes widened when she realized she was not alone and then she flushed, redder than she'd ever been with her rash.

Cade grinned. "Good morning." He kissed her.

"Cade . . ." she began.

"Shhh . . ." He touched his finger to her lips. "Last night was the best night of my life. And I hope you feel the same way."

She nodded beneath his finger. The gold flecks danced in her eyes with the sunlight.

"I'm going to let Dodger take care of business and I'll be right back. Does that suit you?"

"That suits me just fine," she said.

"Good." Cade dropped a kiss on her forehead, pulled on his pants and went to let Dodger out.

Leah sank back into the bed and pulled the covers up to

her chin. She didn't know what to say, or do. She'd been a complete wanton last night. She'd never acted like that. Never! The only man she'd ever been with was Nate and considering that she'd known him since she was thirteen and married him at seventeen it had all been expected. But this. She'd seduced the minister. She was as bad as Pris, throwing herself at the man. So why did something that was so wrong, feel so wonderfully right this morning?

He said it was the best night of his life . . . Leah knew he was not a virgin, although she thought there might be a chance . . . No, a man who loved the way he loved her last night had experience. Now where would an unmarried preacher get experience? Perhaps he'd been called late to the ministry?

No, she remembered Jim talking about Pastor Key's letters. He'd said he'd always wanted to be a minister, and that he'd never married, that he'd dedicated his life and his service to God at an early age.

Another thing about Cade that didn't quite add up. She would not complain. The man in person was much better than the man she had envisioned when it was announced he was coming to town. She'd reserve judgment for his calling when she saw him in the pulpit. If God didn't strike her dead first for her sins.

Cade returned, bringing with him the scent of outdoors and a broad smile. He quickly dropped his pants and slid under the quilts where he pulled her to him. Her nude body was pressed to his wide, smooth chest and his feet felt like blocks of ice between her calves. Yet desire pooled once more in her body as it had repeatedly the night before.

"Ahh! You're freezing!" She squealed at him, just for the pure joy of it. Because he loved teasing her and she loved being teased by him.

"Yes, I am." He grinned devilishly. "And I know exactly what I need to warm me up."

*   *   *

Later that day, after they'd slept some more, and laughed, and recovered what they could from last night's forgotten dinner Cade took Leah's hand and led her into the parlor.

"What is this all about?" she asked. She'd just finished up the dishes, with Cade's help, a nice surprise, as Nate, while helpful and handy, had never lent a hand in the kitchen. He had even taken the time to rub some salve into her hands.

Cade lifted her hands to his nose and inhaled deeply before he turned the rocking chair around to face the fire. She'd always been self-conscious about her hands, as the skin was usually dry and chapped from work. However her days away from the diner, along with Nonnie's restorative concoction, had done wonders for her skin. And she loved the look on Cade's face when he closed his eyes and took in the scent of roses. He always looked so grateful, which was strange, yet thrilling at the same time.

Clouds had gathered in the sky as they'd slept into early afternoon. Leah spared a thought for Banks, that Jake would get him back before the weather got bad again, and then she dismissed it. Banks was safe with Jake. He'd never put him at risk.

"It's Sunday," Cade said in answer to her question. "It's supposed to be a day of rest." He pulled her into his lap and with one foot on the hearth, set the chair to rocking.

Dodger lay beside them on the rug and Ashes clawed her way up Cade's leg and settled into the small space between Leah's hip and Cade's stomach. "Is this your way of getting out of finishing those doors?"

He grinned. "We don't really need them now. I have seen everything, haven't I?" He trailed a long finger down her neck and dipped it into the collar of her dress.

"That and more," Leah said. She hesitated a second,

thoughtful, and then continued. "You know we can't carry on like this when Banks is here."

Cade stopped rocking. His dark eyes were serious when he looked at her.

"I'd never do anything to hurt your son."

And she believed him, this man, this very dear and wonderful man who had stumbled into her life. Was he an answer to a prayer that she'd never given voice to? Was he sent from God to fill her life with happiness? All she could do was hope so.

My Godsend . . .

"I believe you." She laid her cheek against his because she was too overwhelmed with everything that had happened in the past day to do anything else. There were questions she needed to ask, answers that needed to be shared, but that would come later. For today she just wanted to *be,* and be with Cade. She felt the muscles in his thigh flex as he once more set the chair to rocking in time with the ticktock of the clock. They stayed that way, watching the fire, until the voices outside let them know Banks was home.

Finally, after a week away, her son was home once more.

TWENTY-SIX

Cade knew he had to be careful when Banks was around. He couldn't touch Leah as he wanted to, couldn't hold her, couldn't sweep her up in his arms and carry her to the bed and make passionate love to her as he wanted to. He wouldn't be able to sleep with her either. Cade thought he'd miss that the most. He'd never slept beside a woman for an entire night. She exhibited such a feeling of trust when she pressed her body against his. In an odd way, she was at her most vulnerable asleep, more so than when they made love. He wanted nothing more than to protect her from the things that could scare her in the night.

Things like him.

Would he ever stop wanting her? No, but would she hate him for his lies?

Cade carried the wood into the kitchen and dropped it in the box. Banks sat at the table eating a piece of buttered bread while Leah puttered at the counter.

"Mr. Jake taught me how to ride," he said excitedly after he took a long draught of milk. "He said the most important thing was not to yank on the reins, and the horse could figure out where I want him to go if I use my knees. He said the quickest way to a horse's heart is with soft hands. Doesn't that sound funny, Momma?"

"Yes, it does," Leah agreed.

Cade sat down at the table. "Mr. Jake is right," he said. Leah put a slice of bread in front of him and went to pour him some milk from the crock. "A good horse will love you and respect you if you treat him right. It's like having a partner to help you through, when you find a good horse." A pang of pain filled him at the loss of his horse. He'd feel much better about setting out if he still had that horse. Leah gave him a quizzical look as she placed the mug of milk down before him.

"Can I have a horse, Momma?" Banks asked.

"A horse is a lot of responsibility," Leah said. "And they need to be fed. We can't afford one right now."

"But Momma . . ." Banks began.

"Do you want to hear how I learned to ride?" Cade asked, heading off a potentially frustrating conversation between Leah and her son. "It was in an Indian camp."

"Really? You lived with the Indians?"

Leah sat down at the table. Ashes mewed and she picked her up and put her in her lap. Dodger yawned from his corner and settled down for a nap.

"Yes, I lived with the Cheyenne for a while when I was a boy. They treated my brother and me like we were one of them. My mom said it was hard to tell the difference because we spent so much time in the sun our skin was nearly as dark as theirs."

Banks stared at him with his eyes wide and his mouth hanging open.

"We learned how to ride bareback and all we used was our knees to guide the horses. We wrapped our fingers in their manes so we wouldn't fall off." Memories washed over him. "Brody was the best. He rode like he was one with the horse. He had this knack for them, he could gentle the wildest mustang with just a touch."

"Wow!" Banks said. Leah rubbed Ashes and watched him with a gentle smile on her face.

"I remember this one day when we were riding on this plateau. The men of the village had just come back from a big hunt and all the boys went out to meet them. There was a cliff and we were racing like the wind, tearing across the grass like there was no tomorrow. I was certain Brody was going to ride right over the edge of the cliff." Cade shook his head at the memory and smiled. "But he stopped, just in time and then just sat there, on the back of his mustang with his arms spread wide, like he was flying." A wave of emotion washed over him and to his surprise he blinked back a tear. "His face was full of such joy . . ."

"That's a good memory to have," Leah said gently.

"It is," Cade admitted. "It was a good life, before . . ." He stopped. Banks didn't need to hear about the horrors of Sand Creek. But before that he'd had a happy family, full of joy. How long had it been since he'd experienced pure joy? Even the happiness he felt with Leah was tainted because he knew it would not last. That he had to leave.

"How about you help me bring some wood in for the night," he said to Banks. Banks drained his mug and followed him down the hall with Ashes bouncing along behind him. Ashes darted outside as soon as Cade opened the door, despite his best efforts to keep her inside.

"Mind your kitten when we're done," he said.

"Yes, sir." Had he ever been that polite? Yes, when he was in the orphanage, but after that it all just went away.

"Hold out your arms and I'll stack it," Cade instructed Banks. He picked three of the smaller pieces of wood from the pile. "How's that?"

"I can do more." Banks shifted the weight in his arms. "Are you sure?"

"Yes, sir." Cade added two more pieces.

"One more."

"You gotta be able to walk too."

"I can walk."

Cade grinned. "You're pretty strong." He opened the door for him and Banks went in, moving slowly with his load. Cade grabbed as many logs as he could carry and followed. He caught up with Banks in the parlor, and together they filled the basket beside the fire with wood.

"I think that's enough," Cade said. He knelt on the hearth and began to build up the fire. Banks crouched next to him and carefully watched his every move. Cade put a larger piece on the back to relay the heat into the room and the smaller pieces in front. When he was satisfied with the size of the fire, Cade leaned back and dusted off his hands.

"Did you know my daddy?" Banks asked. The boy kept his eyes on the flames. His father's eyes must have been blue. There was a lot of Leah about the boy, the shape of the eyes and the way he talked, but his square face, and his mouth especially, had to be his father's. Nate.

"No. I wasn't here then."

"He was the sheriff and a bad man shot him. Momma said I can't have a gun because guns are bad but Jake says I should learn how to shoot one because we need to be able to protect ourselves and Momma doesn't know how."

"Did Jake teach you to shoot today?"

Banks looked toward the kitchen where Leah was making bread dough. "It's supposed to be a secret," he whispered loudly.

Cade nodded in agreement. This was between Leah and Jake. He had no right to get between them.

"Do you know how to shoot?" Banks asked him.

"Yes I do."

"Have you ever shot anyone?"

More men than he could count . . . Banks didn't need to know that. Cade turned around and sat on the hearth and Banks sat down next to him. "Let me tell you something about guns," Cade said. Banks looked up at him with his blue eyes wide, the realization that this was to be a serious conversation evident on his face.

"Guns aren't bad. Sometimes it's the people who have them that are bad," Cade continued. "Jake and Ward both wear guns, but they aren't bad men. I'm guessing that the man who shot your dad was a very bad man. Sometimes you have to shoot a gun to protect yourself, and the ones you love, from the bad men. I think your mom doesn't want you to have a gun because if you have one, then the bad men think they can shoot at you since you can shoot back. She doesn't want to lose you."

He failed to mention that he was one of those bad men. That it could have easily been him, given the circumstances of his life before coming to town, that shot his father.

"Because my poppa was killed?"

"Even without that. She loves you very much."

"Do you love my mom?"

Leah stood in the doorway, drying her hands on a towel. Cade looked at her and his heart swelled so much that he thought it would burst from his chest. "I love her very much."

And just like that, Banks, satisfied with the discussion, moved on to the next best thing. "Will you play soldiers with me?"

Cade grinned up at Leah. "Sure!" He stretched out on the rug as Banks pulled out his box of soldiers.

Leah went to let Ashes in after hearing her pitiful mews at the door, then watched from the hallway as Cade and Banks lined up the soldiers on the rug. They were both very serious about it until Cade picked up the one with the gun bent to the side.

"I'd hate to be standing next to this guy," he said. "Every time he shoots he's going to hit whoever is next to him."

Banks dissolved into giggles at the comment. Meanwhile, Ashes stalked into the parlor and took up a place beneath the table. She watched for a moment as they lined up for the great battle to come, then with a twitch of her tail, jumped right into the middle of the neat lines. The soldiers toppled in every direction and she turned about in quick jerky motions, in an attempt to keep track of her prey.

Cade made a whistling noise, much like she imagined a cannonball would sound and struck the rug with his hands. Banks raised up and jumped on his back. Cade fell to the rug as if he'd been struck hard. A wrestling match ensued, one full of giggles and squeals. Her heart swelled at the sight as she watched them play in the firelight.

Any fears she had about Cade and her son were laid to rest.

If only she knew his intentions toward her. It seemed strange that the day had passed and he'd not said anything. Maybe it was because it was all new and unexpected. She chose not to worry about it. Instead she joined her two men in the parlor.

TWENTY-SEVEN

"You look like you're feeling better." Ward looked up at Leah as she poured his coffee. Her skin held a rosy glow that had nothing to do with the measles. There was something about her, something different. Something from the inside. He glanced through the window at her house across the street. No sign of the preacher. Did he have anything to do with the spring in Leah's step?

"I am feeling better," she replied. "I take it you're having the usual times two?"

Ward looked down at Lady. "Yes I am," he replied. It was something how having a dog around had so quickly become a habit. He'd never even realized he wanted a dog until she showed up. Now the idea of not having her around was kind of painful.

Leah went off to put his order in. Ward sipped his coffee and looked around the Devil's Table. Everyone was happy, asking after Leah, relieved that she had survived the measles and that the epidemic had passed them by. She answered each person cheerfully, as bright as a summer day.

They were also asking about the preacher. For someone who was supposed to be among them, he sure did keep a low profile. If he didn't know any better, Ward would think he was downright shy. Not a good trait for a preacher. Whatever it was, the man sure did know how to make himself scarce.

Of course he could just be saving himself for the big welcome party coming this weekend. "Nope," Ward said to himself as Leah placed his breakfast on the table. "That is not it . . ." The man had no trouble talking. And he was aces at avoiding. There was something about him . . .

"Something wrong Ward?" Leah asked.

"Not a thing." Ward put Lady's plate before her. She watched him until he nodded his head, giving permission, then she ate.

"Where's the preacher at this morning? Isn't he supposed to eat breakfast here?"

Leah became suddenly busy with a spot on the table that was close to the window. She turned her face away as she worked on it with a vengeance. "He ate at home and then went to work on the doors."

"Sounds like he's making himself right at home," Ward said.

"He's a great help," Leah said, then dashed away to give Zeke a refill on his coffee.

Ward grinned at her vanishing form. So the preacher was a great help. What exactly had he helped himself to? Maybe he'd go see if he could lend him a hand after breakfast.

It didn't take Cade long to work up a sweat. The weather that threatened the day before moved on quickly, leaving behind a few morning snow flurries and a pale and icy sky.

Jim had greeted him before taking off on horseback. He'd turned all the stabled animals out into the corral and they browsed at the sweet grass that grew along the stream banks, pawing their way through the packed snow to get to the tastier blades beneath.

Jim had built the fire up before he left and asked Cade to keep it hot so he could work when he returned. Cade hung his heavy coat on a nail and rolled up his shirtsleeves. Dodger sat in the middle of the shed, curious about the new routine. Cade really could use his short coat, the one he'd left on Timothy's body. He wouldn't desecrate Timothy's frock coat by wearing it out. It brought back too many memories, of both Timothy and his father.

Had Fitch found the bodies yet? Had his ruse worked? When Davis didn't return, Fitch would know something had happened. Davis was too chicken to cross Fitch and too greedy to walk away from a chance at the reward.

The work he did was mindless. The wood was pine, so it was soft and easy to work, with long steady strokes. The job was mindless, nothing more than physical labor. Thinking about Fitch was worrisome and troubling. Thinking about Leah was better.

He'd longed for her company last night. She, in her bed with Banks, and he across the hall in the boy's bed. She came to him, after Banks fell asleep. They'd made love quickly and silently and she'd been nervous the entire time that Banks would wake up and catch them and then she'd have to explain things.

She should marry Jake Reece. Maybe she would after he left. Maybe she'd realize that it was for the best. Above everything, he wanted her to be happy. There was no doubt in his mind that she would hate him when she found out the truth. He didn't want to be around to see it on her face. He was the worst kind of bastard for doing this to her. But he couldn't help it . . . he loved her.

Coward . . . always taking the easy way. Always blaming others for your troubles.

Always alone because of it.

"Good morning."

"Ward." Cade stopped his work as the saloon owner sauntered up to the shed with the dog by his side. Dodger quickly ran to meet his friend and with a woof the two of them took off at a trot, both nipping at the other as they went.

Ward stood by the corral, with his hands in his pockets, and looked at the horses. The chestnut had to be his. It pricked its ears forward and came directly to where Ward stood. He fished a treat from his pocket, a piece of dried apple from what Cade could see and the horse delicately lipped it from his palm.

The donkey, which Jim had christened Libby, trotted up while Ward rubbed the neck of his horse. She stood with her legs splayed and started her hee-haw, deep in her chest, moving her lips back and forth until it finally came bellowing out. Such a big noise for a tiny critter. Cade saw the cross on her spine and withers, a blessing from Christ for carrying him those many years ago, or so his mother had told him.

"Do you think she's trying to tell me something?" Ward turned around to face Cade.

"Could be." Cade was more interested in what Ward was after. "Could be she just misses her family."

Ward nodded in agreement.

"So what brings you around?" Cade went back to his planing, and then ran a hand down the length of the door. He didn't want to waste time with Ward. His time was precious. He didn't want to waste one minute that could be spent with Leah.

"We were worried about you."

"We?"

Ward walked beneath the shed. He poked at the fire

before turning back to Cade. "Half the town was expecting you to show up at the diner for breakfast this morning."

"Hmm," Cade said. "The Devil's Table. I'd think the townsfolk would want me to stay away from a place like that."

Ward pushed his hat back. "Yeah, Dusty does have a wicked sense of humor."

"Kind of like yours, I'd say." Cade put the planer down, dusted off his hands and picked up the sander.

"Well Heaven's Gate did make sense, with the angel and all."

"I can see how," Cade admitted. "I reckon I could use that as an excuse, to drop in and visit. It would make a lot more sense than a preacher going to eat at the Devil's Table."

"You are welcome to come in anytime. No questions asked."

"I might just take you up on that sometime." Cade ran the sander along the side of the door. "So how 'bout you help me carry this door down to the house so I can check the fit."

Cade waited for the excuses. He'd only mentioned wanting his help to get rid of him. The man was way too curious and much too intuitive to have poking around. Jasper taught him the signs and told him to keep his distance from marks such as Ward.

"Why not," Ward said. "After all, we wouldn't want to give anyone an excuse to gossip about the preacher and the widow, now would we?" He picked up an end of the door.

"Let me grab my coat." Cade found the hinges and hardware and dropped them in his pocket.

Dang it . . . Who would have thought Ward would decide to be helpful. Cade picked up his end of the door and they headed for the house. The door wasn't heavy, just awkward. Ward led the way, so he went between the stable and the shed and to the street, another place Cade had been trying to avoid.

"So why *have* you been hiding out?" Ward's voice was casual, as if he talked about nothing more than the weather.

Thank God for Dodger. Cade laughed at the sight. "How do you feel about puppies?"

"What?" Ward looked to where Cade's gaze led. Dodger was mounted on Lady, right in the middle of the street beneath the wings of the angel. His tongue lolled out to the side and he was pretty much having the time of his life.

Someone must have alerted Leah to the situation. She came out from the diner and yelled. "Dodger!"

A woman in a satin robe and an older man came out of the saloon and burst into laughter. A squeal sounded from down the street. Bettina.

Cade looked at Ward who grinned and shook his head. The two of them laughed. The sight of Leah running down the street with her skirts gathered in her arms made them laugh harder. They set the door down and went toward the statue and the dogs, still laughing.

"It's not like we can stop them." Cade grinned.

"Leah looks like she's planning on it," Ward said.

"DODGER!" Leah called out as she reached the dogs. "Shoo!" She clapped her hands. Dodger's eyes rolled back into his head. "Stop!"

"Looks like he's got a purpose, Leah," Ward said.

"Don't touch him." Cade put a hand on her arm and pulled her back. "He's in the throes of passion." He was amazed to see her blush and turn her head away. He checked to see if Ward was watching, but he had his eyes on the dogs. He moved his hand down to take hers. A foolish move, but he could claim he was protecting her if someone asked. Her hand felt right in his. As if a piece of him had been missing all this time. The thing he'd needed without knowing it. A someone to hold on to.

"I bet the pups will be pretty," he said, looking down into

her green eyes. The sunlight brightened them, bringing out the gold beneath her lovely dark lashes.

She rolled her eyes at him. "Cade." Leah laughed just as the pair from the saloon walked up. The woman was pretty with hair the color of strawberries, blue eyes and freckles across her nose. The soiled dove of Angel's End. In another time and another place he would have appreciated her company. But not after Leah. He'd be spoiled for women from now on. Maybe that was a good thing.

"Looks like you healed up pretty good," she said. She sized him up with an audacious grin, cheeky even in the presence of a minister. "But I thought your name was Timothy."

Before Cade or Leah could answer Bettina charged up with her broom. "This is indecent! And in front of the preacher." She jabbed at the dogs. Dodger snapped at her. "Leah Findley *do* something about your dog!"

"They're just doing what comes naturally, Mrs. Swanson," Cade said.

"Oh I'm not sure she would know about that," Ward said.

"Well I never!" Bettina stomped off. Cade put his fist to his mouth to hold back the laughter and Leah was suddenly interested in the schoolhouse as she turned away. Cade squeezed her hand.

"I reckon that is the problem," Ward drawled. He raised an eyebrow at the sight of their joined hands and Leah let go. There would be talk when he left. But there wasn't anything he could do about it now.

"It looks like love is in the air," Ward said.

Dodger dismounted and turned to Leah and Cade with his tail wagging. Cade resisted the urge to say "good dog."

"Oh my goodness," Leah said. "I will never hear the end of this." She would, come next Sunday when it was found that he was gone. There would be something else to talk about besides her dog having his way in the middle of the street. "Come on Dodger," she said and took off, with the dog trotting at her heels.

Lady sat down next to Ward as if nothing had happened at all. "I reckon I need to start thinking about a nursery," Ward said.

Cade laughed again. If the circumstances were different, he had a feeling that he and the saloon owner could be friends. If only the circumstances were different.

TWENTY-EIGHT

"How did you get these scars on your back?" Leah stroked her hand over his back. Cade lay half on top of her, with his head tucked up beneath her chin and over her breast. She'd twisted the ends of his hair between her fingers before moving down to his back.

He held on to her as if he was reluctant to let go. The sun was high in the sky and Banks would be home soon. She should be taking care of her chores, taking care of her son, yet she did not want to move, she wanted to stay where she was, forever. When had she turned into such a wanton? What was it about the way he looked at her, with his eyes full of such sweet desperation that made her melt and fall into his arms?

Was it how he made love to her, as if he would die if he couldn't touch her, as if he needed her as much as he needed air, water and food that made her feel this way? Nate had never needed her like that. Yes, Nate had loved her and she loved him, but this burning passion she shared with Cade was something new, something exciting, something extremely dangerous.

The week had been a blur. Ever since she walked into the house on Monday, after the lunch shift, after getting teased unendingly about Dodger's romance, to find Cade finishing up hanging the door to her room. He had his shirt off, and she watched in wondrous fascination as the muscles moved across his back and shoulders. He'd tested the door, then satisfied with his work, took her into his arms and carried her to the bed.

They'd made love every day since. It didn't matter that she needed to start supper. That she needed to catch up on a week's worth of laundry, or that Banks would be home from school within the hour. All that mattered was that he needed her.

Yet he said nothing about a future, nothing about anything beyond the very moment they were in, and she didn't push him. Still there were things she wanted to know because she wanted to understand him better. So she asked about the scars.

"It happened a long time ago," he said.

"Did somebody beat you?"

He moved then, shifted to his side. Kissed her and then sat up on the edge of the bed with just the edge of the sheet over his lap and his long legs bare to the air. "Yes, somebody beat me until my back was bloody, then they left me tied to a wagon wheel for two days and nights. I was fifteen years old. They adopted me from the orphanage after my father left us there."

Leah put her hand to her mouth to hold back a shocked gasp that somebody could be so cruel to a boy. Cruel to beat him and then cruel to leave him like that. There were so many questions rattling around in her mind. Why would somebody do that? It was too horrible for words. She wanted to take him in her arms, and comfort the boy that had suffered so much when he was so young, but instead she waited for the rest of the story.

Cade scrubbed his hands through his hair, and then jerked his pants on. "You should get dressed. School will be out soon." He picked up his boots and shirt and left the room, with Dodger on his heels, as usual. He shut the door firmly behind him.

Leah stared at the door, in shock, from his revelation and his abrupt departure. The man carried too many secrets, secrets that made her wonder if she had made a big mistake. Secrets that made her think she was in way over her head.

"He overcame it," she said to the wall. "He became a minister." The empty room held no answers, only more questions. How did a boy who survived a massacre in Colorado when he was ten and a beating at fifteen end up back in Ohio, only to come west again? There were too many questions, too many things about Timothy "Cade" Key that just didn't make sense.

Since he was a minister, shouldn't he marry her? It wasn't that she wanted to trap him, but he declared his love for her over and over. Asked her to remember it above all else. And she believed him. She looked into his eyes and she knew it to be true. Could she be wrong? Could he be lying to her? And if he lied about loving her, then what else had he lied about?

Yes, she was in deep, deep trouble, because she was in love with him. She had a feeling things were going to get a whole lot worse before they got better, if they got better at all.

"Maybe he's just worried about Sunday and the first service." Strange, now that she thought on it. She hadn't seen him making any preparation for it at all. Not once had he picked up the Bible, or written out notes, or anything that she supposed a minister should do. He could be doing it while she was at work in the morning.

She knew, deep in her heart, that he hadn't done a thing to prepare for Sunday, just as she knew that something was terribly wrong with Pastor Timothy Key.

It was time to go. Dang it! Cade kicked at a chunk of snow as he stepped off the back porch. He had tried to convince himself all week that he'd figure out a way around it. "God, I've just made it worse."

He never should have touched her, never should have kissed her, and certainly never should have made love to her. His entire life was a litany of never should haves.

But God . . . he loved her.

Cade went to the shed, buttoning his shirt as he walked. The wind caught it and he jerked it back into place, his motions quick with impatience. He needed to find a hat before he left; his was long gone, lost in his flight from Fitch. The chickens scattered as he stalked onward, clucking insults as they ran away from his long strides. Roscoe flew at his ankles and pecked in indignation. Dodger, done with his business, trotted up to Cade with a questioning woof as he put his hand on the door of the shed.

He wanted to rip the door off the shed. Cade wanted to scream his frustration to the mountaintops. He could blame everything that had happened since he arrived in Angel's End on his past, but the truth was he'd dug this hole by himself. He'd wanted Leah and he'd taken her and the consequences to Leah be damned.

He knelt by the door. Dodger must have sensed his despair. He laid his head on Cade's knee and stared up at him with his deep, dark accepting eyes. Dodger liked him.

"You're a good dog," Cade said as he rubbed the dog's head. "A horrible judge of character, but a good dog."

Dodger was content. He closed his eyes and leaned into Cade's hands.

"I'll miss you too," he told the dog. He'd miss all of them, Banks, Dodger, Ashes, even the scrappy little rooster that strutted around the yard. *Leah* . . . His heart hurt. The thought of never seeing her again wrenched at his insides worse than the bullet that led him here.

Did it lead him here? Had Timothy been right when he spoke the words by the fire. *God led you to this place at this time in your life. Did you ever stop to think that perhaps God's answer was not now? To wait and be patient and see where he leads you?*

Had his blind escape from Timothy's camp led him to this place, to this town, to this woman? Why? Wouldn't he have been better off to not know her? Leah certainly would be better off not knowing him . . . unless . . . maybe this was the impetus she needed to marry Jake Reece. Maybe it was all part of God's plan, showing her what could happen to her without the protection of a good man.

The thought of her with Jake Reece would surely kill him.

"It's time to go . . ." Cade gave Dodger one final pat and looked around the yard once more before he went into the shed. He'd make his preparations now and leave tonight, when she lay down with Banks. She'd be better off with him gone and hopefully by Christmas he'd be nothing more than a bad memory.

"You are every kind of fool Cade Gentry . . ." Cade found his stash and pulled out the gun. He checked the load. Fitch was out there somewhere, with his long memory and his need for revenge. He wouldn't stop until one of them was dead. "Maybe this time I'll get lucky and it will be me."

It wasn't often that such a big group rode into town on a Friday. Lady jumped to her feet as Ward played. Her ears, turned toward the door, alerted him that somebody was on the way in. When five men, all of them strangers, walked into the Heaven's Gate he was both surprised and pleased. Unexpected money was always nice. He could only hope they would stay awhile and be free with it. Maybe he could get them into a card game.

"Keep playing and mind your own business," one of them growled. Another one gave a look to his grouchy companion that said *do the same*. Lady rumbled deep in her throat. Ward motioned her down with a finger and went back to playing. Bill always kept a shotgun behind the bar, in case things got rowdy, and he wasn't afraid to pull it out. Ward always lived by the philosophy of not showing his cards until he had to. It served him well when he was playing and it served him well in life. There was no need for these guests to think he wasn't anything more than a piano player.

They had traveled long and hard. They took off their heavy coats and gloves, and threw them across chairs before they bellied up to the bar. Luckily Bill was handy as he'd just come in from the back with a case of bottles. He sat the box down and went to wait on them. Pris must have seen them from upstairs. It was a bit early for customers; still she came down, wearing her best dress and showing an abundance of what God had blessed her with.

"Whiskey," one said and Bill lined up the glasses for all of them. As one they tossed it back and motioned for another. Bill poured the shots and looked over their shoulders to Ward. Ward raised his eyebrows in acknowledgment. A mirror hung over the top of the piano, angled so he could watch the saloon without anyone aware that he was. They had their signals worked out, he, Bill and Pris. Right now they were just going to wait and see. The West was full of men who were hard, and most of them just wanted a place to stop and warm up before they went on their way. There was no reason for them to be in Angel's End other than it was the last town before the country got wild and the going got rough. They'd probably been caught in the past few storms unawares and were anxious for warmth, company and good food to fill their bellies. Hopefully they had money to spend. He wasn't the only one who would prosper by them stopping in town. Dusty and the Swansons could also. All he had to do was sell them a few drinks and rent them some rooms.

That didn't mean he wasn't worried. The men had an edge to them that said tread lightly. *I should have worn my gun . . .* He usually did, and even had it on this morning, but had taken it off when he got back from a ride out to see Jake, who was in a fine mood when Ward told him about the preacher and Leah holding hands. He'd washed up a bit, had some lunch, and then sat down to play as he was still trying to puzzle out the preacher. Perhaps the six who were now moving about the place, all but one of them going to the potbellied stove to soak up the warmth, would be a welcome distraction. Ward often found the best way to solve a problem was to think on something else.

Pris joined the men around the stove. She stretched her hands out to warm them, at the same time sticking her behind out and heaving her chest forward, giving all of them a good view. Her laughter tinkled over his music.

Now was as good a time as any to see what they were up to. Ward stopped with a flourish, stood and stretched with a big yawn while reaching his arms out as if he'd been sitting there for days. He grinned heartily at the man still standing at the bar and then sauntered over to the door. Lady followed, of course. He opened the door to see if she needed to go out, but she just looked at him.

If things got ugly he sure didn't want her to get hurt. Especially since she was probably carrying pups now.

"Harlot," he said to her, loud enough for everyone to hear.

"That's a strange name for a dog," the man at the bar said.

Ward studied the man from beneath his hat brim. From

all appearances he was still looking at Lady but he could size someone up in a hurry. This one was the leader, he had the money and he readily threw it on the bar. The rest were his hired guns. And they were scared to cross him. The one who'd spoken up when they came in stood behind the others, just in case. That meant he had a temper.

Why were they here?

"That's not her name," Ward drawled. He pushed his hat back and flashed another grin. "It's just that I caught her out on the street the other morning, doing the deed for the entire world to see with some trashy stray." Ward casually looked out onto the street before he shut the door. It was empty, except for six wearied horses hitched to his rail. School would let out soon and the little ones would be on the street as they made their way home.

"Right beneath the angel," he added as he pulled the door firmly shut. "I'm surprised the good Lord just didn't strike her and that worthless mutt dead."

"Sounds downright sacrilegious to me," the man at the bar said. The other five laughed. They were well trained. And watchful.

"Well I guess there's just no denying it, when the mood strikes." Ward sauntered up to the bar. He nodded at Bill who took a bottle from beneath. Watered-down whiskey. Very watered down, just enough of it in there to give it the amber color, and the smell, to convince whoever he needed to, that he was drinking. Bill poured the glass extra full and Ward tossed it back with a grateful smile. With luck they would see him as no threat. With even more luck, there would be no need for them to see him as a threat.

I should have put Lady outside . . .

"What brings you to our fair little town?" Ward leaned casually on the bar. Lady stood next to him. She seemed nervous and Ward appreciated her instincts. The man he talked to was shorter than him, thick with muscle, with close-cropped reddish brown hair and small blue eyes that saw everything. They didn't face each other; instead they both looked into the mirror. Behind them he saw the men, sitting around a table, and Pris, chatting them up as she carried them another tray of drinks.

"We're looking for a friend. Haven't seen him for a while. Thought he might have passed this way."

Ward was instantly curious. Maybe this was the guy who'd attacked Timothy. Maybe this group was bounty hunters or a posse of some sort. Unless they were sworn officers of the law, they wouldn't be forthcoming about it. "What does he look like? We don't have many pass through here, and most make it a point to stop in here."

"Tall as you, skinnier, dark hair, kind of long, dark eyes, good with a gun." He tilted his head back as if he were thinking. His eyes stayed on Ward, even though he pretended to search the dark wood beams overhead. "Oh yeah, and he's gut shot."

It was years of experience that kept Ward from reacting to the description. The man he described sounded a lot like the preacher.

"This man have a name?"

"Last time I saw him his name was Cade Gentry."

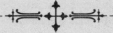

TWENTY-NINE

"**Y**ou're going to get sick if you keep going out without your coat," Leah said, as Cade walked into the kitchen with Dodger on his heels as usual. She checked Banks's homework as they sat at the table. Cade rubbed her son's golden hair when he walked by and got a glass of water. He pumped some into Dodger's bowl also and put it on the floor. Dodger lapped it up and then went to his corner to await his bowl of scraps after dinner. It was funny how they had so quickly fallen into a routine.

"I was in the shed, filling up all the holes. The coyotes have been digging around. You might need to invest in some fencing. With this early winter, they're going to get more and more aggressive. You might wake up one morning and find one sitting on your back porch." He looked out the window over the sink as he spoke. Was he avoiding her?

"Fencing is expensive," she said. "And I missed a week of work." She didn't mention the rest. That the town had yet to pay her for his upkeep. That he was supposed to eat at Dusty's, so she didn't have to bear the expense of feeding him. That he was a drain on her larder. That she didn't know where she stood with him, even though he told her over and over again that he loved her.

Oh God, what if I get pregnant? It was something she should be wary of, but she'd been so caught up in the moment . . . moments.

He sighed deeply as if he were worried. He leaned on the sink and put his head down. Was he praying?

"It's just a thought," he said finally. "I'd hate for Roscoe to lose any more of his harem."

"Dinner will be ready in a few minutes."

Cade nodded and sat down at the table. "What are you working on?" he asked Banks.

"Arithmetic," Banks said. He turned his slate around so Cade could see. Once more Leah's heart swelled at the sight of the two heads bent over, companionably close. Cade hung his arm over the back of Banks's chair as he checked the problem in the book against the one on the slate. The man was so smart. He could have been a lawyer or a doctor, yet he chose to be a minister. It was a powerful calling; yet, again it just didn't make sense. Leah went to her room.

A trunk sat at the foot of her bed. She removed the quilt that covered it and knelt before it. The hinges creaked as she opened it. Within it were some things she cherished. Carefully stitched baby clothes, and blankets, all washed and ironed and folded away in hopes of another little miracle. Leah's cheeks turned fiery at the thought of it. What if she were pregnant by Cade? It would be a blessing in her mind. Would he think so? He made no mention of marriage, no mention of the future. Surely he didn't think they could continue on this way?

On one side of the trunk was Nate's hat. She didn't know why she put it in the trunk, other than it was in the way and she knew that the sight of it hanging on the hook in the back hall, where he always put it when he came in, would tear her heart out every time she looked at it. Leah lifted it carefully and held it before her. She nearly dropped it when a noise from outside startled her, a loud clank, followed by a rattle. The washtub had been blown from its hook by the wind.

The hat was more brown than black, with a pencil roll brim, well creased, and a silk band inside. Nate had been very proud of his hat. The outer band was of braided leather strips with silver pressed around the tips of the ends. It wasn't a hat for a preacher, yet for some reason, Leah felt as if it would fit Cade perfectly. She carried it to the kitchen.

"I thought you could use this," she said as she put it on the table before him.

He looked at it for a moment, his face wistful, and then he carefully picked it up and put it on. He bent his head forward and his fingers settled into the creases naturally. He wiggled it around a bit and it slid into place, a perfect fit. He smiled.

"You look different," Banks said.

Her son was right. Even though Cade quickly took off the hat, she saw the effect. He seemed dangerous now. The eyes not so sad as much as deadly. A chill chased down her spine and she crossed her arms to counter it.

"Thank you," he said. "It will come in handy."

"You're welcome." She went to the stove and dished dinner onto their plates, surreptitiously stealing looks at Cade as she did. Something had changed. Something that scared her. She let Banks monopolize the conversation at dinner and Cade encouraged him as he rambled on about his day. When he was done she sent him to the parlor to do his reading.

"Can we play soldiers then?" he asked Cade.

"Sorry, Banks," he replied. "I've got some reading to do too." Was he finally preparing for his sermon now?

Banks stuck his bottom lip out, ready to protest. "Go," she said. "There's plenty of time for play later. And make sure you feed Ashes."

Banks was sullen when he pushed his chair back. He poured milk from the crock and put it on the floor. Dodger looked at it hopefully as Banks stalked out of the room.

"No," Leah said firmly. She looked around for Ashes, who usually showed up as soon as the bowl hit the floor but she was nowhere to be found. "Was Ashes outside with you?"

Cade stood at the counter, scraping plates. "No, I haven't seen her since you came in. She didn't go out with me." She hadn't. Leah recalled the cat sleeping on the sofa when she started dinner. As Cade left the kitchen he stopped and kissed her forehead. It was strange, how his kiss lingered and how quickly he turned away and left after, going into his room and firmly shutting the door behind him, leaving Dodger sitting in the hall with a strange look on his face. Dodger snuffed beneath the door before lying down with his nose at the crack with a heavy sigh.

Leah went out the back door. She picked up the washtub and hung it back on the hook. "Kitty?" she called out. "Here kitty, kitty, kitty!" There was no sign of her, no answer except the howl of the wind. It was near dark now and downright gloomy.

Leah went back inside. Cade's door was still closed, Dodger still lay in the hall, Banks was pouting in the parlor and she felt ill at ease.

"Are you sure you didn't let Ashes outside?" she asked her son.

"She might have gone out when I used the outhouse," he mumbled.

"Banks Nathan Findley!" Leah's patience was gone. "Put your coat on and go outside and look for her."

"Aww . . ." Banks protested.

"Now!" She had had enough. Between worry over Cade's

actions and Banks's pouting and all the responsibility of trying to make a life for the two of them. And the big question that had suddenly come up to haunt her with a vengeance this day. Could she possibly have conceived a child?

She needed to talk to Cade. She needed to know where she stood with him. The only way she could talk to him freely was if Banks was out of the house. Banks let Ashes out and she was his responsibility. It was time he started to learn what being responsible was all about.

"It's cold outside." He stomped away. "I'm sleepy. I want to go to bed."

"And how do you think Ashes feels?" Leah pointed a finger at the back door. "And no door slamming. Pastor Key is studying for his sermon on Sunday." She didn't mention that their yelling had more than likely already disturbed him. She was surprised that he hadn't come out to see what the problem was.

"Take a lantern," she reminded Banks. "And Dodger."

She stood in the hallway and watched as he sighed and put his coat on. Sighed and pulled on his woolen cap. Sighed and got the lantern from the peg. Sighed when he opened the door and stepped out. "Come on Dodger," he said with a sigh.

Leah motioned for Dodger to go, and he got up, slowly and with his own sigh, as if he were taking lessons from Banks. He walked to the door with his tail firmly down and between his legs as if she had sent him out to be beaten.

"Ashes!" Banks hollered as soon as he shut the door with exaggerated slowness.

Leah rubbed her forehead. A headache was there, just waiting to settle in. She knocked on Cade's door. "Cade?" No answer. "Cade? We need to talk." She slowly opened the door, expecting to find him sitting on his bed, with his Bible open and deep in study.

The room was empty. The Bible sat on the bedside table,

where it had remained all week. She would have thought it hadn't been moved except a folded piece of paper stuck out of the pages. His notes, she assumed, and a marked passage for his sermon. The pegs where his clothes hung were empty of everything except the shirt that belonged to Nate.

She hadn't heard him leave. Did he go out to search for Ashes when he heard her and Banks quarreling? Strange that he didn't say anything, stranger that Dodger didn't go with him, as the dog was devoted to him. And why hadn't Dodger moved from his spot by the door? Did Cade step over him?

Leah put a hand to her heart. For some reason, it suddenly hurt.

Cade was lucky once more. The weather was perfect for his escape. The wind, which was fast enough to rattle the windows and doors, covered any noise he made and the half moon gave just enough light for him to see his way. Occasional clouds scuttled across the sky, which helped him to blend into the shadows. He wore the hat low over his face to hide the pale hue of his skin and the long coat, which moved with the wind, made him part of the landscape, if anyone so happened to come out of the back of their houses or look out the windows.

His horse would be a problem. The animal was light gray in color and dappled. Hard to find in the snow but easy to spot in the moonlight. Since he'd spent so much time around the stables working on the doors for Leah, the animals were used to him. Even Libby, who only tossed her head when he sneaked through the corral door. The cat blinked curiously from her bed when he walked in and his horse, who he had tempted with bits of dried apple all week came to him easily.

"I need to pick out a name for you." He rubbed the long

nose as the animal munched on the apple. "Since we're going to be together for a while I'll have to think on it. Find something that's just right." He quietly saddled up and led his mount out of the stable and down the fence line to a gate that let out at the stream. His saddlebags were stashed on the opposite bank. It was just a matter of tying them on, mounting up, and leaving.

So why was it proving to be the hardest thing he'd ever done?

The town lay peaceful before him. Lights twinkled in the windows as the folk, safe and warm inside, settled in for the night. He'd be long gone come morning, longer still by Sunday. He'd left a letter for Leah, in the Bible, along with most of his money. He told her to buy a fence to protect the chickens. He told her he wasn't who she thought he was, but didn't go into detail. He told her he loved her and he was sorry. He told her to marry Jake Reece. He asked her to forgive him and told her he'd never forget her.

The yip of coyotes sounded in the woods, right behind Leah's house. His horse pricked his ears in the direction and tossed his head nervously. They were close, after the easy pickings of Leah's chickens. He'd done what he could for her and for the chickens.

"Yeah, go ahead and tell yourself that." Cade quieted his horse and put his foot in the stirrup. As soon as he was mounted he heard a screech. *What was that?* Then barking. Then voices calling out.

"Momma!"

"Banks! Dodger! Stop!"

He kicked his horse into a run as the noise of snarls and growls filled the air. The sound of barking dogs filled the air as they all sensed the one-sided battle going on by the stream. Over the noise of the pounding hooves and the angry dogs he heard Leah's screams.

Cade jumped off the horse before he came to a full stop.

Banks was on the opposite side of the stream trying to hold on to Ashes. He backed away from the fight before him. Dodger was a snarling devil, fighting four or five coyotes; they tumbled and moved so fast that Cade couldn't tell. Leah was trying to help. She held a piece of wood in her hands and used it to club at the lighter bodies of the coyotes. She managed to knock one away and Cade shot it.

"Move back!" he yelled. She dropped the wood at his yell, hiked up her skirts and grabbed Banks. She pulled him after her and a coyote gave pursuit. Cade dropped one of the coyotes with a single shot and then quickly shot two more who suddenly realized that their odds were dropping.

"Dodger!" he called out. He saw the darker flashes of Dodger's fur but they all moved so fast that he couldn't be sure he wouldn't hit Dodger. Dodger's answering yelp was filled with pain.

"Help him!" Leah pleaded.

Cade had no choice but to wade in. He jerked one back by its tail, kicked it away and shot it. The other one took off, streaking toward the trees. Cade shot it easily and, without a thought, flipped his gun around twice and dropped it in the holster.

Dodger took a step and fell to the ground with a groan. Sticky blood covered his fur. Cade quickly scooped him up and took off to the house at a run.

"Is he dead?" Leah's voice cried out behind him.

"I can't tell," Cade answered. "Are you hurt?"

"No . . . not that I know of."

"Ashes scratched me," Banks said.

The chickens cackled loudly as he ran into Leah's yard. He heard his horse thundering up behind them, well trained by someone. *Good horse . . .*

Cade kicked the back door open and carried Dodger into the kitchen. Leah grabbed his blanket from the corner and put it on the table so Cade could lay him down. Dodger raised his head and tried to lick Cade. He was still alive but Cade couldn't tell how badly Dodger was hurt until he could examine his wounds. He soothed the dog with his hands while Leah took care of her son.

Leah turned up the lamp and put it on the table. She pulled Banks close. He held the kitten clutched tightly in his hands. The kitten panted its distress. "Is Ashes hurt?" Leah asked. She quickly checked Banks over. He had a scratch on his cheek and a bigger one on the back of his hand.

"N-n-no." Banks's teeth chattered together. A fat tear streamed down his cheek. "Is Dodger going to die?"

"We're going to take care of him," Leah assured him. Her voice was so calm and soothing. "I need you to take Ashes and go to bed," she said. "Ashes is scared and needs to be someplace where she feels safe. Can you take care of her?"

"Yes, Momma."

"Banks," Cade said, stopping the boy as he left. "You did a very brave thing, saving your kitten."

Banks nodded and sniffed. "Dodger saved both of us. Don't let him die."

"We'll take care of him." *We . . . God don't let this dog die . . .*

Leah rubbed a hand over her son's hair and sent him on.

"How bad is it?" she asked when he was gone.

"Hold the light up and keep him still. I need to wash off the blood." Cade quickly filled a pot with water. Leah saw what he was doing and grabbed some towels from the shelf. They worked, side by side, Leah soothing Dodger while Cade washed the blood from his fur. Dodger lay quiet except for occasionally raising his head and looking at Cade when he touched a tender spot. Cade found a long gash on his side and Dodger turned and licked his hand.

"It's going to be fine," Cade assured the dog. He caressed

Dodger's head. Tears streamed down Leah's face and she quickly swiped at them with a towel. "I think he'll survive," he assured her. "We just need to bind the wounds."

"I'll get some bandages." She went down the hall while Cade once more checked for wounds. There was a long gash on his side that wasn't too deep and two bad bites, one on a foreleg and the other on a hip. One of his ears had a tear. He could do with some stitching but Cade wasn't sure if Dodger would let them sew him.

"Your ear is going to be funny looking." Cade leaned down and put his face right by Dodger's ear. Dodger gave a weak thump of his tail. "Good dog. You saved both of them. You are a very good dog."

Just as Leah returned with the bandages someone pounded on the door. Cade sighed and rubbed between his eyes with the back of his hand, hoping he didn't leave blood behind.

He stood in her kitchen in his coat and hat with the gun strapped to his hip. He'd fired five shots that likely woke the entire town. *You didn't really think no one was going to want to know what happened, did you?*

The knock sounded again. Leah put the bandages on the table and turned to look at him. He felt her eyes and felt the incrimination.

"You're not a preacher, are you?"

THIRTY

Things were not going well. Not well at all. The men inside the Heaven's Gate were itching for a fight. Thank God it was Friday and not Saturday. Saturdays were normally full up, with the cowboys and miners all heading in after their long workweek. Luckily, the only one who came by was Zeke, who quickly figured out that the saloon wasn't a friendly place to be tonight.

"Need any help?" he asked Ward, when the leader, who he heard one of the men call Fitch, walked off to talk to his men. Ward almost laughed. Zeke was one of the most unhelpful people he'd ever met, and his skills certainly didn't run to fighting, but he would carry a message to Jim if need be. It was too bad that Jake wasn't around. Jake was downright handy in a fight, whether it was guns or fists.

The sound of gunshots sounded in the distance. Everyone inside turned toward the sound. Ward couldn't help but wonder if it had anything to do with the men inside. Any other night he'd be the first one out to investigate. But not tonight. He had enough trouble of his own to avoid poking his nose into someone else's.

"We'll handle it." Ward turned his back on the gang, making sure to keep an eye on them in the mirror while he talked to Zeke. "Just tell everyone to stay away tonight. I don't want anyone around here to get hurt. And you best have someone find out what all that shooting was about."

"Will do," Zeke said. He tossed back his beer, wiped his mouth on his sleeve, hitched up his pants and left.

Ward waited a moment, made sure Fitch was still with his men, before he walked to the door. Lady, who'd been unsettled since the gang walked in, followed him. She was ready to leave and trotted through the door quickly. She stopped when she realized he wasn't following. Ward quickly shut the door in her face. He heard her whine and then her scratch at the base of the door. He wasn't about to risk her getting hurt. Dang he'd gotten attached to that dog.

The sound of a squeal and the resulting slap spun him around and had him reaching for his gun, only it wasn't there. One of the men had Pris in his arms. She wrestled against him as he tried to kiss her neck.

"Let her go!" Ward saw Bill from the corner of his eye looking at the place where the shotgun was stashed. Ward jerked his finger, just enough for Bill to see it. Bill would get them all killed. He wasn't fast enough for this bunch.

"She was asking for it," one of them said.

"Pris?" Ward kept his voice even. He didn't want anyone getting spooked. "Do you want this?"

"No siree I don't," she said.

"Then come over here with me."

Fitch tilted his head and the man released Pris. She hurried over behind the bar and the safety it would offer.

"I get the feeling that you're more than just a piano

player." Fitch crossed his arms and looked at Ward. His men watched both of them carefully. Ward knew there were at least three guns pointing at him from under their table.

"Piano player, proprietor, protector of women," Ward said. "I go with whatever one suits the moment."

Fitch laughed but his men stayed silent.

"It's time for you to move on," Ward said.

"It's late, and we're not going anywhere tonight," Fitch replied.

"Not until we find Cade Gentry," one of the braver ones said.

"Never heard of him . . ."

"Cade," Pris interrupted. "Isn't that what Leah called the preacher?"

Ward sighed. They were in trouble now. Big trouble.

Leah opened the door to find Jim on her stoop.

"I heard shots," he said.

"Coyotes were after the kitten and Dodger went after them," Cade said from behind her. "I had to shoot them."

Jim's eyes flicked down to the gun he wore low on his hip.

"My horse is out back," Cade added. "I don't want you to think someone stole it."

"Are you all right?" Jim asked. His question was directed at Leah.

"I'm fine," Leah said. Her voice was strange, tight. Considering what just happened, and what was about to happen, it didn't surprise Cade a bit. "Dodger was hurt, but Cade . . ." She stopped for a moment and then continued. "He should be fine."

"Do you need anything?" Jim asked.

"Really Jim," Leah said. "We're all fine. But Cade and I need to talk for a bit. If I need anything I'll let you know." And with that she shut the door in his face. She walked past

Cade into the kitchen and sat down at the table. She looked at him. "It was all a lie."

"Not all of it," Cade said. "The things I told you about me were true."

Leah's lovely green eyes stared at him in earnest. As if she wanted to see what was inside him. She already had, but telling her that now wouldn't help the situation. The ticktock of the clock echoed loudly through the long silence that filled the kitchen, interrupted only by the sound of Dodger, groaning in his sleep as he relived his battle for his family in his dreams, and the howl of the bitter wind.

"We need to talk," Leah said.

"Yes." Cade sighed. "We do."

He sat down at the table and he told her how he really came to Angel's End. Told her he was trying to escape the men who shot him, told her about stumbling into Timothy's camp, about how Timothy helped him, about how Timothy was shot before his eyes and why he had to move on.

"It was never my intent to be him," Cade said. "I just wanted Fitch to think it was me who died that night, so he'd leave me alone."

"Why does he want to kill you Cade? What did you do to him?"

Cade shook his head. "It doesn't matter."

Her voice was angry and her jaw tight. "Yes it does."

"There was this young couple, Bob and Amy Welder. They owned a little ranch, but more importantly they had access to water. Fitch decided he wanted their ranch, and he wanted Amy. He sent me to get both of them."

"What do you mean, sent you to get them?"

"Men like Fitch are never happy. There is never enough for them. And at the time I was just looking for a place to spend the winter. I'm good with a gun."

"Yes, I saw that," Leah interrupted.

Cade sighed. This was harder than he thought. "There

were things about him that bothered me, but I just figured I'd keep to myself, like I always do, and just move on when springtime came. So he sent me to the Welders with orders to kill Bob and bring Amy back."

"Don't tell me that you did it." Leah's eyes flashed with anger.

"I couldn't. I rode up telling myself that I didn't care, that it was just a job, but when I saw them, I couldn't do it."

"It was just a job because you've killed before?"

He didn't want to admit it, but he had to. He watched her face change, watched as her eyes narrowed, and saw the door of her heart slam shut against him. He couldn't look at her. His eyes were drawn to a bit of blue in the wooden bowl on the table. He pulled it out and immediately recognized it as the piece of ribbon he'd picked up, dropped by Amy in their haste to flee. Leah must have found it in his pocket when she washed his clothes. Funny how he didn't notice it lying there until now. He placed it on the table in front of her, as if it was proof of his innocence. A talisman of his attempt to do something right.

"Amy was pregnant. Just barely showing. I gave them all the money I had on me and told them to get. That there wasn't any land worth their lives, and Fitch was determined to have it. They were smart enough to go, and I hoped that the land would be enough to placate Fitch. But it wasn't. He was mad and killing me was the only way he'd feel better. So I ran."

"They got away?" she asked.

"I hope so," he replied. "He wouldn't want me dead if they hadn't escaped. He'd make me watch instead. He'd kill Bob in front of me and then have his way with Amy, all for a laugh and because he thinks he can do whatever he wants, whenever he wants."

Leah shivered. "There are horrible people out there."

"And I was one of them," Cade said quietly.

She didn't deny it. "What about the rest? Your mother's death? The scars on your back?"

"That was all true. After my mother died my father lost his faith. He dumped my brother and me in an orphanage. When I was fifteen a couple came and adopted us. He beat me right after we left the orphanage because another man took Brody and I tried to go after them."

There was genuine shock in her eyes. And pity. Pity was something he did not want from her. He'd pitied himself enough through the years. "Then what happened?"

"He taught me how to cheat and how to steal. And when he saw how good I was with my hands, he taught me how to shoot. He never expected me to get better than he was."

"You killed him?"

"Yes. I did, when I was eighteen. He killed his wife and aimed to kill me next. In self-defense, I shot him." He was relieved that she figured that much out. That he didn't have to tell her about Letty and the horrible things she taught him. Things that he had to keep locked away. "After that I just drifted, getting work wherever I could, and hoping to find a dry, warm place to spend the winter. Everything you know about me is the truth."

Leah slammed her hand on the table. "Everything I know about you was based on the thought that you were a preacher."

"I told you I wasn't the man you thought I was." A poor excuse, he knew.

"But you never said you weren't Timothy Key." Anger flashed in her gold-flecked eyes along with sudden tears. "I can't say you took advantage of me because I wanted . . ." Leah put her hand over her mouth and sobbed.

He wanted to touch her and comfort her. He wanted to make the bad go away. The problem was he *was* the bad. Cade reached for her hand but she pulled it away and put it up to stop him.

"Don't." She took a deep breath. "I'm just as guilty as you are in some respects. I admit it. My sin is great." She looked at him and he saw the hurt in her eyes, mixed with the anger. "And I'll pay for it."

"Leah. Blame me. Please. I'm used to it. Hell, it's the only thing I'm good at."

"And running."

He had no answer for that.

"You were leaving tonight. Leaving without a word."

"I left you a letter. In Timothy's Bible. Along with a letter to Timothy's sister explaining what happened to her brother. I was hoping you could mail it for me."

"Coward." She got up and walked to the sink, stood a moment, looked out the window and turned. "You left it to me to cover your tracks. To have to get up in church on Sunday morning and tell everyone you lied because you're too much of a coward to own up to it." She took two steps toward him and once more anger flashed in her eyes. She raised her hand and he thought she might strike him, and he deserved it, and more. Instead she pointed at the wall. "I have a son sleeping in there." She jabbed her finger for emphasis. "A son who adores you, and you were leaving it to me to explain to him . . ." Her voice broke. Leah straightened her spine and crossed her arms. "That's Nate's gun, isn't it?"

"Yes."

"Take it. I hate guns. Hate them." Her voice was low and toneless for the words she used. "And keep the hat. You'll need it."

It was time to go. Long past. If only he'd left before . . . "Thank you Leah. You saved my life."

Her eyes seemed dead, lifeless. The spark was gone. He'd done that. "You need to go now."

She was right. Cade stood, turned to leave but paused in the doorway. "I love you."

"Just go."

He spared one last look for Dodger, walked out the back door and mounted his horse.

For reasons he could not name, Cade turned his horse to the left and the church. He stopped in front of it and gazed upward at the steeple. He rubbed the silky mane while he looked at the peak of the roof set against the starry sky.

Just like him, the clouds had moved on. At least he had a purpose now. He had a brother out there somewhere. He would find him.

"You did good tonight," he said to the horse. "Stayed put, even though you were scared." He kept talking and the horse pricked its ears as if he understood. "And then you followed, just like you're supposed to." He gave the horse one last pat. "Wish I could say the same."

He was in no hurry to leave. "You still need a name." He studied the church and then his eyes moved back to the sky. Was God sitting up there, laughing at him? *I didn't know how good I had it before* . . . Now that Cade understood love, what it was and how it could twist you up . . . was it better to know what it was and then miss it for the rest of his life?

"Timothy. I know you're up there. I'm sorry for what happened. I'm sorry for a lot of things. I still don't understand why things happened the way they did." Cade shook his head. "Thank you for Leah. Watch out for her, and her boy . . . and Dodger."

A shooting star streaked across the sky. Cade watched it go until it disappeared behind the mountaintops. "I reckon that's a sign," he said. "Of which way we should go." He turned the horse and headed south, down the middle of the street.

"How about Gabriel," he said. "Gabriel is an angel, you know. He's the one with the trumpet. He's God's messenger, not that I've ever met him . . ." The horse twitched its ears. Cade stopped when they got to the statue. "Gabriel it is." He rubbed the pale neck. "Gabe." Gabe tossed his head as if he agreed. "There you go."

They were in front of the saloon. Five horses were hitched to the rail but there was no noise coming from within. It seemed strange. He'd heard the piano music plenty since he'd been here. There was no laughter, no chatter, just silence. Then, suddenly, there was a crash, a scream and a flurry of barking on the porch. Ward's dog dug at the door, beside herself with worry. She wanted in.

Cade jumped from Gabe and smacked the horse on the flanks. Gabe trotted across the street to the stable. He checked the brand on the outside horse, recognized the rig and the horse beyond. Fitch had found him.

Cade pulled out his gun and loaded it. A Winchester rifle sat in the scabbard of Fitch's horse. He pulled it free and checked the load. Full as he expected. Fitch was proud of that rifle and often bragged about killing the man who once owned it.

Lady jumped from the porch, whined and jumped back up, willing him to follow. On silent feet he crept to the door, and then sidled up to the window with his back to the wall.

Thick drapes hung on the inside, but they'd been closed sloppily, as if they'd been jerked closed. A beam of light shone through an opening on the side where they'd been pulled too close in the middle. Cade turned his head and looked, no more than a second. A second was all he needed to see the two who worked for Ward: the older man Bill, tied, gagged and bleeding from a cut on his head; and Pris, held roughly by two men. Ward was tied to a chair. Two men stood behind him with their hands clamped on his shoulders. Another stood at the potbellied stove with a spindle from a broken chair in the fire. Fitch had his back to the window. He punched Ward in the face.

Fitch knew he was here, but he didn't know where. Cade knew Ward well enough to know that even if he knew Cade's real identity, Ward wouldn't give him away, because he wouldn't want to endanger Leah.

That didn't mean that the other two wouldn't. Fitch would kill or maim one or all of them if he thought it would get him what he wanted.

He could ride out right now and leave Angel's End and its people to Fitch and his men. Or he could end it right now. He was tired of running. It felt like he'd been running his entire life. Cade moved to the door, took a deep breath and kicked it open.

He heard Lady barking. He'd surprised them, but it didn't take them long to react. The blur that passed by him was Lady, going straight for Fitch. Pris ran as the men released her and she drug Bill behind the bar. Ward tipped his chair over and kicked Fitch's legs out as the two men who'd been holding him drew on Cade.

Cade shot three times and dove behind a table, flipping it on its side as he fell. The two who'd been holding Pris took cover also and started shooting. Lady had Fitch by the arm and growled furiously as she wrestled it. Ward squirmed around in his chair, trying to get loose. Fitch managed to get his gun loose and Ward kicked it away. Bullets flew, Lady barked and growled and Ward shouted something about a shotgun.

Cade realized quickly that it would be a standoff until someone ran out of bullets. He still had the rifle but it was three against one. He had three bullets left in his .45 and a full load in the rifle. Three men stood between him and freedom from his past. He needed to draw Fitch out.

Fitch managed, finally, to get away from Lady. He kicked her hard, and Lady yelped. Ward was still half tied to his chair, but had broken the legs off. Two shooters were behind him and Fitch was beside him. Fitch went for his gun and

Ward plowed into him with his shoulder. Cade took advantage of the fight being a distraction, holstered his gun and stood with the rifle in his hand, firing it repeatedly as he walked forward to where the other two had taken shelter. He was satisfied with the sounds of bullets hitting flesh just as the chamber finally emptied.

Fitch had won the match with Ward. He slammed Ward against the bar and picked up the gun. Lady growled and hunched down, with the ruff on her neck standing up. She was prepared to attack again. Fitch aimed at her.

"I see you found me, Fitch," Cade said. He tossed the rifle aside. "How 'bout we leave these people out of it."

"Still got that bleeding heart I see," Fitch said. He turned to Cade as Pris crawled from behind the bar and pulled Ward behind it. Thankfully, Lady followed, whining and licking her master's face as he was moved.

"This has nothing to do with them." He heard the shouts on the street, heard people coming. *Stay away. . . . Leah . . . all of you stay away . . .* Heard the pounding of feet as they hit the porch, felt their gasps as they stopped at the door.

"Pastor Key?" a voice asked. Jim.

"Keep Leah out of here," he said. He heard her on the street, calling out.

Fitch laughed. He laughed long and hard. Cade kept his eyes on him, and he was still holding his gun. "Pastor . . . oh that is funny," Fitch said. "You know where you messed up, don't you? It was the boots. I would have thought for sure you were dead and burned up until I saw the shoes on the body."

"I admit I wasn't thinking straight. Since I'd been shot."

"Looks like you recovered well enough."

"Not everybody is a son of a bitch like you. Some people are kind and generous when a wounded man shows up in their town."

"That's pretty big talk," Fitch said.

Why had he ever signed on with this man? He was a
bully. He was mean. He cared for nothing and no one. He
didn't have a thing that he hadn't stolen or killed for. Cade
was tired of him, and tired of worrying over him. "So let's
quit talking, and end it," Cade said.

Fitch laughed again. Cade knew what he was doing. He'd
raise his hand and shoot when he thought he'd distracted
Cade from his purpose. Fortunately, Fitch didn't know how
good he was. Cade had never shown him. He'd held back,
as he always did.

Faster than Fitch could think to raise his weapon and
shoot, faster than anyone could react, Cade drew, shot him
dead and spun his gun back into the holster. Fitch slumped
to the floor.

Without a word Cade walked from the saloon, past Jim,
past Gus and Bettina and several others who stood around,
wondering and waiting to see what was going on. Leah stood
in front of the statue with her shawl wrapped tightly around
her arms. He walked past her to where Gabe stood in front
of the stable.

"Are you hurt?" she called out.

Cade swung into the saddle. "I'm fine," he said. "It's
over."

Without another word he rode out of town.

THIRTY-ONE

His camp had been lonely and cold and he never really slept. He spent the night haunted by the things he'd done and the final words Leah said to him. *You are good at running.*

But he wasn't running anymore. Fitch was dead. He could leave that part of his life behind him, begin anew, and try again. He'd find Brody and together they would build a life that was better than the one he'd been living. Sure he'd left a mess behind, but the people in town could deal with it. They'd hire a new preacher before spring. Leah would move on, and with luck marry Jake Reece. She'd be better off without Cade in her life.

The eastern sun slid over the mountains as he mounted Gabe and rode out from the deadfall he'd sheltered in. It shone so brightly on the snow that it almost blinded him. A valley lay before him, cozily tucked against the mountains.

He heard a dog barking in the distance, and a trail of smoke was the only scar on an otherwise pristine sky.

Which direction should he go? North, east, south? West was out of the question as it would lead into the mountains and the worst of winter was still ahead.

"There you go again, always taking the easy way . . ." Cade stopped Gabe and searched the sky for a sign. There'd been a falling star the night before, what did he expect now?

Cade closed his eyes. "Lord? Are you listening?" He was such a fool. Did he really expect an answer? God was more than likely still laughing at him. A real good laugh.

"Let's go Gabe." The horse took a few steps and then stopped with a grunt. Cade knew the horse had good instincts so he trusted him and waited in silence until whatever it was that spooked Gabe showed itself. He heard a crashing noise behind him. Something was coming. Something that didn't take the time or trouble to travel in silence. Cade drew his gun and turned Gabe to face it. Was it a bear? Elk? Cougar? If it was a danger, Gabe would be nervous; instead the horse just stood with his ears pricked curiously ahead.

A sheep trotted out of the cover of trees. Cade blinked his eyes and looked again. Yes, it was short and thick and covered with dingy white wool. It stood before him and Gabe and baaed loudly before bolting off down the hill into the valley. Had he really seen it? A sheep, out here, in the middle of nowhere, in the middle of cattle country?

Feed my sheep . . .

Cade laughed. He laughed and laughed until he was bent over in the saddle. "I get it Lord," he said. "I get it. I'll take care of it now."

Who would have thought her little house could feel so empty? Leah wandered through the rooms, from parlor to kitchen, from her room back to Cade's. She'd stripped the sheets and put them into the wash sometime during the middle of the night. She couldn't sleep, and used Dodger's wounds as an excuse to stay up so she wouldn't disturb Banks, who slept very soundly after his scare.

When dawn finally broke the sky, revealing a beautiful day, she'd hung the sheets outside to dry and then turned the chickens out. They should be safe now. The coyotes were dead.

She fixed Banks breakfast and sent him off to play with Sam. He asked where Cade was and all she could say was he'd gone off on his horse. She didn't tell him he was gone for good. She was afraid she'd cry and that was the last thing she wanted to do. She was afraid if she started she wouldn't be able to stop, just like she'd been afraid when Nate died.

The events of the night before flashed before her eyes again. Cade with a gun. Cade, really good with a gun. Jim and Ward both agreed that he was the best they'd ever seen. Leah filled them in on the why, and who the men were. The *dead* men. They were laid out now, in Nate's old office, awaiting burial. Maybe the town should look into getting an undertaker too. A sheriff, a pastor, a doctor and an undertaker. If they kept up like this they'd be a big city in no time.

She'd told them about Cade too. Just Ward and Jim. She couldn't deal with anyone else and dreaded having to face Jake.

Cade thought she should marry Jake. He'd said so in his letter. The rest of it held the same things he'd told her, not the details, just that Timothy was dead because he'd helped Cade and that he was sorry.

God, she wished he was here.

Who was she to condemn him? Sure he'd made mistakes, but so had she. God knew she wasn't perfect, so why should she expect Cade to be. He'd had a horrible life. Bad things had happened to him. He should have turned out as evil as the man who wanted to kill him, but he wasn't. He was kind, and sweet, and helpful. He'd been good to her, good to Banks, good to her ever-growing zoo of animals. He'd cared for her when she was desperately ill. He could have left then without a backward glance and no one would have been the wiser.

Dodger looked up from his bed when she returned, once more, to the kitchen. He'd been up this morning, gone outside long enough to relieve himself, and then returned to his warm bed by the stove, to sleep until he was healed. He would be all right, given some time.

"Thank you God for sparing Dodger. Thank you for protecting my child. Thank you for sparing that silly kitten that caused the ruckus in the first place." Her voice broke on the prayer. "Thank you for sending Cade because without him we all would have been killed." Another one of her prayers, shot like an arrow into the heavens.

The church bell rang. Long clanging peals that kept going. Why? It was Saturday. There was no school today and there would be no church tomorrow. No church for a good long while.

Leah went out onto the street. Something was wrong, it had to be. Another disaster on top of the recent many. Banks stood on the stoop of the church pulling on the bell rope with all his strength.

"Banks! Stop this instant." The townsfolk came onto the street, moving out of Dusty's and the store and the other homes and businesses, all of them looking toward the church.

"I can't Momma," Banks said. "Cade told me to."

Her heart jumped. "Cade?"

"He's inside," Banks said with a smile.

Leah looked at the door. It stood open to welcome all. Smoke rolled from the chimney, which meant a fire had been built. Hesitantly, and suddenly full of fear, she stepped inside.

Cade stood at the front, by the pulpit. He looked much as he had the night before. He still wore the gun strapped to his hip but had removed the heavy coat to reveal the frock coat beneath. The hat she had given him sat on Margy's desk. His hair was wild and curled around his neck and ears. He still needed a haircut, something she always intended to give him, but never did. Yet somehow, he looked different.

"Have a seat please," he said.

Leah nodded, still too shocked at seeing him here to ask questions. She slid into a seat.

It's his eyes . . . his eyes were different . . . the sadness and the weariness he carried inside was gone.

Banks still rang the bell. Rang it joyfully because Cade had asked him to. Leah turned and saw the happiness on his face at doing something he always wanted, but never dared to do. She saw the adoration for Cade. *Please, keep him from disappointment Lord* . . .

As Banks pulled the rope he motioned people inside and they came. Dusty and Zeke, Jim, Gretchen, Nonnie and the kids. Bettina, Gus, Margy and the rest of the townsfolk. Then last of all Ward, Pris and Bill. Ward and Bill both wearing their cuts and bruises from the night before. Lady was by Ward's side, sticking close by, as if she were afraid he'd go somewhere without her. The ringing stopped and Banks left. Cade didn't say anything, and everyone milled around for a bit, curious looks on their faces, most of them looking between him and Leah. All she could do was sit there until Banks came running up the aisle with the Bible in his hands. He gave it to Cade, who flipped it open and placed it on the podium. Banks sat down beside her and grinned. Everyone finally sat until the benches were full, except for Jim and Ward who both stood at the back with their arms crossed, waiting to hear what Cade had to say.

Cade grabbed the sides of the small podium and looked out at the crowd.

"My name is Cade Gentry and I'm here to tell you about a man I met. A man named Timothy Key." No one made a sound. They all knew already that Cade wasn't Timothy. News traveled fast, especially in such a small group.

"I met Timothy Key when I was at my most desperate. I was wounded, on foot and running for my life. I'm not a praying man." He stopped for a moment, looked at the podium and swallowed. "I always thought that God didn't care for me. That he wouldn't listen to me. That he thought my prayers were a joke. You see, I went a long time without God answering any of my prayers. But what I didn't know was that he *was* answering my prayers, just not in the way I expected. The night I met Timothy I prayed. I don't even know what I prayed for, all I remember is asking for something . . . anything, to get me out of the situation I was in. And that's when I met Timothy."

Leah looked around. Everyone was listening, enraptured by his words, anxious to hear about the man he'd pretended to be. Would they be angry when they found out what had happened? Jake had come in sometime during Cade's speech. He stood next to Ward and she could tell he was curious. Ward put a finger to his mouth, a sign to stay quiet and listen. Leah turned back to face Cade.

"Timothy was a gracious man. He took me in, without question. He fed me, he treated my wound and he shared a meal with me. He didn't deserve to die the way he did." He stopped again. Swallowed. Looked upward. Was he searching for a sign?

"This is Timothy's Bible. I was looking through it one day. Trying to learn all I could about Timothy, when I happened upon this verse. It's Hebrews 11:40. 'God having provided some better thing for us, that they without us should not be made perfect.' " He looked up. "Now God knows I'm not perfect. I'm pretty certain Timothy wasn't perfect, since he took in someone like me."

There was a guffaw, a laugh, a titter. Leah ignored it. She kept her eyes on Cade.

"It was Timothy's opinion that he was put in my path to take care of me. To help me. To feed God's sheep. That was what he said; those were his last words actually. 'Feed my sheep.' " Cade took a deep breath and let it out. "He said we have no way of knowing where God's path will lead us. He said the Lord will forgive me for my sins. That all I had to do was ask. So this morning, I asked." He looked at Leah. "And now I'm asking you. Forgive me."

No one said a word. It took courage for him to stand up there and admit he had wronged them. More so to do it without any excuses. Tears gathered in her eyes and she willed them away. He wasn't done yet.

"I've been in a lot of bad places, and I've done a lot of things I'm not proud of, yet I can't help but think that in a roundabout way, God led me to this place, and to you." Leah knew his words were for her and only her, yet he spoke them for the town to hear. There would be no more secrets.

"God knew what I needed before I did. It was you, Leah. I don't want to leave you, but I will, if you think that is for the best. I want to be a better man. I promise I will be, whatever you say, stay or go. But I'd sure like to be a better man for you."

"Momma?" Banks said.

What should she do? What could she do? She was madly in love with the man, no matter what his name. She'd fallen in love with the real man. She knew he was good and he was good for her, and her son.

"Yes." She stood up and went to Cade. She heard Jake's gasp, heard him stomp out but she didn't care. "Yes. I love you. Stay."

Cade put his hands on her shoulders. His eyes were full of hope. It was such a beautiful thing to see. "Are you sure?"

"I'm sure." She kissed him then. The entire town saw it.

She didn't care. All she needed was right here. Banks pulled on her arm. Cade picked him up and placed him between them and Banks puts his arms around both of them.

"Can we go home now?" he asked.

"Yes." She smiled. "Let's go home."

"Wow, it's big," Banks said.

Cade stood the tree up in the corner of the parlor. The top brushed against the ceiling and the branches poked out in every direction, filling the room with the scent of pine. "I believe I told you that when you picked it out. But you said it was the one you wanted."

"It is," Banks said. "Can we decorate it now?"

"Ask your mom," Cade said. They both looked expectantly at Leah. Their cheeks were flushed with cold and their hair damp from the snow. Both of them had wide grins on their faces and their eyes danced with excitement. It was Christmas Eve and joy filled her house once more.

"I don't know which one of you is worse," she said. "If I didn't know any better I'd think you were six years old too."

"That was the last time I had a Christmas tree." Cade shrugged sheepishly.

Leah felt her heart jump, as it always did when she looked at this man—her husband now, thanks to the circuit preacher coming through last week—and thought of all he'd suffered through in his life. But he'd survived it. He'd never lost his soul, although from what he'd told her, it had been a hard battle fought and he'd had to keep it hidden for so very many years. Now he wanted to find his brother and she would help him as best she could.

"The box of decorations is on the table in the kitchen."

Banks let out a whoop and ran to get them. He set it on the table before the sofa and immediately went to work. Ashes sniffed around the base of the tree and jumped onto the trunk and disappeared into the branches. Dodger woofed at her one time and then lay on the rug before the fireplace.

Cade came behind Leah, wrapped his arms around her waist and put his chin on her shoulder. "It looks like the decorations are all going to be around the bottom," he said. She shifted a bit. The sheriff's badge that hung on his shirt jabbed her.

"It doesn't matter," Leah replied. "I'll spread them out when he's done. He'll get tired of it soon." She didn't move, as she enjoyed the feel of Cade's arm around her, while his body stood solidly behind her. Through the window she watched as big fat flakes floated down, once more covering the town of Angel's End with a beautiful snowfall. It was welcome, as the streets had been muddy lately, from a recent thaw. The world would be clean and new when they woke up Christmas morning.

Leah put her hand over Cade's and slid it down to her belly. "I have a present for you."

He spread his fingers over their child and kissed her cheek. She felt dampness as his cheek touched hers and she knew it wasn't from the snow, but from tears of joy. "It's a gift from God," he whispered in her ear. "Thank you so very much."

Keep reading for a special preview of
the next historical romance by Cindy Holby

COLORADO HEART

Coming November 2012 from
Berkley Sensation!

"Stop right there!" a gruff voice called out.

Jacob Reece cursed himself for a fool for getting so lost in his musings that he didn't see anyone coming their way. He looked up the trail and didn't recognize the small appaloosa or the rider who was currently pointing the business end of a Spencer rifle at his head. The rider was small and new horses turned up all the time. Could it possibly be one of Jim's older twin boys? But surely the twins would recognize him. And why would they be robbing him?

Jake raised his hands, but he kept a hold on Libby's lead. He heard Dan and Randy pull up behind him.

"Boss?" Randy asked.

"Let me see what's going on," Jake said. "There's no need to punish foolishness with waste." He knew the three of them could take whoever it was but he wanted to avoid bloodshed if it was possible. It was too pretty of a night to have to shoot someone, even if they were stupid enough to try and steal from him.

"Turn loose of that donkey," the rider said. The voice wasn't as gruff this time. It was a boy trying to disguise himself by speaking lower than natural. Then the words sunk in to Jake's mind.

"Wait." Jake tried to keep a straight face. "Are you trying to steal my donkey?" He stretched out Libby's lead. "This donkey?"

The rider cocked the rifle to let him know he meant business. "No. You are stealing my donkey."

"What the hell?"

"Watch your language. And let her go."

"I think there's been some sort of misunderstanding," Jake started to say.

The rifle raised a notch. "I'm guessing you understand *this*, don't you?"

"You want us to do something?" Dan said quietly from behind him.

"I got it," Jake responded. "The last thing I want to do is kill some fool kid." He raised his hands higher so the idiot with the rifle could see that he wasn't holding a weapon, and with a squeeze of his knees, Skip, his mustang, moved forward, slowly, with Libby walking along by his side.

The rider, whoever he was, wore a coat that was way too big for him. It reached from neck to ankles and was made of heavy wool. He wore a wide-brimmed, flat-top Stetson that was pulled low over his face and a heavy knit scarf wrapped around his neck that covered any hint of skin. The rider was so laden down with trying to stay warm that Jake knew he could take him out before he had a chance to twitch his finger on the trigger.

"Take it easy," Jake said as they approached. "I'm bringing the donkey, although I don't know why anyone in the world would want to steal the fool thing. She's more trouble than she's worth."

"Like I said before. It's my donkey."

The rider sat on a small rise in the road. The moon was directly overhead and his features were lost in the shadow of his hat but the gloved hands on the rifle were small, albeit steady, and the tips of the boots that stuck out from beneath the folds of the coat barely showed.

"What are you? Twelve?" Jake asked as Skip stopped about a head's length from the appaloosa.

"What are you?" the thief said after he cleared his throat. "Stupid?"

Jake tapped his heels and Skip charged full bore into the appaloosa. The appaloosa reared and Jake wrenched the rifle from the rider's hands as he tumbled backward from the saddle.

Libby hee-hawed and kicked out, and the appaloosa, spooked, took off up the trail toward Dan and Randy, who quickly cut the horse off and grabbed its reins. Libby trotted a few steps away and turned to watch.

Jake jumped from Skip's back and jabbed the business end of the rifle in the chest of the kid who lay sprawled in the snow.

"Ow," a much more feminine voice said. Jake used the tip of the rifle to push the hat away from his . . . no, her face. The moonlight spilled down on delicate features and skin that looked like it should be on a porcelain doll. Her mouth was pursed into a pout that made his lips twitch with the urge to press a kiss against their fullness. Lush lashes formed crescent moons on her cheeks before she opened them to stare up at him with light blue eyes that captured the moonlight. Her hair was short and wispy, and its color was as pale as the moonbeams. It stuck out in every direction like tufts of grass.

"Who the hell are you?" he asked.

"Language," she said as she pushed the rifle away.

"What are you, a Sunday school teacher?"

In the next instant Jake was lying on his back in the snow and she was standing over him with a .45 pointed at his chest. He heard Randy and Dan chortling in the background. He had to admire her. Tiny as she was, she'd managed to sweep his legs right out from under him with one of the slickest moves he'd ever seen.

"I'm the owner of that donkey that you stole," she said vehemently.

"I didn't steal her. She came to me."

She raised a skeptical eyebrow and the pistol she held in her left hand did not waver a bit. She was so petite he wondered how she could get her hand around it, but she did, and it was obvious she knew which end meant business.

"Yeah, Libby is madly in love with him," Dan said.

"You're fired," Jake said. He didn't take his eyes off the woman. He wasn't worried for his life and he knew Dan wasn't worried about his job. Jake knew his two men could take her out if they wanted to and were just cutting up, as he was, to put her at ease so she didn't do anything stupid.

She raised the gun and took her finger from the trigger. "You do know her name . . ."

"And now you do too," Jake said. "That doesn't mean you knew it before."

Her pale eyes changed. "What is that supposed to mean?"

"Do you mind if I stand up? My ass is freezing."

"Do you always talk like this?" she asked with a sigh.

"Only when someone tries to rob me and then dumps me in the snow."

Randy and Dan snorted with laughter. The woman backed up a few feet but kept a tight hold on the pistol as Jake clambered to his feet and made a production of brushing the snow from the back side of his duster. She picked up her rifle while Jake cleaned himself off and stuck the pistol in the pocket of her oversized coat.

"You can put the rifle away too," Jake said as she stepped far enough back so that she could keep the rifle leveled on all three of them. "If I wanted to hurt you I would have done it already."

"Well excuse me if I've heard that before."

Jake found his hat and brushed the snow from it. "Lady, I don't know who you are and where you are from but I can tell already that you have an attitude problem. So I suggest we both go to town and clear this up."

"I'm not going anywhere with you," she said indignantly.

"Then tell me who sold you the animal." If she said Jim's name he'd gladly turn Libby over to her. But he wasn't about to give the donkey up just because some woman waved a gun in his face.

Her tone turned defensive and her hold on the rifle slackened. If Jake wanted to, he could jerk it from her hands. "I got her last fall from the livery in town. I don't know his name as it was a friend of mine who bought her."

"Well that sure does prove a lot," Jake said. "How about we both go to town and we'll see what the sheriff has to say about this.

"What?" she spouted. "Like I said, I'm not going anywhere with you."

"Suits me," Jake said. "If this donkey is indeed yours then you can pick her up tomorrow at the livery. If she's not . . ."

"Oh she's mine," she said. "And maybe I'll have a word with the sheriff about how you wound up with her."

"Fine," Jake said. "You can both find me at the Heaven's Gate." As he didn't trust her with the rifle he kept his eyes on her as he spoke to his ranch hand. "Randy, you can give her back her horse now."

The tiny woman gave an exasperated sigh and clicked

her teeth together. The appaloosa responded by shaking her head. Randy let go of the reins and the little horse trotted over to her owner. "Stand back," she said.

"Gladly." Jake raised his arms wide. She guided the appaloosa to a rock buried in the snow and used it to gracefully swing into her saddle. "Believe me, I plan on staying as far away from you as possible," Jake added.

She slammed the rifle into her scabbard. Without a backward glance she took off up the trail to Sam Parker's spread.

"Well now, don't that beat all," Randy said as they watched her move up the trail.

Jake let out a heavy sigh before he slammed his hat onto his head and mounted Skip. "Boys, I am in desperate need of a drink."

"Compelling and beautifully written."

—Debbie Macomber, *New York Times* bestselling author

FROM *NEW YORK TIMES* BESTSELLING AUTHOR

JODI THOMAS

THE COMFORTS OF HOME

A HARMONY NOVEL

Twenty-year-old Reagan Truman has found her place and family in Harmony, Texas. But with her uncle taken ill and her friend Noah lost and disheartened with his life, Reagan is afraid of ending up alone again—and she's not the only one. When a terrible storm threatens the town, the residents of Harmony are forced to think about what they truly want. Because making the connections they so desperately desire means putting their hearts at risk...

penguin.com

From the award-winning author of Open Country and Pieces of Sky
KAKI WARNER

Heartbreak Creek
A RUNAWAY BRIDES NOVEL

From Kaki Warner comes an exciting new series
about four unlikely brides who make their way west—
and find love where they least expect it . . .

Edwina Ladoux hoped becoming a mail-order bride would be her way out of the war-torn South and into a better life, but as soon as she arrives in Heartbreak Creek, Colorado, and meets her hulking, taciturn groom, she realizes she's made a terrible mistake.

Declan Brodie already had one flighty wife who ran off with a gambler before being killed by Indians. He's hoping this new one will be a practical, sturdy farm woman who can help with chores and corral his four rambunctious children. Instead, he gets a skinny Southern princess who doesn't even know how to cook.

Luckily, Edwina and Declan agreed on a three-month courtship period, which should give them time to get the proxy marriage annulled. Except that as the weeks pass, thoughts of annulment turn into hopes for a real marriage—until Declan's first wife returns after being held captive for the last four years. Now an honorable man must choose between duty and desire, and a woman who's never had to fight for anything must do battle for the family she's grown to love . . .

Praise for the novels of Kaki Warner

"Emotionally compelling."   —*Chicago Tribune*

"Thoroughly enjoyable."   —*Night Owl Reviews* (Top Pick)

penguin.com

**Enter the rich world of
historical romance
with Berkley Books . . .**

Madeline Hunter

Jennifer Ashley

Joanna Bourne

Lynn Kurland

Jodi Thomas

Anne Gracie

Love is timeless.

berkleyjoveauthors.com

Discover Romance

berkleyjoveauthors.com

See what's coming up next from your favorite romance authors and explore all the latest Berkley, Jove, and Sensation selections.

See what's new

~

Find author appearances

~

Win fantastic prizes

~

Get reading recommendations

~

Chat with authors and other fans

~

Read interviews with authors you love

berkleyjoveauthors.com